WHERE
HIDDEN
SOULS LIE

BOOKS BY D.K. HOOD

Her Bleeding Heart

Chase Her Shadow

Now You See Me

Their Wicked Games

D.K. HOOD

WHERE HIDDEN SOULS LIE

bookouture

Published by Bookouture in 2023

An imprint of Storyfire Ltd.
Carmelite House
50 Victoria Embankment
London EC4Y 0DZ

www.bookouture.com

ISBN: 978-1-83790-388-7
eBook ISBN: 978-1-83790-387-0

To my readers. I write these stories just for you.

PROLOGUE

He's buried me alive.

Panic gripped Wanda Beauchamp as the heavy weight of damp soil pressed down on her. Disoriented and in total darkness, she moved her outstretched arm. She'd enjoyed enough time in her garden to recognize the touch and smell of soil as the unmistakable crumbly dirt moved through her fingers. Something covered her face, a cardboard box maybe, and had given her a small gap filled with lifesaving air. Had he wanted her to suffer or couldn't he look into the eyes of his victim? Terrified, the need to be free gripped her, and biting back a sob, she moved her fingers, walking them up through the loose dirt. When they broke through the surface, she waved her arm around and dirt spilled over her pushing down the edges of the box onto her shoulders. Horrified of the soil slipping down to cover her, she tried to move her other arm but couldn't feel her fingers. Her hand was trapped beneath her.

She pictured the position of her other arm. It was above her shoulder, and if she'd managed to bend her elbow to push it through the ground, the soil above wasn't too deep. The will to live gripped her and she sucked in a lungful of damp air and rolled, surprised to discover soil moving above her. Ignoring the waves of pain wracking her body and using the box covering her head like a battering ram, she pushed hard with her knees. The soil above her was so heavy, like a massive log across her shoulders, and it pushed down on the box, crushing her head and neck. Relentless, and terrified as soil closed in tightly around her like quicksand, she gathered her strength and thrust upward. The second her head broke through the soil, cool air seeped beneath the edges of the box. Gasping deep breaths, she tossed it aside, dragged out her numb arm, and surveyed her prison.

The smell told her she'd been buried deep in a pine forest, and the icy chill and distinct smell of snow meant somewhere in the mountains. It was quiet, apart from the usual sounds of a forest at night—the odd screech of an owl and other wildlife out hunting. Waist-deep in the ground and waving unsteadily, she stared around a small clearing. Beside her was a newly dug shallow grave, and close by a soil-encrusted shovel leaned against a tree. Was the man who'd dragged her from her bed coming back to bury another victim? Trembling, she scanned all around. How long had she been unconscious? It had been dark when he attacked her, but she had no memory of what had happened next. Her head throbbed and she lifted her hand to examine her scalp. Her fingers came back bloody, the sticky substance black in the moonlight. She peered around searching for any signs of life. Only the full moon above filtering through the dense pines illuminated the area. If he was coming back, he'd use a flashlight, so she must be safe for now. Shaking out her numb fingers, she pressed her hands on each side of the grave and pushed up with her legs. In one almighty effort she rolled onto the forest floor. Panting as her senses slotted back into place, she sat up slowly. Nausea gripped her but she swallowed hard, fending it off. If she had any hope of escaping unnoticed, she must cover up the grave.

Heart pounding, she pushed the box open-side down into the grave and, standing on shaky legs, grabbed the shovel and scraped the dirt back into the grave. She looked at her footprints in the disturbed soil, evident even in the light of the moon. She walked a few steps into the forest, ripped a small branch from a tall pine and brushed away her footprints, leaving the large man's prints undisturbed. She'd just replaced the shovel against the tree, when the screech of an owl made her turn and search the forest. Fear gripped her by the throat and she stared in disbelief. Way in the distance, a light bobbed. *He's coming.*

ONE

MONDAY

Sheriff Jenna Alton leaned back in her office chair, looking back on her time in Black Rock Falls. So many things were happening it was difficult to believe that her life here had begun only six years previously. Her world had been turned upside down when she'd been placed in witness protection. It hadn't been easy, moving from DC to an alpine region in the West with no family or friends. With a new name and face, DEA Special Agent Avril Parker no longer existed, but with law enforcement soundly behind Jenna, putting her name forward as sheriff of the backwoods town had seemed a normal progression. She had employed a rookie, Deputy Jake Rowley, a tall strong Montanan, who over the last six years had become a fine deputy, and along with his wife, Sandy, a very close friend. Jenna had become godmother to their twins, Cooper and Vannah. This wasn't why Jenna was reminiscing. It went so much deeper than that. Her life was about to change again in a wonderful way. She and husband Deputy Dave Kane, an ex-special forces sniper and later a Secret Service agent, had passed all the checks necessary to adopt four-year-old Tauri.

Now all they needed to do was wait for the judge to call them back to court to sign the paperwork.

Tauri's previous legal guardian was one of their best friends, Native American tracker Atohi Blackhawk. After he'd been tossed from one foster home to another, DNA testing had linked Tauri to Blackhawk's ancestors and, more surprisingly, another person had shown up on the ancestral chart: Kane's dead wife, Annie. Her ancestors were also descendants of the same Native American. Five years previously, pregnant Annie had been murdered in a car bombing, which left Kane seriously injured and with a metal plate in his head. As Kane had a bounty on his head, his appearance had been changed too and his real name had never been revealed to Jenna, not even after they'd married.

Although Blackhawk had agreed to become Tauri's guardian, from the moment he'd met them the little boy was convinced Jenna and Kane were his parents. He'd insisted they were his mommy and daddy. Discovering Tauri's link to Annie had been a shock, and Jenna had weighed up the consequences but couldn't resist the chance to have Tauri in her life. They'd fallen in love with the little boy, seeing him as a wonderful gift, and agreed to foster him to see if they were a fit as a family. It had been a long and tedious experience for Jenna, jumping through the hoops necessary to prove she and Kane were worthy to have a child. In truth, she'd longed for her own baby but had instantly felt a deep loving connection to Tauri.

The background checks for the adoption had been a nightmare. Although their cover stories had held, in truth neither had lives that went back more than six years. Although Tauri was four-years-old, he was very intelligent and tall for his age. He craved knowledge, so after speaking with the local kindergarten, the coordinator agreed he could enroll—and he loved it. Jenna stared at the picture of Tauri on her desk. She missed him when he attended kindergarten, and the three weeks' vacation they'd taken when he'd arrived to live with them hadn't been enough. She glanced over at Kane. "Do you figure we'll hear this week?"

"Adoption takes time, Jenna." Kane looked up from his desk. "Don't worry. We've got this. Think about it. Tauri has been moved from one foster home to another all his life and they gave him to Blackhawk as a last resort." He checked his watch and pushed to his feet. "I need to relieve Rowley. With the rodeo in town, people are using Main as a racetrack."

With difficulty, Jenna dragged her mind back to the open file on her computer. "Okay. By the way, Blackhawk found another grave in Stanton Forest. I think we should head out to Bear Peak in the morning and observe Norrell and her team excavating it." She smiled. "It isn't often we get to watch a forensic anthropologist do their thing."

"Hmm." Kane stared at her. "I have to admit, having Wolfe as our ME was special, but getting Dr. Norrell Larson to join his team was pure genius."

Dr. Shane Wolfe had his own secrets. He just happened to be Kane's handler and reported weekly to the White House, although he lived in Black Rock Falls under his own name with his three daughters: Emily, a medical examiner in training; Julie, at college; and Anna, the baby of the family, now eight years old.

Jenna stood and went to the counter to fill a Thermos with coffee. "I agree." She glanced up at the door as Deputy Zac Rio, who'd come to them from LA as a gold shield detective, poked his head around the door and knocked. She smiled at him. "Ah, good you're back. Why don't you take a break now and then you can take over from Kane in an hour or so?"

"Ah, sure." Rio frowned. "Two women have been reported missing in Bozeman. I know it's some ways away, but I've added them to our files and sent them on to the sheriffs' offices out of Blackwater and Louan."

"Any signs of foul play?" Kane pulled on his sheriff's

department jacket and checked his weapon.

"Nope they just vanished... as in like, poof, not a clue." Rio shrugged. "Both close together in the same local area. The women are not known to each other. It's freaky."

After grabbing energy bars from a carton under the counter, Jenna handed the bars and Thermos to Kane. She looked at Rio. "That case isn't our problem, thank goodness, but I'm glad you told me."

"Sure." Rio backed out of the door and his footsteps echoed on the staircase.

Jenna smiled at Kane. Six-five and handsome, he made her want to smile every time she looked at him. "Two-hour shift, maximum, okay?" She went on tiptoes to kiss him on the cheek. "I'll call you if any news comes through from the court."

"It's only paperwork." Kane smiled at her. "Tauri is our son. We just have to make it legal. Remember, you're picking him up today. Just don't be late collecting him from the kindergarten or we'll get a black mark on our record."

Laughing, Jenna walked him to the door. "As if. I'm just staying here to wait for the nanny to arrive or I'd be down there volunteering."

"You worry too much." Kane grinned at her. "It's not as if he's going to be bullied. He's the biggest kid in the class." He shrugged. "He gets on with everyone. I just hope he likes the nanny."

The phone on Jenna's desk rang and she waved Kane out the door. "Sheriff Alton."

It was Magnolia "Maggie" Brewster, their receptionist. *"Dr. Wolfe is here, and he has a woman with him. They want to speak to you."*

Jenna smiled. "Oh, that will be our nanny. Send them up." She waited eagerly to see who'd been chosen for their nanny. "Thanks, Maggie." She disconnected.

Being as both Jenna and Kane were on the hit list of terrorists and drug cartels, everyone they came into contact with or employed was cleared by the federal police. She stood as a Native American woman walked into the office with Wolfe behind her. She smiled. "You must be Raya Clark. I'm Jenna Alton. You likely passed my husband, Dave, in the lobby."

"Yes, I've met him." The nanny eyed Jenna speculatively. Her rich dark eyes had smiling lines at the corners. She was in her late fifties, a widow, and had once been very beautiful. "It's Nanny Raya. I like to establish my role in a family from the get-go."

Jenna glanced up at the white-blond Dr. Wolfe, towering over her like a Viking marauder, and smiled. "Thanks for delivering Nanny Raya. We're still waiting for the final paperwork for Tauri."

"It's in the bag." Wolfe smiled at her. "Nanny Raya has had a tour of the house and I've dropped off her bags." He pushed a hand in his pocket and pulled out a set of keys. He handed them to Nanny Raya. "The keys to the house and vehicle in the garage." He turned back to Jenna. "I'd better get back to the office. Call me when you have any news."

"I sure will." Jenna waved Nanny Raya into a seat. "Is everything to your liking?"

"It is indeed." Nanny Raya frowned. "This is the first time I haven't been living with the family of the child. I understand there are security issues? Will they cause problems for Tauri?"

Shaking her head, Jenna leaned back in her chair. "Not that we're aware, but where you are is very secure and right next door to the office." She leaned forward on her desk. "We'll be raising Tauri, as in spending all our downtime with him, taking him to kindergarten or school. We want his life with us to be as normal as possible. However, we want his time with you to be beneficial too. Although Atohi Blackhawk has offered to instruct him in his culture, he will benefit greatly from your help as well. We don't want to ignore his Native American heritage, the same as we want him to embrace his American heritage."

"If he is with you all the time, how can we achieve this goal?" Nanny Raya opened her hands. "Where will there be time?"

Jenna stood. "Coffee?"

"Yes, thanks." Nanny Raya smiled at her. "Black."

As Jenna made the coffee, she looked over her shoulder. "We'd like you to collect him from kindergarten each day and care for him until we finish work. During school breaks, we'll try to get vacations, but it will depend on the caseload. In fact, we'll need to rely on you to care for him whenever we're working long hours on a case. We've spoken to him and he understands. He is looking forward to meeting you." She placed cups on the table and sat down. "Come with me this afternoon to collect Tauri. We'll take your truck so he'll recognize it. I'll spend some time with the pair of you. If there's ever a problem, I'm usually here in the office or you can call Blackhawk."

"What happens if you decide to have your own child?" Nanny Raya gave Jenna a long look. "I hope Tauri isn't a for-now substitute?"

Horrified, Jenna shook her head. "No, Tauri is our son and has been from the day we laid eyes on him. If, God willing, one day Tauri has a baby brother or sister, I hope you'll still be around to help us. From the information Dr. Wolfe gave me, you're qualified to care for babies as well." She eyed her critically. One of her criteria was plain speaking. She didn't ever want anyone hiding the truth when it came to her son. "Because it's classified, I can't explain our reasons for the security, but you can trust me that we are doing everything possible to adopt Tauri."

"That is good enough for me." Nanny Raya grinned, showing perfect teeth. "I believe you and I are going to become great friends, Jenna Alton."

TWO

Kane leaned against the back of his black tricked-out truck, affectionately known as the Beast, and smiled at his bloodhound, Duke, who was currently lying on his back under a tree on a patch of grass, legs in the air, no doubt watching the butterflies dancing by. He'd given out three speeding tickets and aimed his radar gun down Main. A truck came speeding toward him and he stepped out to wave it down. Sure, some might risk driving on by, but his truck had a camera that recorded speed, time, and the license plate of all speeding vehicles. This was a boring part of life in Black Rock Falls, although breaking up brawls in the Triple Z Bar on weekends was something he secretly enjoyed.

The vehicle slowed and stopped. Kane dropped his mirrored sunglasses on his nose and held out his hand. "License and registration."

He dipped his head to look at the man inside and everything inside him froze. The man gave him a dismissive stare and handed over the paperwork. Following procedure, Kane slid into his truck to check the documents on the mobile data terminal but pulled out his phone, took photographs, and then called Wolfe. "Are you secure?"

"Yeah, I'm in my truck. What's up?"

Kane rubbed the back of his neck. "I've just pulled over someone I killed. You recall the terrorist I took out by the name of Hudson Driver? There could be no doubt I took out the target. He's sitting on Main not ten feet away from me. His name on the license is Brice Johns."

"I'm on my way. Make some excuse to delay him or get prints." Wolfe disconnected.

Slowly climbing from the Beast, Kane took out his notebook and opened it to a clean page. When he reached the man, he handed him the notebook. "I'll need the name of the person and approximate date you purchased this vehicle."

"Why?" The man glared at him. "Just write me a darn ticket and I'll be on my way."

Shrugging, Kane dropped down his sunglasses to look at him. There was no doubt, Hudson Driver was sitting right in front of him, a little older, but it was him. "I'm sorry, your vehicle came up as stolen. I'm just doing my job, Mr. Johns."

The man took the notebook and scribbled the name of a car showroom in Billings, Montana, and a phone number before handing it back. "I purchased it new. It's not stolen. Just ask them." He held out his hand. "Call them. You can use a phone, right?"

The traffic streamed by, but just in his periphery, Kane made out Wolfe's white truck, lights flashing, coming up the wrong side of the road. He held up a hand and waved the traffic down a side road. The vehicles followed like sheep. He walked back to the truck and looked at Johns. "Get out of the vehicle, Mr. Johns."

"This door is a little stuck." Johns gave a small shrug. "Give me a second."

The man scooted over to the passenger door and jumped

out. He smiled at Kane and held up something in his hand. One of his thumbs hovered over a red button. *He's got a detonator.* As Johns ran away, Kane turned and waved down Wolfe, alerting him with a hand signal to the danger. A cloud of dust billowed into the air as Wolfe turned into the park entrance and slid to a halt. Moving fast, Kane scooped up Duke and dived into the Beast. An explosion shook the truck and turned the air fire red. Burning-hot and flaming vehicle parts rained down, pinging on the roof as Kane lay across the back seat. Seconds later, another explosion rocked the Beast as the gas tank on the other vehicle exploded. Billowing black smoke surrounded them as Duke trembled in his arms.

Glad the president of the United States had supplied him with a bombproof, practically indestructible truck, Kane kept his head down until the falling debris had subsided. He made soothing sounds to Duke, who turned his head and licked him on the cheek. As long as it wasn't a storm, a bath, or a visit to the vet, Duke could tough his way through most situations. Through the ringing in his ears, Kane heard Wolfe's distinctive Texan drawl calling his name. The door behind him was yanked open and he turned to look at Wolfe's distraught expression. "We're fine. You?"

"Yeah, it missed me. No one was hurt. It's lucky you diverted the traffic and no one was walking by at the time." Wolfe stood back to look at the Beast. "Well, I'll be. There's not one dent in your truck. Man, they sure built this to protect you."

Wiggling out backward, Kane signaled to Duke to stay. The ground was strewn with twisted metal and he couldn't risk the possibility of him cutting his feet. He turned to Wolfe. "There's no doubt that was Hudson Driver." He scanned the smoke-filled area. "Did you see which way he went?"

"Nope, he's a skilled operative and will be long gone by now. We can't put out a BOLO on him if he plans on blowing up every cop who detains him for a traffic violation." Wolfe shook his head. "Unless he came here to kill you? Did he show any sign of recognition?"

Kane picked debris from the top of the Beast and piled it beside the curb. Although being his handler, Wolfe had only known Kane by his codename Ninety-eight H, and likewise, Kane had known Wolfe as Terabyte before they'd met in Black Rock Falls. He straightened and shook his head. "Not a chance. Apart from my size and eye color, I don't resemble my other self. I had scars on my face, wrinkles from being in the desert for years, a small tattoo between finger and thumb. Every distinguishing feature has been removed. My own father wouldn't recognize me." He smiled. "My accent has changed. I sound like a Montanan. That was deliberate and I worked on it some before I arrived here."

"Yeah, I noticed." Wolfe smiled at him and then indicated to the road behind him. "Jenna is heading this way and I hear sirens. If we can clear the road around the Beast, we'll get you out of here. I'll contact the White House and see what they want to do about Hudson Driver." He sighed. "Are you one hundred percent sure you eliminated him?"

Wolfe had never doubted him before and Kane stared at him. "I'm darn sure I killed the given target. I used an RIP between the eyes, and you know as well as I do, a direct hit with a radically invasive projectile would blow his head right off his shoulders. There's no chance he survived. There's only one possible solution. Someone leaked information before the mission. He knew I was coming for him and used a doppelganger. We both know there's a leak in the White House and since the change of administration, we can now be sure it's military." He held up his notebook. "I have his prints." He pulled a scanner from his pocket and collected them.

"Whoa, hold on." Wolfe plucked the scanner from his hand and negated the reading. "I'll do that in a safe way back at my office." He took the notebook from Kane. "We can't go alerting

POTUS if it's just another crazy."

As Kane had the faces of everyone he'd taken out during his missions cemented in his memory, he rubbed the back of his neck. His gaze settled back on Wolfe's face. This news would hit like a magnitude-nine earthquake. People could die. He nodded. "I'm one hundred percent sure it was him, Shane. The prints will confirm, but that's not our immediate problem. We can't call in another team to handle this or it will break my cover. I'll have to handle this alone."

"We'll handle it alone." Wolfe frowned. "I'll go straight to the top with this. We'll need to move around without restriction. We don't need to be running foul of local PDs." He rubbed his chin. "Do you still have that US Marshal badge I gave you?"

Nodding Kane smiled. "Yeah."

"Okay, let me make a few calls and arrange a chopper." Wolfe frowned. "We can't use the ME's chopper or I'll be identified. When the debris is cleared, go home and pack a bag. You know the deal. Bring your gear but no weapons, no ID. I'll have a replica of your rifle and an arsenal of everything we'll need at a safe house. I'll come to you. I'm afraid you'll need to leave the Beast behind this time. It's too easily traced. I'll arrange federal Marshal IDs. It will take me a couple of hours." He blew out a long sigh. "You can't tell Jenna. It's need-to-know."

Kane turned to see Jenna running toward him and his gut twisted. He'd promised never to leave her or lie to her and now he had no choice. Hudson Driver was a highly trained rogue black ops turned assassin and he was right here in Montana. No one else could stop him. Kane could anticipate his every move. Good men would die, *had died*, in an effort to stop him, but it was his mess to clean up. He thought for a beat. Why Montana? The enemy would only utilize an asset like Driver for something to shake up the world. Kane moaned as the realization of why Driver was in Montana slammed home. POTUS would be making a speech in Helena later in the week. He shot a look at

Wolfe and frowned. "Driver must be heading for Helena. He's targeting the president."

"Well at least we have a destination." Wolfe stared at Kane grim-faced. "We'll need to take him down before he gets the chance."

Possible scenarios running through his head, Kane nodded. "Copy that." He turned as Jenna picked her way through the debris. Behind her, fire trucks wailed to a stop and men jumped out.

"What the heck happened here?" Jenna stared from one to the other. "Are you both okay?"

Taking her arm, Kane led her to the shade of a tree. People milled around but stern shouts from Wolfe kept them well away. "This is old business and I need to go with Wolfe to deal with it. Don't ask me any questions because I don't want to lie to you. I'll be going dark, so I won't be taking my phone. If by chance I can get to a payphone, I'll call as Mr. Jones. So go with the flow."

"I understand." The color drained from Jenna's face. "What if we get called back to court about Tauri?"

A knot formed in Kane's stomach. "Talk to the lawyer. Ask him for an adjournment. Tell him I've been called away on urgent private business. It's up to him to make an excuse to the court. Tell him it's sensitive and he'll think of something." He touched her cheek. "I'm hoping I'll be back way before then."

"What's the cover story?" Jenna stared at him. "For everyone else."

Kane thought for a beat. "I'm going with Wolfe to a conference in Helena. Keep it simple."

"When are you leaving?" Jenna moved closer to him. "And what about Duke?"

Smiling, Kane tucked her against his side. "In a couple of hours. I'll take Duke back to the ranch and I'm leaving the Beast behind too. Take him with you when you go with Norrell to excavate the gravesite. He'll enjoy a run in the forest." He pressed a kiss to the top of her head. "We knew this might happen one day and is always a future possibility. Now smile so I can keep that memory of you in my mind."

"You too." Jenna turned to face him and smiled. "Stay safe."

Pushing down the need to crush her against him, Kane matched her smile. "Always."

THREE

TUESDAY

Rolling over in bed and finding the sheets cold startled Jenna awake. She'd had trouble sleeping, her mind drifting to Kane and wondering just how much danger he was facing. At least he had Wolfe beside him. As well as being a doctor and medical examiner, Wolfe's years in the Marines meant he was well trained for combat. He kept himself in good shape and Kane was at his physical peak right now as well. The problems that dogged him since the initial car bombing and a subsequent bullet to the head and a knee injury had become things of the past. Sure, the metal plate caused headaches in extreme cold, but it was summer now and heat didn't worry him.

Being a mom took preference over everything right now and Jenna slipped out of bed and headed for the bathroom. Without Kane to help with the chores and make breakfast, she'd need to get a move on. She turned out the horses and had the stalls mucked out before Tauri stirred and was able to shower and have breakfast well on the way before he came into the kitchen, hair tousled and rubbing sleep from his eyes. "Morning. It's orange juice and eggs for breakfast. There's bacon too if you want some."

"When is Daddy coming home?" Tauri climbed into a chair and his eagle-colored eyes moved to her face. "Did you fight? I was in a home once and the adults fought all the time. He used to drink too much and fall around and she'd hit him with a frypan." He frowned. "My daddy doesn't drink like that does he?"

Tossing a strip of bacon to Duke, Jenna chuckled. "No, he's strictly a one-glass-of-wine man. We didn't fight. He's gone to a conference with Uncle Shane. He didn't know until yesterday, so didn't have time to tell you he'd be gone for a few days." She filled a plate and placed it in front of him before filling her own. "I'm sorry we didn't find you sooner, Tauri. It was sad you had to live with nasty people."

"It's okay." Tauri smiled at her. "I knew you'd come. When I was waiting to go to live with Atohi, an elder from the res came to see me. I don't remember his name. He said I was an old soul with great wisdom and my parents would find me." He smiled. "I like Atohi and his mom. They were very kind to me, and Atohi took me to see the elders."

Always surprised how a four-year-old could communicate so well, she smiled. "That would have been nice. They have wonderful stories to tell."

"I told them I didn't belong with them on the res." He pointed to his heart. "In here, I could feel you and Daddy calling for me. I knew you'd come for me soon."

Intrigued, Jenna sipped her coffee. "What did the elders say?"

"They said we are family and my destiny was to bring people together. I must keep one foot on both sides and know them and know you." He dug into his eggs and shrugged. "Sometimes I don't understand them, but Nanny Raya said she'd tell me stories."

Nodding, Jenna was surprised he'd accepted the new person in his life without question. "Do you like her?"

"Not like Atohi's mom, more like my teacher." He grinned at her. "Don't worry, I love you the best."

Heart clenching, Jenna forced food down. This child was a wonderful gift and she treasured him. "That's good to know." She cleared her throat. "I'm going into the forest today with Atohi and Norrell. I'm taking Duke."

"Are you hunting down old burial sites?" Tauri gave a knowing nod. "Atohi mentioned them to his mom. Some of them need to be preserved before hikers disturb the spirits."

His detailed information stopped Jenna in her tracks. This was just a little boy and he absorbed knowledge like a sponge. It seemed he'd not forgotten anything about his past life in foster care or anything else. She'd need to remind Kane not to discuss any case-related matters within his earshot. She nodded. "Yeah, we're going to look around Bear Peak. Nanny Raya will collect you from kindergarten and take you to her house, but I shouldn't be late."

"Why do you bring the horses in at night?" Tauri sipped his orange juice. "They have food and water. It's nice and warm. They enjoy their freedom. It would save you work if they stayed outside in the paddock. Atohi says horses need to run if you're not riding them."

Thinking through his words, Jenna nodded. "I guess that would be okay. Your daddy likes to groom them every day. He says it keeps him connected to them and he can check on their health, but as he's away it would cut down on the chores. We'll leave them out tonight and see how they go."

After dropping Tauri at kindergarten, she headed straight for Wolfe's office to meet Norrell. They'd made plans to go together and she'd leave her cruiser at the ME's office and ride in Norrell's truck. They'd follow the firebreaks to the local area where Atohi would meet them and guide them to the burial site. Jenna had only met Norrell's team once before but they seemed to be nice. Her assistants, Matty and Leo, had followed her from the Helena medical examiner's department and both were top in their field. They set off in a convoy, Norrell leading the way.

Jenna turned in her seat to scratch Duke's ears. The dog was missing Kane and spent his time searching the house and then returning to lean on her leg. He liked Tauri and sat in his room each night until the little boy went to sleep, his big head resting on the sheet watching him. When Kane was at home, he'd play with Tauri in the yard as if keeping watch over him. It warmed Jenna's heart. "You are going to have so much fun in the forest, Duke. Blackhawk will be there too and he might bring one of your friends with him."

"You talk to that dog as if he understands you." Norrell chuckled. "Although, he does do everything you say. Kane has trained him well."

Smiling, Jenna turned to look at her, all white-blonde hair and drop-dead gorgeous. She had the same Viking look as Wolfe, and although he was some years her senior, they'd become close. Wolfe's wife had died of cancer five years previously. Although Wolfe was old-school and took relationships at a snail's pace, Norrell didn't seem to mind. "That was all Blackhawk. He raised him, sold him to a tracker who passed. Duke went to the shelter and was taken by a brutal serial killer. He tried to starve him to death. When we found him, Kane adopted him. We discovered his link to Blackhawk later. Duke has some serious phobias but he's a great tracker dog and a trusted friend."

After following the GPS instructions, they arrived at the end of a fire road to find Blackhawk sitting on a stump, waiting for them. He'd ridden on his dirt bike and left it behind when they set out along an animal trail. As they walked, Jenna fell into step beside him. "No dog today?"

"Nope." Blackhawk smiled at her. "I'm training one of the pups to track. He gets distracted and wants to play with other dogs. On the trail, I need him to concentrate, so he can play at home today." He frowned. "The weather looks fine but dry storms are around. They come in so fast there's no warning. Try to keep out of open spaces. Lightning seems to find people."

Jenna nodded. "Okay. Can I talk to you about Tauri?"

"Anytime." Blackhawk smiled at her. "We're family now."

Jenna nodded. "We are and I'm very happy about it. It's just that Tauri says things he's too young to know about. It's strange. Was he like that when he arrived at your place?"

"Yes. He asked questions constantly and gained knowledge from the elders." Blackhawk shrugged. "He is an old soul, torn between my people and yours." He squeezed her arm. "I'm happy he is with you, but I do miss him. He was a breath of sunshine in my home." He sighed and looked ahead into the forest. "My mother reminds me it is time I took a wife and had children of my own." He gave her a sideways glance. "Finding love isn't that easy. I haven't met anyone in Black Rock Falls to form a relationship with and many of my friends are the same. A few of us might take a vacation to see if we can meet anyone special in other towns but I'm not too confident."

Trying not to stare, Jenna nodded. Atohi Blackhawk was a very handsome man, with a kind and gentle soul. He owned a thriving tracker and guide business. He would be quite a catch. "My mother once told me there was a Jack for every Jill, so I guess, like me, you'll just have to wait until she shows."

"That is what I keep telling my mother." He laughed. "She is not convinced of my sanity." He led the way into a small leaf-strewn clearing and pointed. "There's the grave alongside the rock. It is barely visible but it's clear the ground has been disturbed."

They all crowded around the small mound and Jenna turned to Norrell. "What do you think?"

"We'll clear some of the leaves and take a look." Norrell

waved her team forward and they put down the equipment they carried and sprang into action.

The sound of running water came from close by, and seeing Duke head in that direction, Jenna followed him. She stopped in awe at the beauty in front of her. A fast-flowing river fed by the mountain tumbled down the valley, where it would join many more to become Black Rock Falls, the magnificent waterfall the town was named after. Rainbows danced across the surface and dragonflies zipped in and out of patches of sunlight. Beside her, Duke snuffled through the vegetation growing thick between the trees. Fed by the constant water vapor from the tumbling river, the edges of the river were deep green and glossy, dripping with water. Jenna sat on a boulder to absorb the scenery. It was so peaceful and she hoped it hadn't been sullied by a killer burying a body close by.

A loud crack came from deep in the forest. A gunshot? Jenna pulled her weapon. Where they were working was a no-hunting area. Another loud crack split the silence, followed by a roll of thunder so loud it shook the mountain beneath her feet. Duke howled and took off running blindly but before Jenna could follow him another crack came and something whizzed past her face. Was someone shooting at her? She stepped backward as the top of a tree snapped in half and tumbled toward her, the stump blackened and smoldering. The branches slapped against her, knocking her weapon from her hand and thrusting at her with force. Balanced precariously on the edge of the boulder with the river tearing past below her, Jenna windmilled her arms trying desperately to get her balance. Suddenly airborne, she hung in the air for a long second before ice-cold water covered her. Instantly cold with bubbling white water all around, she stared in shock. Which way was up? Her wet clothes dragged her down to certain death. Currents pulled at her, but remembering her backpack, she relaxed and allowed it to drag her to the surface. Seconds later, she burst into the light gasping for air. She tried to swim but water dragged her down, her boots like leaden weights on her feet. There was no time to scream for help as the misty river engulfed her and swept her away into its freezing swirling depths.

FOUR

Helena

It had been years since Kane had received direct orders from POTUS. The man he once knew was no longer in charge, but the new president had been read in about Kane before the old administration departed. His own situation was more serious than "need to know." In fact, apart from POTUS, Wolfe, and one contact within the Secret Service, the fact he existed at all was classified. His missions during his time as a black op sniper had removed enemies of the USA and now many terrorist organizations had placed a bounty on his head. The people who wanted a piece of him didn't want him dead. They wanted to extract information from him—and then likely sell him to the highest bidder.

After taking the chopper to Helena, Wolfe had secreted Kane in a safe house, a place only Wolfe knew, and using a bunch of codes on a secure device, Kane had been patched through to POTUS. He apprised him of the situation. "How do you want me to proceed, sir?"

"It's been some years, Ninety-eight H, are you up to the task?" POTUS sucked in a deep breath. "Just say the word if there's any doubt. I have teams at my disposal ready to roll."

Kane glanced at Wolfe and shrugged. "I'm always ready to serve, sir. In this case, unless you're prepared to risk massive collateral damage, allow me to bring the target in, or take him out. It's your call, sir."

"You do know you'll be risking exposure? If he reports back to his HQ with your details, every enemy of the US will be on your tail. All the years spent creating a new life will be in vain. You'll be hidden and will never see your family again. Do you understand?"

The image of Jenna and Tauri flashed through Kane's mind. He caught an expression of doubt in Wolfe's eyes as he listened in to the conversation and smiled at him. He sucked in a deep breath. "He won't see me coming, sir. If he does, he won't have time to report to anyone." He rolled his shoulders. "Just give me the order, sir."

"Take out that SOB and I want visual confirmation. Put Terabyte on the phone. You'll need supplies."

A surge of adrenaline spiked Kane's heart and, pushing Jenna and Tauri to the back of his mind, he nodded. "Yes, sir." Handing the phone to Wolfe, code name Terabyte, he walked into the kitchen.

After pouring coffee from a bubbling machine, he opened a secure laptop and scanned the maps between Black Rock Falls and Helena, estimating the time to drive from one town to the other along the way. If Driver planned to take out POTUS, he'd arrive two days before the speech, scope out the area, and find the best and most secure place to take his shot. Driver, like him, worked alone. He likely had a handler equipped with all the latest technology to assist using satellite technology or even a small drone to watch his back. As Wolfe came into the kitchen, grabbed a cup of coffee, and joined him, he explained his theory. "We have to outthink him."

"I've had nothing else on my mind." Wolfe added sugar to his cup and stirred. "First, we locate him. Just remember that the Secret Service will have agents everywhere for the speech. You'll need to be a ghost to get past the security. They'll have snipers on every rooftop. They won't know you're on the job, which makes you a possible threat." He smiled. "We'll have the advantage of knowing exactly where everyone will be, so the man who is the odd man out will be your target."

Kane scratched his chin. "He might not use a rifle. He likes bombs. Don't think he won't use a child or an old lady as his killing machine. He's done that before. All areas under and close by POTUS must be checked and rechecked prior to the speech. Don't forget his vehicle and all along the walk to and from the podium."

"You know as well as I do that's normal protocol." Wolfe stared at his cup as if in a trance. "One man in a crowd. It's going to be difficult."

Ideas flashed into Kane's mind. Knowledge he'd gained along the way came back to him as if his last mission was hours ago. "First, we find him. We'll backtrack. We have the ability to blend into the towns along the way; he's an outsider. His Boston accent is noticeable. We have US Marshal creds, and people will talk to us. Once we find him, we'll track him. I'm assuming you've ordered the usual gear, surveillance, and other gizmos we'll need, right?"

"Yeah, they'll be at various pickup spots around town." Wolfe looked interested. "You do know he'll have the same equipment and a handler watching his every move. He'll spot you following him. Remember he's as good as you and maybe has a few new tricks up his sleeve."

Kane chuckled. "Then we'll go old-school." He looked at

Wolfe's blank expression. "Trust me." He took a notebook and pen out of his pocket and made a list. "Make sure everyone of our guys on the ground has one of these. Including us. If this goes down like I imagine, they're going to need them."

A slow smile crept across Wolfe's face as he read the list.

"Old-school, huh? You got it." He pulled out his phone and made the call.

FIVE

Stanton Forest

On her face in the bubbling water, Jenna twisted and grabbed air. Her backpack was keeping her afloat but tipped her face down as she rushed along the river, moving through giant boulders so fast the riverbank was nothing more than a green flash of color. Ahead she glimpsed only blue sky. Panic gripped her as she hurtled toward one of the smaller falls. In seconds she fell in a thick body of water and plunged deep. In the turbulent water, she unclipped the waist strap of her backpack and slipped out of it, grabbing hold as it rose up behind her. Lungs bursting, she clung onto the shoulder straps, looping her arms through them. The water carried her along and above her white water bubbled. She kicked her feet and, using the push of the water against the backpack on her chest, risked letting go to secure the straps around her waist. She fumbled with the straps, her fingers numb from the cold and awkward in the leather gloves. Heart racing with lack of oxygen, she finally pulled the strap tight as starbursts danced across her vision and the air rushed from her lungs. Kicking desperately, she broke the surface gasping.

Waves covered her head, and out of control in the rapids, she sped along the river. The end of this journey could only mean death. Almost all the rivers joined to create Black Rock Falls, a few others turned to flow out west, traveling through miles of virgin forest. Hanging onto the backpack, she dragged in air between being smashed against moss-covered rocks. On each side of the river, the mountain rose up in vertical granite walls. There was no escape. Just trying to breathe, Jenna sped along, learning she could lean one way or the other to miss boulders. She had one slim chance to survive if she didn't drown. To avoid Black Rock Falls, she'd need to keep right to be swept into one of the arterial rivers flowing toward the west. They would pass through forests and give her a slight chance to get out of the fast-flowing river.

Teeth chattering, she looked up and gaped in horror as the Bison Hump Bridge came into view. The next, bigger falls was close by and she'd never survive it. She tried to recall the river system, but the freezing water was numbing her brain. Her hands had frozen into fists around the backpack handles, but she wouldn't give up. Ahead, the river went around a massive boulder. Her heart ached for Kane, when the memory of him in this very river, battered and bruised as he tried to retrieve a body, drifted into her mind. She couldn't leave him alone. No, she darn right refused to die. Kicking like mad, she headed straight for the huge boulder. Her shoulder slammed into the granite, numbing her arm, but she kicked again and like a piece of flotsam was scooped up and she shot past the right side.

It was like being on a rocket. Tipped one way and then the next. Twirled over onto her back and gasping for air, Jenna watched the forest at the tip of the ravine flash by. She dropped suddenly, legs flying out behind her and like a ball in a pinball machine, bounced off smaller boulders as the river carried her onward. The freezing water numbed her extremities but hadn't stopped her elbows and knees from screaming with pain. Exhausted, she searched ahead and, seeing the end of the ravine give way to dense forest, she fought the rapids to get closer to the riverbank. When a fallen tree offered her a slim chance to get out of the washing machine, she took one arm from her backpack and, as she flew toward it, looped one arm over a branch. It was like fighting a giant, but she hooked one leg over the trunk and then dragged her soaking body very slowly onto the tree. She didn't care when the spiky dead branches scraped her face, and just lay there breathing.

It seemed like a lifetime before she moved. Teeth chattering, she sat up, legs dangling in the water, and rearranged her backpack. Kane had selected their backpacks. All the survival packs in the office were waterproof and could be used as buoyancy vests. The extra expense had been worth it. It had saved her life. Crawling along the fallen tree, she reached the riverbank and dropped onto a rock. Numb with cold and aware of the chances of hypothermia, she looked around trying to get her bearings. She didn't recognize anything. All around was just more and more trees. She needed to walk and warm up, but in what direction? Sore and battered, she jumped up and down and windmilled her arms, but the freezing wind rushing down from the mountains pressed the wet fabric of her clothes to her goosebump-covered flesh. Pushing trembling hands into her pockets, she found nothing. The river had picked her clothes bare of possessions. Her satellite phone was gone, along with her badge and cred pack. She had no weapon and pulled off her soaked gloves to feel along her belt. Her knife was still locked inside its leather sheath. It had been a gift from Blackhawk. The handle, beautifully crafted to fit her hand, was made from an elk antler with delicate silver decoration. She stared into the sky. "Thank you!"

She opened the backpack. Inside were the usual things Kane had packed but she'd added extras. More water and energy bars. A large slab of chocolate and ten brownies all in ziplock bags. Not having any idea which way to go, Jenna had few options. No one would have any idea where she'd ended up. She could be miles from Black Rock Falls. She looked around, thunder still rolled across the mountains and lightning strikes were common. Night would come way before anyone found her, so her first priority would be to make a shelter, get warm, and dry her clothes.

Using her knife, she cut long branches from the fallen tree and arranged them over a tall bush close to the riverbank. Under the bush was dry and offered a cave-like space. The extra tree branches would keep out the wind and rain. Next, she collected a pile of dry wood and made a firepit beside a huge smooth boulder by digging a hole in the sand and then building a fire just the way Kane had shown her. His survival techniques filled her head as if he were standing beside her. The fire would keep her warm and the smoke would act as a signal to her rescuers. All three Zippo lighters from the backpack worked just fine and the dead pine branches ignited in a whoosh of orange flames. She fed the fire until the logs glowed red and then stripped off her clothes, socks, and boots. Shivering, she used sticks driven into the sand to dry her underwear and socks close to the flames. If they got singed, she didn't care. She just wanted to be warm again. She placed the boots beside the firepit, wrung out her other clothes, and hung them over the heated boulder beside the fire.

Trembling with cold, she dragged two of the silver survival blankets from the pack. She placed one blanket on the ground and, after wrapping the other around her, sat down to warm her chilled flesh in front of the fire. She had food and water, and apart from bruising, she'd survived. But where was she? If she'd ended up in the virgin part of the forest, there'd be very few cabins. No one hunted in these parts at this time of the year, if at all. It was too far from the nearest town. She looked around and suddenly the feeling of being completely alone hit her. She could die here and no one would ever find her body. A lump formed in her throat. She'd never see Kane again or hug her sweet Tauri. After waiting so long for a real family, it was trickling between her fingers like sand. What was she going to do? Kane and Wolfe were gone for an unknown length of time. Would her team be able to find her without them? *I'm in big trouble.* Dragging her backpack toward her, she contemplated her supplies. Kane would eat them in a day, but she could be lost for weeks. How long before someone even noticed her missing?

SIX

Black Rock Falls

The howls from Duke caught Atohi Blackhawk's attention. He turned in a full circle to discover where the noise was coming from. Moving away from the crowd around the open grave, he continued to search until he noticed the thick tan and black tail sticking out from beneath the branches. "Was it the thunder? Come on out, Duke. You are safe now."

When the dog came to his side still trembling, Blackhawk placed a hand on his head. "Where's Jenna?"

It was obvious the dog knew the name very well and peered around the clearing. After sniffing the ground, Duke headed toward the river's edge, nose snuffling through the dead leaves. Blackhawk followed close behind and stopped dead at the site of the smoldering tree. On one side, Jenna's pistol lay in the dirt. He searched all around the tree, lifting branches to make sure she wasn't trapped beneath them. Concerned, he cupped his hands around his mouth. "Jenna! Jenna!"

He listened intently but no sound came above the roar of the water. Moving slowly along the edge of the ravine, he examined the ground from the fallen tree. In between two of the boulders he found a small collection of things. A hair tie, a few coins, and a bag of doggy treats. As he retrieved the items, realization slapped him in the face. He stared into the fast-flowing river, searching downstream, but all he could see were the white-capped fast-flowing rapids. He turned on his heel and ran back to the camp. He touched Norrell's shoulder. "Jenna has fallen into the river."

"What?" Norrell gaped at him. "When? Just now?"

Blackhawk pulled out his satellite phone. "I don't know. I believe a tree was struck by lightning and knocked her into the river. I'll need to notify Rio and Rowley." He made the call. "They'll need my help."

"Wrap it up, people." Norrell turned to her team. "Cover the grave and we'll come back another time. We have an emergency. Jenna has fallen into the river. We need to get back to town and organize a search."

With his mind on the implications, Blackhawk called Kane, and when the call went to voicemail, he frowned. "Can you contact Shane? Kane isn't picking up."

"We won't be able to contact them for a couple of days." Norrell frowned. "It's one of those high-tech conferences. No phones allowed. I'll try and call them later. What do you want us to do?"

Wishing for an instant he could transform into an eagle and search for Jenna along the riverbank, Blackhawk lifted his chin. "Rio can organize a search and rescue team in seconds, but we need more than one chopper. I'll call Carter. When he arrives, I'll go with him. There are places we'll need to search that others won't know about." He looked at her. "What about Tauri? Both his parents are away now."

"Nanny Raya collects him from kindergarten and takes him

to her house. Jenna and Dave have emergency protocol in place. He'll be fine there until we can contact Dave." She gave him a long, concerned look. "What are her chances?"

Unable to form the words, Blackhawk shook his head. He gathered himself and swallowed the lump in his throat. "If she went over the falls, we'll find her body by nightfall. The water is fast flowing and bodies always end up in a fishing hole on the bend just before town. If not, she could be trapped anywhere among the boulders between here and Black Rock Falls or if she's lucky, she has traveled along a smaller river toward the west. If so, there's a chance she washed up on a riverbank deep in the forest. If this is so, the sooner choppers are in the air, the best chance she'll have to survive." He looked at Duke. "I'll take you back to the fire road and then go home and get my truck. Take Duke with you. We'll need him to track Jenna. See if you can find anything belonging to her. Place it into a plastic bag and give it to me. I'll be back within the hour."

Heavyhearted, he led the way back to the fire road and called Carter. After explaining and mentioning both Kane and Wolfe were out of range, he took a deep breath. "We need your help searching the arterial rivers. There are many, and if luck is with us, she'll be out there alive somewhere."

"We're on our way, but Atohi, you know as well as I do our chances of finding her are a million to one." Carter's footfalls sounded on tile as he moved around.

Shaking his head, Blackhawk touched his chest. "I don't believe she's dead. I can feel her like a light in my chest. We have to search for her. I'll never give up and neither will Dave. Please hurry."

"Copy that." Carter disconnected.

Blackhawk gave his head a shake. Kane couldn't have picked a worse time to go away. He dragged in a deep breath. *Hang in there, Jenna. We're coming.*

SEVEN

Helena

"Is there any chance we can take him out before he reaches Helena?" Wolfe sat at the kitchen table of the safe house beside Kane, stripping weapons and reassembling them. "Stop him and we can go home."

Kane slipped a clip into an M18 pistol and slid it into a shoulder holster. "It sounds fine in practice, but in truth, I could have shot him in the head in the middle of Black Rock Falls. Problem is everyone would have seen me, the press would have gotten involved, and the next thing, some terrorist cell would be holding Jenna as a hostage so I'll give myself up." He gave Wolfe a long look. "When I started in the military and became a sniper, my commanding officer pulled me to one side and told me that every action has a reaction—so don't be the reaction."

"Like killing someone won't cause a reaction." Wolfe frowned and shook his head. "That makes no sense."

Shrugging, Kane smiled at him. "It makes perfect sense. He

means if no one can see you coming, no blame can be credited to either side. As the people we deal with have multiple enemies, the idea is to shift the blame to one of their factions." He reassembled the sniper rifle and then broke it down and replaced it in its box. "First, we locate him, next we follow him. He's on his way here, so will be staying in a town close by. Only a fool would take a room in Helena. When he makes his move, I'll be ready for him. I figure he'll go for a headshot, which means he won't be where the Secret Service will be watching. He'll be maybe two thousand yards away, but to make sure he hits the target my guess is one thousand yards away."

"So, we look for tall buildings one thousand yards away from the town hall?" Wolfe pulled the laptop toward him and opened the maps app. "We have three different locations." He turned around the laptop to show Kane. He indicated as he spoke. "This building is under restoration, and then we have an office block, and there's a lower building, but he'd be able to make the shot from any of them. They all have a clear line of view to the podium in Helena."

Scanning the page, Kane enlarged the buildings and then sat back in his chair. "I don't figure Driver will arrive early. He'll be holed up in a small town tonight. We've got time to drive to these locations. I'll scope them out. One of them will have already been chosen, which means a spotter has been there. You'll need to bring your forensic skills into play. If Driver is doing this, it will be a walk-in, walk-out deal. It will be set up by now, and on the day, he'll be getting instructions through a headset, same deal as me. His backup team will be most likely in an aircraft and feeding him information. He'll trust them to be watching his back and he won't be expecting to be disturbed." He pushed to his feet. "Let's go."

Kane took the wheel of the white Jeep and followed the GPS to explore the buildings Wolfe had found. After spending way too much time trying to establish a way inside the first two without tripping alarms or gaining undue attention, they headed for an old building. The outside was covered in metal scaffolding. Contractors walked back and forth like ants over a sweet bun. "This looks promising." He smiled at Wolfe. "Let's see how easy it is to get inside." He went to a van parked out front used by the site manager as an office and poked his head around the door. It was empty. He snagged two helmets from a table inside the door and tossed one to Wolfe and then picked up a clipboard. "You know the deal. We walk in like we own the place."

"I'm not usually in the field, Dave." Wolfe tossed his hat inside the Jeep and pushed on the helmet. "This is your field of expertise."

Kane removed his Stetson and plonked the helmet on his head. "Just follow my lead. We're architects from the city. Don't worry, when contractors see a guy with a clipboard, they usually scatter like rodents from the pest guy."

Not one person challenged Kane or looked his way as he made his way through the building and climbed up the hundred or so winding stairs to the roof. He bypassed the areas where the men had been working and kept on climbing until he reached the top. He stopped and pushed open an old door with brown paint peeling from years of neglect. In front of him, footsteps in dust on the aged wooden floor led to the crenulations around the rooftop. An old office chair seemed out of place, set before a dilapidated bookcase pushed hard against the wall overlooking the town. Neither had a coating of dust, so had been taken there for a reason. He turned and smiled at Wolfe. "This is the place."

Kane sat on the chair, rested his elbows on the bookcase, and using his scope peered through the gap in the crenulations. "He'll set up here to take the shot." He stood and waved the papers on the clipboard over their footprints, hiding them from sight. "We know the time of POTUS's speech, so all I need is a place to hide."

"You won't have to worry about the contractors." Wolfe pointed to the paperwork on the clipboard. "That says work will cease for three hours during the president's speech." He pointed out the door and onto the landing. "One floor down is a decent-size closet. It's empty. I checked it on the way up." He looked at him. "It's risky taking him out at the last second. What if we make a mistake and POTUS is killed?"

Surprised that after knowing Wolfe so long he'd question his judgment, Kane shook his head. "You know darn well I won't let that happen. Trust me, I'll die before allowing Driver to pull the trigger." He waved Wolfe back down the steps. "Show me this closet."

The plan was dropping into place, and once they'd established Driver's whereabouts, Kane would be able to plan ahead and then relax until the day. He followed Wolfe down the steps, opened the closet door, and smiled when he noticed a key protruding from the lock. "Perfect. I'll go inside and lock the door, just in case Driver checks it on the way to the roof." He headed down the steps and looked back over his shoulder at Wolfe. "If the site is going to be closed during the speech, I guess I'd better keep the hat."

EIGHT

Stanton Forest

Trying to work through outcome possibilities, and stay positive, Jenna wrapped the blanket around her. The crackling Mylar space blanket made by NASA in 1964 wasn't very comforting, but it kept out the wind. She'd found six of them in her backpack. They each came in a tiny packet she had to rip open with her teeth. She could clearly remember Kane telling her how more is better, now she knew why. She had a spare T-shirt and socks, but had decided not to wet them with her soaking hair and body. Drying herself was a priority and she leaned closer to the fire, finger-combing her hair. It was a strange, frightening experience to be naked in the forest, watching her socks and underwear hang from sticks to dry in front of the fire. It had taken a couple of hours, but her underwear, socks, and her T-shirt had at last dried. After pulling on the warm garments, she stretched out her sweater between two sticks and placed it closer to the flames. Building the fire close to the boulder was a trick Kane had taught her. The granite retained heat and meant she could spread out her wet clothes over it and keep turning them to dry. This idea was working just fine. Her jeans were almost dry, and her boots were hanging upside down on sticks drying close to the flames with steam rising from them. At night she'd snuggle close to the boulder and have double heat to keep her warm.

The idea of spending a night in the forest alone scared her. She had a can of bear spray in her pack, and if she kept the fire going, most wildlife would keep away. Her food was all packaged and relatively safe inside her backpack and wouldn't attract bears. Thank goodness she'd packed the brownies in a sealed container. Strange thoughts rattled around inside her head. Were people searching for her? How would they find her?

She had a general idea of where she'd come ashore but how far had she traveled? She'd been in the river for what seemed like forever and, traveling at high speed, she could be miles away from town. In the west there was nothing apart from fire roads and the odd forest warden's lookout. Finding one of them would be a miracle. She hugged the silver plastic around her and stared at the river. If the team had noticed her missing, Rio would take over and have search and rescue out, but they didn't know her location. First thought would be she'd gone over Black Rock Falls. It was, after all, less than a fifty-fifty chance she made it to an arterial river. She imagined they'd use ground teams to search the inlets and fishing holes, where bodies usually showed. They'd likely find some of her personal items along the way. That would take them most of the daylight hours. During this time, they'd get a chopper up to search the riverbanks. One chopper would never cover the massive area in one afternoon, but remaining on the riverbank with a fire going gave her a good chance of being spotted. She stared at the pile of green leaves she'd collected to drop onto the fire to make smoke the moment she heard the sound of a chopper.

If nothing happened and no one came, she'd finish drying her clothes, use logs and rocks to make the initial *J* and an arrow to indicate which way she'd gone, and then head downstream. Sooner or later, she'd reach a fire road or a highway. Happy with her plan, she got to her feet and walked up and down the sandy riverbank collecting anything she could find for a sign. She laid out the rocks in the letter *J* as big as she could make it and stood back to admire her work. As she bent to gather long sticks to make an arrow sign, a cloud of nosy birds rose in a flock scattering in all directions. Jenna straightened, dropped the logs into a pile, and scanned the forest. Birds were a great warning sign of approaching danger.

Heart racing, she moved into the shadows. A thumping noise came from deep in the forest, and twigs snapped like gunshots in the silence. Someone or something was coming, and they weren't too worried about making noise. A search party couldn't possibly have gotten to her that fast and they'd be calling out her name. A bear? When a bush turkey squawked, she estimated the distance and figured she had maybe five minutes to grab her clothes and run for her life. She dashed back to camp, dragged on her damp jeans, socks, and hot boots. The inside of her puffy jacket was dry, and she pulled it on and grabbed her backpack. With only her knife as a weapon, she slid into the dense forest. The noise was closer now. Too close to risk running away. If it weren't a bear heading her way, she might be in more trouble. Dangerous or unstable people hid off the grid deep in the forest and they usually chose the spartan life for a good reason. Jenna swallowed hard. If so, they'd know she'd built the fire. She'd left the blankets scattered around, and her sweater still hung between two sticks. Maybe they'd seen the smoke. A bear would be the better option. Taking deep breaths to calm her rising panic, she slid into the shadows and pressed her back against the rough bark of a tall pine—and waited.

NINE

Black Rock Falls

Rio sprang into action the moment Blackhawk called him. He'd alerted search and rescue and set up a command post in the office. The usual volunteers had arrived and were set to man the hotline. News that Jenna had fallen into the river would be all over the county in the next few minutes. He stood on the office steps as the media gathered. When everyone was in place, he cleared his throat. "This morning, Sheriff Jenna Alton fell into the river alongside Bear Peak. We're asking for volunteers in all areas between Bear Peak and town, including anyone who uses the rivers heading west, to join in the search for her. We are organizing search parties along the riverbanks. Please call the hotline for the name of your local coordinator. If you locate her, or anything belonging to her, please call the hotline. The lines are open now and will be until she is found."

"Deputy Rio. Troy Leman, Mountain View TV News." He

stuck a microphone in Rio's face. "Are you looking for a body? Where is Deputy Kane? Did she fall or was she pushed?"

Rio stared at him. "Deputy Kane left town with Dr. Shane Wolfe, the medical examiner, yesterday morning. The sheriff was alone when she fell. A lightning strike hit a tree close by to where she was standing. It broke in half, and we believe that she was struck by falling branches and fell into the river. We're holding out hope of finding her alive. That is all at this time." He turned and walked inside the glass doors.

People with somber expressions sat at desks waiting for the phones to ring as he made his way through the office. He pulled out his phone and punched in Kane's number. It went to voicemail again and he tried Wolfe with the same result. Jenna had mentioned that Kane and Wolfe would be out of range for some days, but what was he to do in an emergency? He called Emily. It seemed ages before she picked up. "Has your dad left any instructions about contacting him in an emergency?"

"Why, what has happened?" Emily's footsteps could be heard on the tiled floor at the medical examiner's office.

Rio rubbed the back of his neck. "Jenna is missing. She fell into the river out at Bear Peak and we can't find her."

"She what? Oh, that's a disaster. Dave will go ballistic."

Rio let out a long sigh. "I can't contact him either. He's the first person I called."

"That's because they turned off their phones." Emily sighed. *"Dad's instructions were to contact Jenna, you, or Rowley if anything happened. They will only be out of reach for a day or so, but that's not going to help us now, is it? Has anyone contacted Jo and Carter?"*

Heading for Rowley's desk, Rio nodded. "Yeah, Blackhawk called them earlier. They should be on their way. Did your dad mention where they would be staying or give any information about their whereabouts? We could call the motel on the landline."

"Nope, when he goes away, he doesn't give details, but then he usually checks on us nightly to make sure everything's okay. Although he didn't call last night or this morning. This isn't unusual behavior for my father. When I was younger, he used to be gone for days at a time and never mentioned the reason why. I don't think I need to ask him now. His work takes him all over." Emily sounded annoyed. "You know as well as I do they could be working a case for the FBI. It could be need-to-know and we don't need to know or ask any questions. He works with a wide variety of police departments all over Montana. They could be anywhere. I think it's best you don't ask when they return."

Shaking his head, Rio stared into space. "I don't give a darn where they are or what they're doing, but Dave's wife is missing, presumed dead, and he needs to know. If you hear anything from your father, please give him the information. I have to go. We have people arriving for the search parties." He disconnected and realized he'd stopped beside Rowley's desk.

"Do you really think she's dead?" Rowley looked distraught. "When Blackhawk contacted me earlier, he mentioned if we don't find a body in the next twenty-four hours, there's a chance she traveled down one of the arterial rivers heading out west." He stood and pointed to a map of the county pinned to the wall. "There are five arterial rivers that run from the main river feeding Black Rock Falls. If she was conscious, she had five opportunities to get to the other side of the river and make it into an arterial flow." He frowned. "Did Blackhawk mention seeing any blood at the scene? We have to hope she didn't hit her head."

Staring at the map, Rio used his retentive memory to store all the information he needed. "Norrell called me as well. She scanned the scene with her forensic eye and only noticed heel marks, as if Jenna had been thrust backward. She believes a tree branch struck her. She dropped her weapon, so was startled before the event. Norrell figures there was dry lightning around at the time, and when it hit the tree, it sounded like gunshot." He sighed. "It's a straight drop to the river and it's deep enough that she doubts Jenna would have been seriously injured entering the water. It all depends if she lost consciousness before she went under." He stared at Rowley. "We have to hope she didn't get a jolt from the lightning strike. You do recall when Kane was close to a tree that was struck? He was unconscious and lost his memory. Right now, all we can do is search for her, taking in all possibilities."

"She knows how to survive in the forest." Rowley nodded as if to himself. "She and Kane both trained me as well. If she made it out of the water, she'd stay alongside the riverbank, light a fire, or leave a sign she was close by. Kane always insisted that if we get lost in the forest, we try and find a river and follow it down the mountain. Sooner or later, we'd run into a town or a road. Most towns are built alongside a water supply. You can survive for a time on water, if necessary, although at this time of year there are tons of huckleberries and gooseberries all over." He turned to him. "What's the search plan?"

Running his mental list through his mind and using his unique ability to see everything at once, Rio shrugged. "It's logical. We'll send search parties to all catchment areas and places where bodies have washed up before. I've estimated, at the speed the river is running, if she drowned, she'd be through the falls and in one of the catchment areas within the next half hour. I'll send out search parties there. The search and rescue chopper and Carter will be scanning the riverbanks. She is a strong swimmer and fit. She could have made it out of the river at any point. It's over a hundred miles of winding river from Bear Peak to the final stage of the river that heads out to Blackwater and countless miles through arterial rivers heading west." He gave Rowley a long look. "Let's face facts, she isn't a superhero. She'll be soaking wet and freezing cold. Unless she carries a Zippo in her pocket, she doesn't stand a chance."

TEN

Helena

Kane smiled, catching a glimpse of himself in the reflection of a storefront window. He hadn't shaved and his five o'clock shadow was looking fashionable. Dressed in a brown suede jacket and Wranglers and without his signature black Stetson, he didn't recognize himself. With rodeo cowboys filtering through the towns, he blended in with the crowd, and beside him Wolfe had dressed casually. The ball cap and the red and orange plaid jacket was so not him it was laughable. They'd wandered through three towns during the afternoon without spotting Driver. The bartenders had been talkative and when Kane asked them if they had seen their friend Hudson with a Boston accent passing through, none had paused for a second before shaking their head. Kane strolled up to the bar and ordered a beer from an attractive bartender. He gave her a wide smile and beckoned her a little closer. "I'm looking for a guy by the name of Hudson. You can't miss his Boston accent. He had a misunderstanding with the boss man and left without his pay." He pulled a wad of bills from inside his jacket pocket. "He said he'd be here in town somewhere. I need to give him this." He waved the cash in front of her nose. "Seen him around?"

"Can't say that I have but cowboys pass through here all the time." She smiled and leaned forward allowing Kane a view of her ample breasts. "You staying around? If I see him, I'll tell him you're looking for him. What's your name, honey?"

"Deke." Kane dropped bills on the bar and, leaving the beer untouched on the polished wood surface, headed for the men's room.

He used the bathroom and walked past three scruffy-looking men in the hallway and headed for the back exit. Wolfe was waiting for him out front across the street. As he stepped outside into the alleyway, someone pushed him hard from behind. He sucked in a deep breath and turned to face the three scruffy men from inside. The last thing he needed was to cause a ruckus and draw attention to himself. "What can I do for you, boys?"

The men had formed a semicircle. One with black greasy hair was the spokesman. Another, grinning a yellow smile on his left, could be his brother and a man with the face of a rat rested one hand on a weapon riding on his waist. Kane's M18 pistol was under his jacket and the weight of it pressed comfortingly against his ribs. He could kill them all before they drew down on him but that would bring the local law enforcement running and he didn't have the time for explanations.

"Hand over the cash, we'll see that Hudson gets it. He's a good friend of ours." Black Greasy Hair held out a hand.

Kane shrugged. "He never mentioned you. I'll pass, thanks." He turned to leave.

"Laura is my girl." Yellow Smile glared at him. "We all saw you staring at her. We don't like strangers talking to our women."

Grinning, Kane couldn't believe his ears. Were these guys just spoiling for a fight? "Well, she's in the wrong job if you don't like her talking to men. Not that any man has a right to tell a woman what she can and can't do." He snorted. "And I didn't ask her to show me all the pretty skin right down to her navel. That was her choice." When the man's mouth opened and closed like a freshly caught trout, Kane frowned. "You sure she's your girl? Seems to me like she's advertising for a replacement."

When the men looked at each other and nodded, Kane dropped his hands to his sides and took a step backward. He had a brick wall behind him, metal garbage cans to his right and left. There wasn't too much room for him to maneuver. Would they draw down on him or try and mess him up? When Yellow Smile and Black Greasy Hair both ran at him, he grabbed the garbage lids one in each hand and, twisting at the waist, swung them at their heads. He moved right and then left so fast the men didn't have time to blink before hitting the ground. Rat Face went for his weapon, and Kane clanged both lids together around the man's head like cymbals. Rat Face fell backward over the unconscious bodies of his friends and didn't as much as moan. Shrugging, Kane replaced the lids and then checked the men on the ground. They were all out cold. "Thanks for the workout, boys. I needed to relieve some stress."

Smiling, Kane adjusted his hat, put on his shades, and headed for the truck. He slid into the passenger seat and looked at Wolfe. "No one has seen him."

"You look pleased with yourself." Wolfe narrowed his gaze at him. "What happened in the saloon?"

Kane shrugged. "Nothing. I helped a bartender put out some trash, is all. It was my good deed for the day." He dropped down his sunglasses and raised one eyebrow. "Can we eat now? I'm starving."

. . .

After stopping at a greasy spoon for a meal, Kane sighed with contentment as he finished his double order of burger and fries. "We've checked out every bar and motel in town. He's not here."

"There's a roadhouse with a motel close by, about five miles away." Wolfe peered at the laptop screen. "It's only a tiny spot on the map. Anyone could have missed it. We need to sleep somewhere. That's going to be it."

Kane nodded and sipped his coffee. "We can gas up the truck and spend some time in the roadhouse. If he's there, he has to eat. We'll take a booth if they have one and try and be inconspicuous." He raised one eyebrow at Wolfe. "He's seen me before. I don't want him making us."

"If he shows up there, I can't see any reason why you can't take him out before he gets to Helena." Wolfe gave him a long considering stare. "It sure would make life easier."

Wolfe had never understood the process Kane went through to validate his reason for killing someone. He wasn't a serial killer. Sure, he followed orders, but it took more than that. He needed proof that someone was guilty of a crime. He gave Wolfe a long stare and noticed his friend become uncomfortable. "What?"

"I'm not your enemy, Dave." Wolfe closed the laptop. "I can see your mind working. What did I say to upset you? They say 'if looks could kill' and you just shot one right my way."

Kane shrugged. "Sorry. It was unintentional I can assure you. The thing is, I need justification before I take a life, Shane. I'm not the machine everyone thinks I am. When Driver makes an attempt to kill the president, I'll take him out. If I did this before he makes his move, in my eyes it's murder." He leaned back in his chair. "You recall before I went on missions, I requested every piece of available info on my targets. I needed to know the threat they posed and how many people they'd killed. I didn't want any mistakes."

"You already know what this guy has done and how many good people he's murdered." Wolfe shook his head. "So, what's different now? You figure he's changed?"

Shaking his head, Kane leaned back in his seat. "I know who I shot, Shane. What I don't know is if this guy is his twin. We know zip about him, don't we? The fingerprints were inconclusive, and you know darn well that identical twins can have similar fingerprints." He sighed. "For me to live with myself for killing someone in cold blood, I need to know." He swallowed his coffee. "I'm fully aware this is high risk. The roof is all skylights and air-conditioning units. It doesn't leave much space for hand-to-hand combat and he's good, very good."

"Why fight him?" Wolfe opened his hands. "You never miss. Shoot the SOB. We'll have a cleanup crew there before anyone sees anything."

"It's not going down that way." Kane cleared his throat. "If I shoot him, we have two problems."

"Which are?" Wolfe closed his hand around his cup of coffee.

Kane placed his cup on the table and met Wolfe's inquisitive gaze. "The odds are he'll have a backup shooter, so if they hear a gunshot coming from the rooftop, he'll deploy, and I'll have no chance of neutralizing a second shooter in time. I can't use a suppressor, it won't work. Noise is amplified up there. He'll hear it I guarantee." He leaned forward in his seat. "I figure the second shooter will be in the hotel, probably on the roof. It would be my second choice."

"So POTUS gets gunned down no matter what we do?" Wolfe removed his ball cap and ran both hands through his hair. "This is a disaster."

Smiling, Kane waved to the server. He needed more coffee and a slice of pie. He looked at Wolfe. "Oh, ye of little faith."

ELEVEN

Stanton Forest

Hunching down in the lush vegetation, Jenna tried to slow her breathing. The noise was getting closer and within seconds she could hear gasping breaths and sobs. A woman's sobs. She stood slowly and peered through the branches as a mud-splattered woman came hurtling through the trees. Blood caked one side of her face and a long cut was evident on her forehead. She ran to the riverbank and threw herself down at the edge to scoop up handfuls of water. Once satisfied, she just lay there panting as if all the fight had gone out of her. Not wanting to startle her, Jenna remained hidden and waited for the young woman to sit up slowly and then stagger to her feet. When the woman noticed the firepit, she walked backward, eyes wide and fearful.

Jenna moved a few steps out of the trees and keeping her voice low looked at the distraught woman. "Are you okay?"

The woman's gaze shot to her and then she sank to the floor and, sobbing, just stared at her. Jenna edged out of the trees.

"I'm Sheriff Jenna Alton. You're in my county of Black Rock Falls. What's your name?"

"Do you have a gun?" The woman wiped her face on grimy sleeves and stared at her. "He'll find me. He buried me alive."

Alarmed, Jenna peered into the forest and listened. Birdsong told her all was well and she went to the woman. "No, I'm afraid I don't and I don't hear anyone coming. You're safe for a time. Maybe you should sit down."

"Okay." The woman blinked at her. "My head aches real bad. Am I bleeding? My face feels all stiff." The woman rubbed at her blood-covered face and then pushed a mass of long dirty hair from her eyes.

There was so much blood, most of it dried and congealed on her face. "You have blood on your face and hands. If you're feeling okay, why don't you wash up in the river? It will make you feel better and then I'll dress the wound for you. I have a brownie I can share with you if you're hungry?"

"Okay." The woman looked at her hands and grimaced. "A hot shower would be nice, but the river will do for now." She staggered back to the river and spent a long time washing her face and hands.

As she seemed to be coping, Jenna headed back to the fire. She needed to help this woman but didn't want to reveal the extent of her food supply. She took one brownie and cut it in half with her knife and laid both pieces on one of the rocks. She added two bottles of water and pulled out the first aid box and then zipped up her backpack. She'd need to ration the supplies. If the team didn't locate her in the morning, there was no telling how long it would take them to get back to civilization. When the woman came back to the fire, Jenna dressed her wound and noticed another scar along her hairline. "Have you injured your head before? You have a scar along your hairline."

"I don't remember hurting my head at any time." Wanda

touched her scalp gingerly and looked at Jenna. "I have dirt all through my hair. Do you have a hairbrush in your bag?"

Jenna pulled a comb from a pocket in her backpack and handed it to her along with the hair tie she kept around her wrist. "It's all I have but it's better than nothing. I lost my phone and weapon when I fell into the river."

"You fell into the river?" The woman gaped at her. "Does anyone know you're here?"

Shaking her head, Jenna tried to keep her voice comforting. "Not here exactly, no, but they'll be searching for me. Where did you come from and what happened to you?"

"I don't know where I came from, but I've been walking for hours." The woman stared all around. "There's nothing here but forest. I figured I would die of thirst."

Jenna handed her the water. "We're west of Black Rock Falls. This part of the county is remote. What's your name and can you tell me what happened to you?"

"I'm Wanda, Wanda Beauchamp, and I'm from Bozeman." She waved a hand around. "Black Rock Falls? How did I get here?" She took the comb and pulled it through her hair, spilling dried soil over her shoulders like dandruff. "I don't remember anything apart from a man's voice yelling at me and then waking up in the grave."

After waiting for Wanda to hand her back the comb, she indicated to the brownie. "You should try and eat something and rest awhile. We'll need to move at first light. I'm going to head downstream and see if I can find a road out of here."

"Not me. I'm not going back that way. You'll run straight into him. He'll be out there somewhere." Wanda shook her head. "He buried me alive. He wants me dead."

Needing more information, Jenna nodded. "It's a big forest. We can avoid him. Can you recall which direction you came from? Did you follow the river?"

"No. I was deep in the forest and I didn't see a house or

even a light anywhere. The trees went uphill and I could feel a cold breeze like from the mountains. I walked that way. I figured if I could climb high enough, I could figure out which way to go." Wanda nibbled at the brownie and the color was coming back into her face. "Are you sure someone is looking for you?"

Nodding, Jenna smiled to comfort her. "Yeah, I have a great team and they'll have missed me by now. I'm only staying here in case I hear a chopper. They'll have one at least out searching for me by now and I'll add green leaves to the fire the moment I hear it coming this way. They'll see the smoke." She indicated to her sweater hanging near the fire. "I was soaked through and freezing. My first priority was getting warm and making a fire before nightfall. I've covered that bush close to the boulder to sleep under tonight, if nobody comes to rescue us." She leaned back against a tree. "If you can't remember what happened, how do you know he's following you?"

"I don't." Wanda shrugged. "Not for sure. I covered my tracks best I could and just ran. There were three graves, mine and another freshly dug one. That one was empty. I pushed the box he'd placed over my head inside my grave and covered it. I used the shovel he'd left behind. I'm hoping he doesn't know I'm alive. If he discovers the grave is empty, he'll come after me."

Frowning, Jenna recalled the recent reports of missing persons cases coming out of Bozeman. Maybe this was one of the women that Rio had mentioned. "Do you know how long you've been missing? It's Tuesday. What's the last date you remember?"

"I thought it was Sunday." Wanda gave the date.

Concerned as the date Wanda mentioned was more than four years ago, Jenna sucked in a deep breath. She needed to tell her the truth and hoped it wouldn't be too much of a shock. "I'm afraid, somehow you've lost time." She gave the date and year.

"That's not possible." Wanda gaped at her. "I must have amnesia or something if the last date I remember is almost four years ago." She looked down at her clothes and boots. "I don't recognize my clothes or the boots. Do you figure I've been kidnapped?"

Running her gaze over the young woman, Jenna stared at the bruises on her bony wrists. She'd seen similar bruising from people restrained and a dark mark around one of her boots would suggest she'd been shackled. She'd had cases involving sex slaves, and by the state of Wanda, it was possible she'd been held for a time. Perhaps she'd blocked everything from her mind? It was possible. People who'd suffered traumatic events often never regained the memory. She ate her brownie and sipped water. "Maybe. Can you tell me anything about yourself? Your home and family?"

"Yeah, I'm fourteen and I lived in Bozeman with my aunt, but she got sick and they put me into foster care because my dad couldn't return to the states because of his work." She blinked and pressed one hand to her chest. "Oh, that means I'm almost eighteen."

Frowning, Jenna stared at her. Her father refused to do anything and allowed her to go into foster care. What kind of father was he? "Did your dad have a good reason not to take you with him?"

"I guess. My dad recently remarried." She paused a beat as if struggling to remember. "He works in renewable energy and moved to the UK." She sighed. "You see, I don't get along with his new wife. She's really young. My mom passed five years ago. Well, that's almost nine years ago now." She let out a long sigh. "I remember waking up in the middle of the night. I was afraid that someone was in my room. The next thing I was in the grave. I was kind of stunned and then really scared. If it hadn't been for the box over my head, I'd have died in there."

Trying to keep the woman calm, Jenna kept her voice

conversational. "What time of the day do you think it was when you climbed out of the grave?"

"It was dark but there was a moon." Wanda ate her brownie.

Jenna nodded. "It was almost a full moon last night. Whereabouts was the moon when you saw it? Was it high in the sky above you or lower?"

"Low. Like on eye level." Wanda sipped water and sighed. "It didn't take long to get light after I started running through the forest." She stopped chewing and frowned. "I tried to keep moving all the time, but I wasn't running all the time. It was uphill all the way, so I walked some of the way. I started running faster when I heard the river. I was so thirsty. Earlier this morning I licked water from leaves on bushes."

Calculating that she'd probably run for about two hours, Jenna's stomach clenched. She'd heard the woman coming, so she'd left a trail behind her, and it wouldn't take a tracker to notice the broken branches and her footprints in the soft soil along the way. The half an hour the woman had been there could mean someone was close behind her. She swallowed the rising fear and looked at Wanda. "Did you see the man?"

"Nope." Wanda licked chocolate from her fingers. "I saw his flashlight coming toward me but I'd refilled the grave and brushed away my footprints by then. I figured he was coming back to bury another body. He had the grave all ready and left the shovel."

Getting up to check if her sweater was dry, Jenna peered into the forest. The birds still chirped and moved from branch to branch blissful in their security, but she'd need to move Wanda before nightfall just in case the man who attacked her had found her trail. She turned to look at Wanda. "I'm going to the riverbank to destroy my sign. If no one is following us, I'll make another one farther downstream. If someone is searching for me from a chopper, they'll see the arrow and my initials and head in that direction. Maybe not today or tomorrow because they won't expect me to have come this far. When my body doesn't show up downstream, my husband will widen the search. He'll never give up. I just hope he'll be home soon. In the meantime, my deputies and search and rescue will be looking." She gave Wanda a long look. "We have to move as soon as you're able. You've left a distinct trail and if the man you mentioned finds it, he'll easily follow it here."

"I thought you said we'd be safe here." Wanda's face drained of color.

Jenna shook her head. "Do you really want to risk it?"

"No." Wanda went to the river to refill her bottle. "What do you want me to do?"

Pointing to the footprints where Wanda ran into the camp, Jenna looked at her. "I'll put out the fire and cover all signs I was here. You go back to your footprints and wait while I brush the sand. When I'm done, continue across the clearing and back into the forest and head for the river. Take off your boots and jeans and wade into the river and then walk downstream but go past this clearing and get back onto the riverbank but make it about twenty yards to be safe." She pointed downstream. "He won't be expecting you to double back and maybe believe you ran into the river and drowned. I'll do the same. I'll meet you downstream."

"I'll help you first." Wanda looked distraught. "I know how to cover my tracks. What about finding shelter for tonight?"

Jenna folded the foil blankets as small as possible and stuffed then into her backpack. "We'll find somewhere under a bush and use the foil blankets. Right now, we can't risk a fire. We're dry and we have food and water. We'll be fine. I have bear spray. There's plenty of fish in the river for the bears to eat, and I don't think we'll be worth their trouble."

They worked together cleaning the camp, and Wanda took off through the forest. Five minutes later, Jenna heard her splashing toward her along the river's edge and waved as she went past. She removed her boots and hung them around her neck, rolled up her jeans and pushed them into her backpack. After dragging a dead pine branch behind her to cover her footprints and then sending it into the fast-flowing river, she slipped into the water and caught up with Wanda.

They headed downstream, climbing from the river on a rocky river's edge, legs cold and blue from the freezing water. After sitting in the sun for a spell to dry their legs, they dressed. Jenna had taken the time to explain how to walk with care and not break any tree branches. "Ready? Keep your voice to a whisper all the time. Sound carries, and if he is looking for you, he'll hear us. Keep listening, watch for signs someone is around. Usually, the birds take off or stop singing if someone disturbs them. If we're very quiet, they won't see us as a threat."

"Okay." Wanda's eyes were huge. "I still think we should be heading up the mountain."

Jenna shook her head. "My husband knows how to survive just about anywhere, and he told me, if ever I was lost in the forest, to follow the river downstream. So, if he's looking for me, he'll be heading toward me. If not, we'll run into a road sooner or later. Keep a look out for gooseberries or anything else we can eat along the way. There's no rush. Keeping at a steady pace is more productive."

Jenna led the way through the forest. They'd traveled alongside the river, sticking to animal tracks for about an hour when the squawking of crows followed by the distinct sound of a horse's hooves moving fast stopped Jenna in her tracks. Pushing Wanda under a bush, Jenna dived into the vegetation and held her breath just as a man on horseback burst through the trees, not twenty yards from them. His horse was slick with sweat and white foam fell from its neck as it tore past. In that few seconds, Jenna noticed the mud clinging to the man's boots and jeans, and one of his sleeves was unmistakably soaked in blood. The man would reach Wanda's trail to the riverbank soon and then where would he go? He wouldn't search forever. Would he believe Wanda had fallen into the fast-flowing river and been swept away to her death? Would he backtrack, search the riverbank, and find them? Heart pounding, Jenna stared around. She needed a place to hide—fast.

TWELVE

Black Rock Falls

Deputy Jake Rowley ran both hands down his face as the reports came in one after the other. It was after six and Rio had estimated that, taking into account the current speed of the river, if Jenna had gone over the falls, her body would have washed up in one of the fifty or so catchment areas alongside the Black Rock Falls River. That wasn't to say she hadn't been wedged between boulders or washed up alongside any part of the river system. He figured just about every person in Black Rock Falls had volunteered to search, and the call out to Blackwater and Louan would mean that replacements for tired searchers would be on their way at first light. Despair gripped him and he slammed his fist down on his steering wheel. This was happening and Kane had no idea his wife was missing. Where the heck was he? He pulled out his phone and called him for the hundredth time. Nothing.

When Atohi Blackhawk's truck pulled up beside him, he buzzed down his window. "Any news?"

"I was about to ask you the same question." Blackhawk slipped from his truck and stared at him. "How many teams have called in?"

Rowley swallowed the lump in his throat. "All of them. Most are heading home and will start again fresh in the morning."

"It's a good thing they haven't found a body, Jake." Blackhawk stared at him. "There's a good chance she's still alive. She was wearing her backpack and it would act as a flotation device."

Shaking his head, Rowley stared at him. "It would tip her on her face."

"You underestimate Jenna." Blackhawk stared at him and raised both eyebrows. "She is strong. You know she works out with Kane every day. She is a strong swimmer. Last summer, you recall we all went white-water rafting? We overturned in the rapids and all swam to safety. She was the first to the river-bank. That's not the first time we've all been swimming in strong currents. She is smart, she knows how to survive."

Recalling the day, Rowley shrugged. "Yeah, but she was wearing a lifejacket. I know she's a strong swimmer, but even Jenna couldn't survive the falls. No one has and she's human like the rest of us."

"I've been thinking about what would happen if I fell into the river." Blackhawk stared into space. "She understands how the rivers flow and knows the positions of the waterfalls. If it were me, I'd try to get to the right side of the river, and hope I'd be carried down one of the arterial rivers that go west. They have no waterfalls—rapids, yes, but the chances of survival are greater. There are no canyon walls to worry about and leaving the water would be easier."

Rubbing the back of his neck but seeing the possibility,

Rowley nodded. "That would be logical, and Jenna is very logical. The only problem I see is if she's injured. We have to assume the tree hit her and knocked her into the water. Norrell is sure that's what happened."

"Maybe knocked her back into the river but I searched all over with Norrell and her team." Blackhawk shook his head. "We climbed all over and checked the tree branches. There wasn't a spot of blood anywhere. Norrell believes when the force of the tree branch hit her, it would have thrown her in an arc into the middle of the river. She would have gone under and by the time she surfaced she'd have been swept away. She didn't have time to call out."

Leaning back in his seat, Rowley nodded. "She didn't make it out anywhere along the riverbank before the first falls. The search and rescue and Carter have been up and down there for hours. She knows to leave a sign and if she still had her backpack, she'd have Zippos inside and space blankets. If she couldn't light a fire, she could just spread out a foil blanket and the choppers would see it."

"Then first light, you ask them to search the five arterial rivers." Blackhawk glared at him. "You're not giving up are you, Jake?"

Blowing out an exasperated sigh, Rowley looked at him. "Never. Not until we find proof either way. If she hasn't left a sign, she's okay. We must assume she's alive but injured or she lost her backpack. I'd search all night if I had my way, but people need to rest. The search parties will be out until sunset and start again first light."

"Where is Tauri?" Blackhawk gave him a direct stare. "I have Duke in my truck. He'll stay with me."

Nodding, Rowley sighed. "He's with his nanny. He likes her and understands his mom and dad are busy working right now. He'll go to kindergarten as usual in the morning. Nanny Raya said we should keep things as normal as possible. He was aware Kane was going away for a few days and Jenna would be working late."

"If you need to keep him away from gossip"—Blackhawk frowned—"my mother will care for him. We are his family too. He is always welcome at our home." He scratched his cheek. "I'll go for a visit before heading home to make sure everything is okay. Will he have enough clothes? Carter has access to the ranch house. He and Jo are holed up in the cottage at the moment."

Rowley shrugged. "You should ask Nanny Raya. Carter is still in the air. He won't give up until his fuel is low. Call me and I'll patch you through to him."

"Okay, thanks. I'll go now." Atohi headed for his truck, and as he drove away, Duke's face appeared at the window.

Tears pricked the back of Rowley's eyes. *Where are you, Jenna? Please be safe.*

THIRTEEN

Stanton Forest

Every hair on Jenna's flesh stood at attention as the rider came to a halt alongside the river and dismounted. He searched around, moving low branches and cursing. With her heart pounding hard, Jenna crawled slowly through the bushes and cottonwood trees using the rush of water to cover the sound of her movement. She peered at the deranged man but could only see the bottom half of him. Mud caked his boots and jeans, and when he turned in her direction, she shrunk back in terror. Blood spatter covered his legs and boots. Whatever he'd done, it had been a frenzied attack, and from the string of curses he wasn't finished yet. A baseball bat, protruded from a rifle holster on his saddle and bloody fingerprints smeared the handle. Pushing down rising panic, Jenna took in the size and approximate age of him, but with his hat pulled down over his eyes and a full beard, she couldn't make out his features enough to identify him. He was tall but not Kane's build, smaller, maybe six foot, and wiry not muscular. He looked anywhere between forty-five and sixty. The skin on his hands was leathery, as if he'd spent a good deal of time outside. His full beard had streaks of white discolored to yellow, as if he'd smoked for a long time.

What had made him so angry? Serial killers usually murdered and left bodies behind, but this guy was on a mission. He was stalking his victim, so maybe Wanda had witnessed a crime and finding her grave empty must have sent him into a frenzy. Jenna duckwalked to the next tree and hid under the bush growing at the bottom. A chill slid over her. Wanda had mentioned another grave. How many people had this man murdered? Or did he get his particular twisted satisfaction from burying people alive? Hands trembling, Jenna pulled her legs under her and sat perfectly still. The backpack crowded her, making the small confines under the bush claustrophobic, but she pushed the feeling aside and rested her face on the leaf-covered ground. At least it was dry. This close to the river, the sandy soil held little moisture. She hoped Wanda had remained curled up under the bush safe and sound. The man was twenty yards from Wanda, and if she remained very still, he'd go right past her. A horse whickered, and dread gripped Jenna. The man had turned around and was heading straight for her.

Sweat trickled down Jenna's back as she took deep calming breaths to slow her heartbeat. Kane could do it so easily, but she'd never been able to master the technique. He'd instructed her many times, and she'd wanted to feel time slow and be able to plan her actions a split second ahead like he did in a crisis. *He's getting closer.* Even above the noise of the rushing water, she could hear the man's heavy footfalls. How close was he now? Unable to risk moving, Jenna watched a spider knit a cocoon around a helpless butterfly. Moving back and forth, the spider weaved white silk to wrap the insect in its eternal shroud. The spider was a strange reflection of the man stalking them, as both had captured something beautiful and then inflicted intolerable suffering.

Jenna's blood ran cold as branches swished and twigs cracked as the stranger headed in her direction. Moving in slow motion and holding her breath, she slipped the knife from the sheath at her waist. It was all she had for protection but dug her other hand through the sandy soil and grabbed a handful. Throwing dirt in a person's eyes would slow them down long enough to get away. She didn't intend to stand and fight a man twice her strength determined to kill her. Running and hiding was her only option. Staying alive until help came was the idea. She'd need backup to take down this maniac, that was for darn sure. Breathing through her nose, Jenna trembled. Alone and curled under a bush made her vulnerable. It would be an impossible position to fight anyone, especially someone swinging a baseball bat. Heart pounding in her ears, she peered through the gaps in the branches as the man came so close, she could smell the sweat and blood on him. When he tied his horse to a pine tree, the animal turned his head toward her and blew through its nose. It was a friendly gesture but not one she needed right now.

"Wanda. Get your butt where I can see it right now." The man turned in a slow circle. "I'm over playing games with you. Look, when you fell and cut your head, I thought you'd died—okay? What else was I supposed to do? I couldn't leave you to stink up the place, could I?" He walked a few yards deeper into the forest, stood for a few seconds and then turned back. "You'll die out here. I shot the dog. I didn't know he'd jump on you and knock you down the stairs. It was my bad. He should never have been inside the house." He paced up and down. "I know you're here. When you ran your hair caught on the pine trees and you lost the scrunchie from your ponytail. Come out now and I won't use the manacles again. I promise. You can trust me, right? I've looked after you for four years and I need you to train another girl for me. Think about it. When I'm satisfied, I'll do the same as I did with Della. I'll find your relatives and take you to them." He waved a hand around. "Out here, the bears will eat you or you'll die of starvation. There are no roads or towns for hundreds of miles. Look, I'm going down to the river. You have five minutes and then I'm going back to the cabin."

Jenna recalled with horrific clarity a case where a man had kept children as sex slaves, killing them by mistreatment or if they became too old for his perverted tastes. This man would never return Wanda to her family. She understood how his mind worked. He'd be worried Wanda would tell someone about him and what he was doing. He wouldn't think twice about killing her. To him, she was disposable. He felt nothing for her. She was like the wrapper of a candy bar he'd enjoyed. People like him preyed on young vulnerable kids all over the world and not just in her town. The knowledge that men like this existed made Jenna sick to her stomach. Often girls taken as young children had grown to believe living as a slave was normal. Some were too afraid to leave because their captors had filled their minds with horror stories about outside their prison. She held her breath, hoping that Wanda would remain hidden and not fall into the monster's trap, and then she heard a small sob. The man turned, grinning, and hurried back to his horse. Jenna watched in horror as he slid the baseball bat from the gun holster and turned in the direction of Wanda's sobs. *He's going to kill her.*

Horrified as the man walked past, so close he brushed the bush, making the spider run into the corner of its web, Jenna watched him move through the trees and then she rolled out. Alone against him she had no chance. Wanda was under his spell, but Jenna had an ally and headed toward the horse. The animal was well fed but his head was down with exhaustion. She'd noticed the man hadn't allowed him to drink from the river and dried sweat coated its neck and flanks. "It's okay, boy. I need you to help me. She rubbed the horse's muzzle and untied him. The stirrups' leathers were long, which made it easier for her to mount. She gathered up the reins and headed down the path. Her intent to ride at the man was short-lived. The sickening sound of the baseball bat hitting Wanda's head would stay with her forever. There was no scream, no sound at all apart from the constant crushing sound as it hit home over and over again. Jenna reined up the horse and gaped in horror as the man dragged the unrecognizable body to the edge of the river by her hair and tossed Wanda into the fast-flowing stream. In seconds, she disappeared into the bubbling firmament and was carried away.

Blind panic gripped Jenna and she turned the horse inland and taking the first path she could find, kicked the horse into action. The exhausted mount trotted forward but not fast enough to avoid detection. She urged it on. "Come on, boy, just a little farther and we can double back to the river."

Fear crawled up her spine when a bellow came from behind her. She turned to see the man running toward her bat held high over one shoulder. The tired horse would never outrun him. Jenna squeezed her legs willing the horse to go faster. Behind her the man's voice carried on the wind.

"I see you and you're next."

FOURTEEN

Outside Helena

The rusty old truck sliding in beside the gas pumps almost went unnoticed by Kane until Hudson Driver climbed out from behind the wheel. He kicked Wolfe under the table to get his attention from his laptop. They'd been sitting for hours, eaten enough for ten men, and consumed enough coffee to keep them awake for the next forty-eight hours. "He's here. Old red Ford pickup. He's dressed differently and must have been to the charity store to get that outfit." He tipped his hat down a little more over his eyes. "Coming through the door now. Get ready to leave."

As Wolfe closed his laptop, Kane waited for Driver to walk to the counter and then they slipped out behind him and hustled back to the motel. Wolfe had already disabled the light outside their room and installed a tiny camera in the window to watch the courtyard of the only motel for miles around. They'd spent the entire afternoon watching the parking lot on his laptop. He'd sent Wolfe to check in and they'd taken a room with two single beds. Kane could sleep anywhere but was pleasantly surprised by the room. It smelled fresh, as if it had been aired recently, and didn't have the ashtray or sweat smell he'd come to expect. It was clean with thick towels in the bathroom and had toiletries supplied in tiny plastic bottles. Whoever owned the place had pride in their establishment. They slipped inside and took turns watching the laptop screen for Driver to arrive. It was the only motel in this part of town, so unless Driver planned to spend the night in his truck, this was the place to be. The one thing Kane needed to do the moment Driver went to sleep was to sneak outside to his vehicle and attach a tracking device. They knew where he was going, Kane was sure he'd discovered the correct place for the assassination attempt but they didn't need to be discovered following him. Driver would spot a tail in a second, no matter how good. They'd leave early and make sure they arrived on scene before their target arrived.

It wasn't late but to pass the boring time on a stakeout, Kane and Wolfe took turns sleeping in two-hour shifts. Waking five minutes before his time was up, Kane rolled off the bed and went to the bathroom. He washed his face and headed for the coffee plunger he'd pushed into his bag. They'd be working most of the night. For him snacks and coffee were a must. Although on the morning of a mission he never drank coffee. The adrenaline pumping through his body was all the stimulation he needed. He made the coffee and poured two cups. They had no fixings, but black was better than nothing.

"Here he comes." Wolfe peered at Kane over the top of his laptop. "He's two rooms down from us."

Kane checked his watch. "He spent a long time in the roadhouse. Maybe he had a few calls to make?"

"Maybe, but I doubt it." Wolfe shrugged. "You've all had the same training. He'd go dark the moment he set out and was probably watching for a tail. I'd say he had vehicles placed all along the way to Helena, so he could switch them out at will. Don't be surprised if he changes his ride again before the hit."

The thought had crossed Kane's mind. "Maybe, but the old Ford is a good cover. It would be great to know his location, but we know where he's heading. If he suddenly heads out to Bozeman, we'll know he's swapped out his ride. I'm sure we have the right place. Everything is preset for him and the site is closed for the morning of the speech. It's perfect and the second shooter will be right where I said he would be. If I'd been guarding POTUS, I'd have snipers on buildings two hundred yards from the target, watching for shooters."

"There's been no intel, nothing, not even the slightest suggestion of an assassination attempt." Wolfe sighed and pushed a hand through his hair. "If you hadn't seen Driver, we'd never have known this was going down."

Sipping his coffee and wishing for cream and sugar, Kane narrowed his gaze as he stared at the screen over Wolfe's shoulder. "Lights out. I'll give him an hour and then slip out." He straightened. "Why is POTUS in Helena anyway?"

"I believe it's to visit the fire station. He's talking about government assistance to fight wildfires." Wolfe yawned. "I need a shower." He headed for the bathroom.

Kane filled up with some of the brownies Jenna had made. She did make great brownies and cookies. His mind went to her and his fingers itched to call to see if she was okay. It was different now, being away from home. He missed her and his son. He smiled. *His son.* Tauri would be theirs legally very soon. He had everything in place and had secured the best representation available in family law to make sure everything went smoothly. He understood the regulations and timeframes required to make sure a child was a fit with a family, but all the visits by social services had given glowing reports. Tauri insisted to everyone that he and Jenna were his parents. He'd slipped into their lives like he'd always been there. Nanny Raya was a wonderful woman, kind and giving. How Wolfe had plucked her out of the ether never ceased to amaze him, and then there was Atohi Blackhawk. A dear friend, he'd become the uncle, and his mother, the grandmother Tauri needed. He sighed. One more day and he'd be heading home to his family.

After watching Driver's dark room for almost two hours, Kane set up the tracking device and slipped outside. He aimed a laser pointer at the streetlights, and they blinked out. Silently, he made his way across the courtyard, looking in all directions for any signs of life. He reached the old Ford and dropped down to slap the magnetized tracker under the body above the front wheel. As he went to move away, a door opened. Kane froze on the spot as footsteps came toward him. He dropped down to look under the truck as denim-clad legs with brown boots walked toward him. There was no place to hide. He heard the unmistakable slide of a pistol dropping a round into the chamber as Driver moved toward the back of the Ford. Kane crawled behind the front wheel just as Driver peered under the truck using the same method as he had to look for someone before straightening. Kane eased around the front, keeping low, and kept moving as Driver circled his vehicle. Heart thumping, Kane reached the back and peered under the truck. Driver was standing outside his door staring at the Ford. Cigarette smoke drifted toward Kane and minutes passed by without a sound. Not moving, Kane kept his breathing slow and regular, his attention fixed on the man's feet. A cigarette butt dropped to the ground and Driver squashed it with a twist under his boot. The door to his room opened and then closed. Kane let out a long breath but remained still. Only a fool would move now. Driver would be watching, just like he would, to make sure no one was there. He waited an hour and then moved away in the opposite direction to his room. He circled around the motel, glad to relieve the stiffness in his legs and then made it back. He looked at Wolfe hunched over the laptop. "That was close."

"Too close." Wolfe checked his watch. "We'll rest for two hours and then get the hell out of Dodge." He smiled. "That's when most people set out to go fishing."

Kane smiled. "I'm planning on catching me the one that got away."

FIFTEEN

WEDNESDAY

Black Rock Falls

Distraught, Rio disconnected and stared at the screen of his phone for a long minute. He took a deep breath and stood, making his way to the control center he'd set up to run the search for Jenna. Rowley was organizing another search party and Carter had just walked into the office awaiting orders. He indicated to both of them that he wanted to speak to them alone and led them to the back of the office. "A couple of fishermen found a body washed up on one of the arterial rivers running west. The place is known as Cottonwood Creek." He turned as Blackhawk arrived and waved him over. He explained. "The body is female. It's in bad shape. Someone needs to go and identify and collect it. Anyone hear from Kane or Wolfe yet?"

"Not a word." Carter narrowed his gaze. "I've used every contact I know to track them down and came up empty. What the heck are they doing?"

"I'll go with you." Blackhawk stared at Rio expressionless. "I don't believe Jenna is dead. You need to keep searching for her."

Rio stared at him. "You figure it's a coincidence we found a body in a river when we know she fell in? It has to be her." He dashed a hand through his hair. "I don't like it either, but we must face facts."

"I'd know if she was dead." Blackhawk touched his chest. "In here, and Tauri would know too, and he is fine apart from a bad dream last night. He misses both of them." He looked at Carter. "Tell them they must keep searching."

"Come with me and we'll check out this body." Carter moved a toothpick across his lips. "Do you know this place?"

"I do. It is the first river that branches from the main one and heads west." Blackhawk nodded. "I can show it to you on a map. I figure where they found the body is where the river leaves the forest and runs into a lake. It is grasslands there and good fishing. You'll be able to land the chopper there without a problem."

"Okay." Carter turned to Rio. "I'll need a body bag."

"What's going on?" Emily Wolfe came up behind them. "Body bag? Please don't tell me you've found Jenna's body?"

Concerned, Rio placed an arm around her shoulder. "We don't know for certain but it's not looking good. Carter and Atohi are going to retrieve the body now."

"I'm going too." Emily lifted her chin. "Don't any of you dare tell me I can't go. That's my best friend out there and I'm the only one of you qualified to handle a corpse." She looked at Rio. "You know what we'll need. Go and grab it and I'll inform the morgue to get ready for an arrival." She pulled out her phone.

Rio sighed. He looked at Rowley, who was ashen. "Keep the search going. We won't give up until we have a positive ID. I'll go with Carter. Kane will have my badge if the retrieval isn't witnessed by a deputy."

"Yeah, I'll stay here and keep the search parties going." Rowley gave himself a shake. "I know what you need, Em. I'll go and grab everything from the supply room." He hurried away.

"Okay, I know where to go." Carter turned away from the map on the office wall and used his phone to get the coordinates. "Is everyone ready? My chopper is on the ME's office helipad. I'll take Atohi with me and get the chopper ready. I'll meet you there in ten." He strode out of the office.

Mind running through procedure for body retrieval, Rio collected the forensics kit and body bag from Rowley and followed Emily out the door to his ride. He watched her closely, waiting for the tears to fall, but Emily was professional all the way. He admired that in her, but if this was Jenna's body, he hoped she would allow herself to cry. Holding grief inside wasn't good. On the way to the ME's office, he had no idea what to say to her. The devastation that clutched his heart actually hurt. He couldn't imagine breaking the news to Kane. As third in command, he'd left him as Jenna's backup, and he hadn't been with her when she fell. Would Kane blame him?

"Are you okay?" Emily squeezed his arm. "There's always a fifty-fifty chance it's not her. Hold on to that thought until we see the body."

Loving her positivity, he nodded. "This is going to be tough, whatever the outcome."

"What did the caller say?" Emily turned in her seat to look at him.

Running the conversation through his mind, Rio took a deep breath. "He'd given his details to Maggie and she patched him through to me. I took down the location of the body and asked for some details." He shot her quick glance and his heart sank at her distraught expression. She was trying hard to be professional. "I asked him if he believed the body was the sheriff and he said she was unrecognizable but she had a ponytail the same color as Jenna's hair, she's the same size." He cleared his throat. "She washed up on the bank and the fishermen dragged her onto the sand. I asked what she was wearing and apart from the puffy jacket, it sounds the same: sweater, jeans, and boots."

"That could be anyone." Emily frowned. "I'm wearing the same, so are hundreds of women around town."

They headed for the ME's office and Emily used her swipe card to gain entrance. Rio held open a forensics case as she hurried to collect a few things she'd need for a preliminary examination. "Are you sure you can do this alone?"

"Yeah." She indicated to a light burning over an examination room. "Norrell has taken over for Dad while he's away. She's doing an autopsy for a sudden death of a hospital patient right now but will be done by the time we get back." She gave him a long look. "I'm qualified to collect a body, Zac. I've only two years left on my medical degree before I start residency. I already have a forensic science degree. You need to trust I can do this professionally, even if it is Jenna." She looked around. "It's me or Webber, and right now he's prepping the room for the body."

Rio nodded. "Okay. I'm just considering your well-being, Em. This is Jenna we're talking about. My stomach is in knots thinking about going to collect the body."

"That's a normal response." Emily squeezed his arm. "I feel the same, but we have a job to do and as sure as heck we owe it to her to bring her home with dignity."

They headed up the stairs to the helipad. Rio nodded to Carter and Atohi as they climbed inside. Nothing was said, apart from Carter informing the local flight control of his movements. They headed over the great Black Rock Falls, seeing from above how the many rivers and lakes sprung from the one massive waterfall to spread throughout the county and beyond.

"That one." Atohi pointed to a small river branching off and heading deep into remote forest. "Follow that one, the lake is at the edge of the forest and spreads into the lowlands. You'll be able to land there."

Vast areas of trees spread out beneath them, and later the perimeter of the forest gave way to a glistening lake. A short distance away was a small town Rio hadn't known existed. "What is the name of that place?"

"Cottonwood." Atohi turned to look at him, his voice sounding strange through the headphones. "All along this river cottonwood trees mix with the pines. It's the only place in Black Rock Falls we see them in abundance. Maybe because of the lower altitude." He turned to smile. "Most of the fish you eat at Aunt Betty's come from Cottonwood Lake."

"I'm never eating fish again." Emily shot Rio a glance.

Below, two men stood beside pickups and were waving frantically as Carter put down the chopper. Rio collected their equipment and handed it to the men. A stretcher and the body bag seemed so final it gave him a lump in his throat. He approached the men. "We have all the details, so if you'll wait here, we'll examine the body. How far was it in the water?"

"Only the legs were in the water. We pulled it out only a foot or so." One man wearing a red ball cap frowned. "I didn't see any footprints or anything around the body. There were no other vehicles in the area when we arrived."

Rio nodded and followed the others to the edge of the lake. He steeled himself for the sight, but his legs went weak at seeing the faceless mass of blood and bone before him. The woman was unrecognizable.

"Here, take notes for me." Emily stared at him and thrust her iPad into his hands. She started to list temperatures. "Air temperature goes in the first box, water in the second, and body in the third. Weather is sunny, clear sky, wind is from the north." She bent down and lifted the woman's sweater, and after making a small incision, inserted an instrument to take the temperature of the liver. She gave him the temperature. "Hmm, same as the water. That isn't much help at all to establish time of death, but looking at the rate of decomposition and the skin on her hands, I'd say she's been in the water less than twelve to fifteen hours."

"Jenna was wearing leather gloves when she went into the river, the thin ones she wears to protect her hands." Blackhawk was crouching close to the body. She wouldn't remove them in the river and this poor woman isn't wearing a wedding band. Jenna's ring was a snug fit—I recall her mentioning it—and look, her hands are in fists. She didn't lose the ring in the water and there's no mark she ever wore a ring. This isn't Jenna."

Nodding and hoping he was correct, Rio glanced at Carter. "Do you have an opinion?"

"Not until I see the body." Carter rubbed the back of his neck. "This didn't happen in a fall or due to her ride through the rapids. This is murder. I want to see if there are any defensive wounds for a start." He swung his gaze toward Emily. "You do have Jenna's DNA on file, right?"

"I have no idea." Emily stood and shook her head slowly. "Let's get her back to the morgue." She looked at Rio. "I suggest you keep the search going. I'm not convinced this is Jenna yet either. The problem is we have no teeth to check dental records either. If we haven't a DNA sample, we'll have to wait until Kane returns. No doubt, Jenna has some distinguishing scars or something we're not aware of."

Snapping on gloves and covering his face with a mask, Rio bent to assist Carter roll the body into a body bag and then onto the stretcher. He turned to Emily. "Who is going to tell Kane that Jenna is missing?"

"I'll tell Dad and he'll tell him." Emily removed her gloves and mask. "If he goes nuts, Dad will be able to handle him, both being Marines and all."

"Rather him than me." Carter shook his head. "I'm barely keeping my head on straight. She was like a sister to me."

"And me." Blackhawk looked from one to the other. "Which means we need to find her. This poor woman isn't Jenna. You might need DNA to prove it, but I can still feel her in here. She's alive and likely needs our help. We need to get back to searching, every hour of daylight counts."

"Okay. When we're done here I'll refuel, and you can come with me." Carter looked at Rio. "Is that okay with you?"

Exhausted by the chain of events, Rio nodded. "Yeah. I trust Atohi's instincts. Let's go."

SIXTEEN

Helena

Time seemed to drag but Kane relaxed on the sofa watching Wolfe pace up and down. He prepared himself for missions by moving his normal thought processes into a combat zone. It was a remote feeling but one that kept him focused and his mind safe. His state of calm meant he never suffered PTSD. He could place his missions and any bad memories into boxes in his mind and shut them away. The only time he'd fallen apart was when his wife Annie had been murdered in a car bomb meant for him. He'd dropped his guard with Annie. He'd known being in a dangerous occupation was risky and should never have dragged someone he loved into his world. His heart had ruled his head, and after meeting her on a mission, he'd tried desperately to forget her, but destiny had forced them together. He'd married her, and lost her and the son she carried.

He'd grieved for years, closing down his emotions and not allowing anyone to break through his shell until Jenna. If Annie hadn't been murdered, he'd never have been sent to Black Rock Falls. He'd fought against forming another relationship so hard, but right from the first time he'd met Jenna, there'd been an unbreakable connection between them. One he'd never understand. His love for her held no bounds. She was never out of his thoughts, and even now, as he went to risk his life to save his president, he could almost feel her close to him. He might fall into the zone, become the machine the military had created, but Jenna was always there, just hovering on the edge of his mind. His need to get back to her had become his incentive to get the job done. He rubbed his wedding band, suddenly wanting to see her face and smell her hair. The sudden wave of emotion startled him, and he pushed harder into the zone by taking long deep breaths and slowing his heart rate. When he deployed, he couldn't have anyone with him. In that moment, he'd be alone and in charge of his fate.

"It's time." Wolfe stopped pacing and stood in front of him. "Ready?"

Cool and calm, Kane nodded. "Always." He followed Wolfe from the safe house to the truck.

Wearing a liquid Kevlar vest under his sweater and an M18 pistol in a shoulder holster under a baggy jacket that gave him room to move with ease, Kane left the passenger side door of the truck. He pushed on the helmet and slipped inside the building. All was quiet as he made his way silently through the building and up the stairs. He went past the closet and onto the roof to scan the area for any additional obstacles or building materials left there since his last visit. He mapped out the area in his mind. He found a place to wait before creeping up behind the shooter and estimated the time to neutralize him. He peered across the buildings, making mental calculations. He'd have seconds to take out the second shooter. Sure of his mission, he backtracked and slipped into the closet using the key he'd taken the previous day to lock himself inside. He tapped his earpiece. "Tell me when you have eyes on the second shooter. If he doesn't show, check the second location."

"Copy that." Wolfe sounded calm as usual. *"I have full visual of both positions but not yours."*

Kane smiled. "I hear footsteps. Driver has no idea he's been compromised. Radio silence now."

He could hear Wolfe but replying would be a problem with Driver so close. He would have the same skills as Kane and hearing a pin drop would be one of them. The noise as Driver walked by was louder than expected and Kane frowned. He should be able to move without making a sound, even carrying his sniper rifle. Taking a few deep breaths, he envisaged Driver setting up his rifle, getting the settings right, and then settling in to wait. It wouldn't be long. Snipers didn't wait around. Everything was timed to the last second. The moment the president stepped into his line of vision it would be over.

He unlocked the door opening it a crack and listened. As expected, the wind rustling the plastic coverings was the only sound apart from the crowds gathering way in the distance. He slipped out, moving up the steps, and paused at the entrance to the roof. He took in the location of Driver, his sniper rifle in position and right beside him an unexpected complication. A spotter.

As a highly trained enemy operative, Driver would have satellite surveillance. The moment Kane stepped out onto the roof Driver would know via his handler, but Kane had expected that small complication, but not the spotter. Kane tapped his earpiece and dropped his voice so low only Wolfe could hear him. "Spotter."

"Deploy. Blackout in five, four, three, two, one." Wolfe wasn't pulling the mission for any extra complications.

Shrugging, Kane reevaluated his course of action. His new

plan gave him a very short window of opportunity. Alone now, as Wolfe had just initiated a total blackout of all wireless, satellite feeds, phones, TV, and all modern types of communications, in fact the whole ten yards. It was risky, and one mistake could cause untold repercussions around the world. He, Wolfe, and the six Secret Service agents surrounding the president were carrying old-style walkie-talkies for emergencies. Kane eased out of the door and onto the roof, keeping hidden behind giant air-conditioning units. Both men were involved in the final preparations and waiting for the command to go, which was muted for a few precious seconds, but if Kane failed, there'd be no turning back for Driver. Kane had his orders, but the spotter was a complication he hadn't expected. He took a dime from his pocket and flicked it across the rooftop. It made a hardly perceivable noise, but Driver spun around. With no intel coming from his earpiece, he'd assume all was well.

"It's probably a bird. I'm on target and waiting for the countdown. Go and check." Driver waved the spotter away.

Silently, Kane moved to a different location. As expected, the spotter placed his scope on the table and headed to where he'd tossed the coin. Driver had his back to him, and moving swiftly, Kane ran at him, pulled back his arm, and smashed Driver in the side of the head. The punch would have killed most men, but Driver dropped his hands from the rifle and staggered to his feet, his eyes widened at the sight of Kane. Driver wouldn't have recognized him, but seeing someone else there had surprised him. Driver would believe his handlers were watching over him, and normally it would be impossible for anyone to creep up on him during a mission. The curse from Driver's lips had the spotter running toward them, Kane ducked a punch from Driver and took a step back as the spotter ran at him, knife in hand. He shoved Driver away and the assassin staggered back, tripping over the chair and sprawling on the floor, but he wasn't out and was already getting to his feet.

The spotter ran at Kane and he turned just in time to miss a fatal blow from his knife. As the blade came down way too close, he grabbed the man by the wrist and, bending the knife away, slid one arm around his waist and, using the spotter's momentum, hip-tossed him over the edge of the roof. The man's cries sounded like a seagull swooping down on to a fish. *One down.*

Before he had the time to face Driver, a punch like steel rammed into Kane's exposed ribs. He rocked on his feet, but the Kevlar vest had taken most of the shock and he spun on one foot to land a devastating elbow strike to Driver's throat. In the restricted space, the man couldn't avoid the blow and grabbed his throat gasping for air. Blood bubbled from his mouth, but he wasn't finished yet. Concern flashed across Driver's face and he struggled to straighten and staggered across the roof before turning and aiming a sloppy kick at Kane's head. Kane ducked away and laughed. "You're too slow, old man."

Aware that time was moving at a deadly fast speed and the second shooter would be ordered to deploy as soon as Wolfe lifted the blackout, Kane moved in, ducking and weaving but pushing Driver ever closer to the edge of the roof. Heavy blows rained down from Driver's kicks to his thighs, but Kane kept on his feet, using fists and elbows to take the man down. Driver fought like a deranged grizzly. Shooting him would have been so much easier, but when Driver pulled a knife, Jenna's face flashed into Kane's mind. Enough was enough and time was slipping by like the last grains of sand in an hourglass. He took two steps backward and spun to land a roundhouse kick to the head. The force sent Driver stumbling and the back of his knees hit the unfinished roof surrounds. Kane stared at him. "That's for the president and the USA."

"Ahhhhh!" Driver's arms windmilled and in a strangled cry he toppled backward over the edge to join his friend.

Breathing heavily, Kane pulled out his radio. "Neutralized. Confirm second shooter's position."

"As predicted. Blackout lifted in three minutes. Go!"

Bruised and battered, Kane limped back to Driver's sniper rifle. It was the same as his own and like an old friend. He spun it around and, after making swift adjustments, picked out the second shooter on a roof not fifty yards from his position and too far away to be noticed by the security surrounding the president. Without delay, he checked the wind, took a few deep breaths, and dropped into the zone. He didn't need a countdown and took the shot. He counted the seconds for the bullet to strike the target and then pressed the button on his radio. "Second target neutralized."

The com startled him as the blackout ended and Wolfe's voice boomed in his ear.

"Satellite will be back online in four minutes. Get the heck out of Dodge. Cleanup crew on the way."

Heart thundering, Kane ran, tossing the helmet as he dashed down the stairs. He had no idea who else was involved on the ground or how many terrorists lurked in the shadows, but once the satellite feed came online, he'd be seen and they wouldn't stop until they'd identified him and taken him out. He did not intend to become a target. Not now, not ever again. Blocking out the pain, he took off and sprinted out of the building. He dashed across the road and ran along a side street filled with dumpsters. Seconds later, Wolfe pulled up at the end of the road and Kane fell into the truck, gasping for air. Driving slowly, they headed to a gas station a few blocks away and drove inside a garage. The doors closed behind them and they waited for ten minutes before changing vehicles. As they drove away, Kane leaned back in the seat, allowing the adrenaline to drain away as they headed straight for the airport.

Twenty minutes later, Wolfe's secure phone buzzed, and he glanced at it and tossed it to Kane.

"That will be for you." Wolfe smiled at him. "Be nice."

Kane didn't say a word as the president's voice came through the speaker.

"Thank you. I won't forget your commitment to our country." He chuckled. *"You really are as good as they say."*

Thrilled, Kane smiled at Wolfe. "I'm here to serve, sir."

"I'd prefer to have an asset like you beside me in the White House but I understand your circumstances and having a top-secret black ops team on standby is the edge we need. Carry on, soldier." He disconnected.

Smiling, Kane handed the phone back to Wolfe. "I wasn't expecting a call."

"Well, you're kinda special." Wolfe chuckled.

They dumped the vehicle in the airport parking lot and hotfooted it to the chopper and climbed aboard. As the bird climbed into the air, Kane pulled on his headset and grinned at Wolfe. "Well, that was an interesting mission. Can we go home now?"

"Sure." Wolfe shook his head slowly. *"Interesting huh? Some days you scare the heck out of me, Dave."* He smiled. *"It's just as well you're on our side."*

Suddenly exhausted, Kane yawned. It had been a long couple of days and all he wanted to do was hug Jenna and Tauri. "Always."

SEVENTEEN

Stanton Forest

Numb from remaining in the same position for hours, Jenna listened to the sounds of the forest. Curled up under a bush for the entire night, she hadn't moved even when the sun had risen. Shaken from last night's encounter with a baseball bat-wielding maniac, she'd used the horse to get away, but the poor thing was so exhausted she'd dismounted and slapped it hard on the rump before heading in the opposite direction. It had been almost dark when she rolled herself under the bush and, using her backpack as a pillow, curled up and waited, heart pounding. The man had followed the hoofprints and gone in the opposite direction. He had a cabin somewhere close by, and the horse, given its head, would have likely headed home. She assumed the man would have gone home for the night but would likely be back searching for her at dawn. Leaving the safety of her bush too early might place her in his line of sight.

The forest sounded normal, the birdsong happy and

unthreatened. Her mind went to Tauri waking up at Nanny Raya's and her stomach clenched with worry. She missed him so much and needed to get back to him and Kane. Forcing herself to be strong and keep fighting to get out of the forest, she crawled out and sat in a beam of sunshine, glad her puffy jacket had kept her warm. If it had been winter, she'd have frozen to death within the hour. She checked the contents in her backpack and pulled out an energy bar and a bottle of water. If the man hunting her down lived off the grid, he would still need to go into town for supplies. He managed to abduct women as well, so there must be a road close by his cabin and he'd need a water supply. Jenna shook her head, realizing just how dependent she'd become on her smartphone. Maps and information were no longer at her fingertips, and she tried hard to visualize the map of Black Rock Falls on the office wall. She'd referred to it so many times, and now as much as she tried, she couldn't recall a darn thing. She looked up at the pine trees surrounding her and recalled seeing cottonwoods alongside the river. There was only one place they grew, Cottonwood Creek.

Washing down the energy bar with the water, she stood and stamped the cramps from her legs. Cottonwood Creek led to Cottonwood, a sparsely populated area set around Cottonwood Lake. She brushed the crumbs from her leather gloves and, taking the wrapper and empty bottle with her, swung on her backpack. She stood for a few minutes getting her bearings. It was easy to get lost in the dense forest. The wind in Stanton came down the mountain, so that was north. She stood with the wind at her back and held out her arms. West would take her deeper into the forest; east would take her back to Cottonwood Creek. The sun rose in the east, so she turned toward the sun and, avoiding wider trails, followed narrow animal pathways through the forest. She turned at every sound, checked she'd left no footprints, and eased between obstacles, making sure she'd left no sign of her behind. Thinking about Tauri for the millionth time, sorrow gripped her. Her little boy would think she'd left him. Right now, he had no one. With Dave goodness knows where and on a dangerous mission, would he even know she'd gone missing? Had he returned yet? What would happen when they didn't find a sign of her? They'd be thinking she'd drowned in the river. Finding her body would be a problem over such a vast area of waterways. How long would they search?

Concerns for her family fled at the sound of a horse, and Jenna scanned the forest for a place to hide. Panic had her by the throat as the thundering hooves came closer and she dived into the undergrowth. Suddenly glad the dark brown puffy jacket blended with the rich leaf-covered forest floor, she pulled up her hood and kept her face facing the dirt. The horse went by throwing up clumps of dirt, and heart pounding, Jenna lifted her head to see the murderer's back as he walked along the trail, swishing the baseball bat at bushes as he rode by. She had to keep moving. He could turn and come back at any time. He was retracing his steps upstream to where he'd found Wanda and likely believed she'd be heading back in that direction. He'd have no idea where Jenna had come from and might believe she had a camp close by.

She needed to get to the river. She'd lay out one of her silver blankets as a sign of her position and keep moving downstream. It was her only chance of survival. It would reflect in the sunlight and a chopper pilot would see it and send help in her direction. If only Kane were back, he'd know she'd travel downstream and he'd come and find her. He would be frantic with worry. *I'm okay, Dave, come and find me. Please come.*

She weaved through the forest, avoiding all paths and not stopping until her lungs burned. She gave her head a shake and leaned heavily against a tree. She needed water and a two-minute rest to get her breath back. Gasping, she fumbled for the water bottle in the side of her backpack and took a few sips. She had two bottles left. The river water would need to be boiled. She ran through the contents of her backpack. The brownies were inside an aluminum container, and she had a cup. She could boil the water and let it cool but lighting a fire would alert the murderer with the baseball bat. She had evidence bags. If she could find a safe place to rest, she could put one over a leafy bush and seal it with a bandage. Water vapor would form during the day, but she'd need a whole day for one sip of water.

Hunger gnawed at her belly and she noticed how high the sun had gotten. It would move to the west soon and she'd need to keep it at her back. The river must be close by. She seemed to have been walking for miles. Deciding to rest, she slid down a tree and sat down. She'd just opened her backpack when she heard a sound. She closed the zipper and pulled it over one shoulder. The smell of male sweat came to her on the breeze and fear had her by the throat. *He's found me.* Terror gripped her as she crawled on hands and knees to get away. The crashing sound as the man swung the bat through the bushes made her spring to her feet and run for her life.

Behind her she heard him swearing. He'd seen her. Jenna lifted her knees and sprinted. With each step, bushes clung to her clothes and branches scratched her face. Sobbing with relief as she broke through the trees and onto a sandy path, she ran faster. In the distance she could hear the river. She'd take drowning to being butchered by him and, lungs bursting, increased her speed. As his footsteps gained on her, Jenna broke through the cottonwood trees alongside the river gasping for air. She'd come to a rock plateau and below the river moved swiftly downstream. He was gaining on her and she needed to make a decision: stay and die or risk the rapids. Trembling with fear but determined to survive, she pulled her arms through the backpack handles and buckled the strap behind her. As the maniac broke through the trees swinging the bat and laughing maniacally, Jenna leapt into the water.

EIGHTEEN

Wolfe had dropped over the mountains when a call came through his headset from the control tower at Black Rock Falls airport. He gave his call sign and listened.

"FBI Agent Ty Carter is searching heaven and earth for you. You need to contact him urgently. It's a life-or-death situation, over."

Wolfe frowned. Had something happened to one of his kids? He glanced at Kane. "We'll need to stop in town. Carter is trying to contact me and my phone is in my office."

"Not a problem." Kane smiled. "I'll drop by the office and get a ride home with Jenna. I'll be able to collect Tauri from kindergarten."

As he landed on the helipad, he stared at the FBI chopper. "It looks like he's here already."

"Maybe we have another serial killer in town." Kane frowned and slid from the chopper. "I'm dog tired. That's all I need right now."

Concerned, Wolfe rubbed the back of his neck and followed Kane down the steps and into the morgue. The corridors were empty but a light over an examination room meant a body. He glanced at Kane. "Suit up, Norrell is probably working on a victim in my stead. If Carter is inside, it's a problem."

They pulled on scrubs, gloves, and face masks. Wolfe scanned his card and the door opened. All eyes turned toward them, and Carter ran at them and pushed Kane into the hallway. A scuffle ensued and Kane had Carter against the wall by his throat. Wolfe pushed at Kane's shoulder but couldn't dislodge his hold. "What's going on here." He glared at them. "Y'all gone mad?"

"He didn't want Dave seeing the body." Emily came out the door and it shut behind her. "Dave, look at me."

"What?" Kane turned his head slowly.

"Jenna fell into the river at Bear Peak." Emily's face had drained of color. "We found a body but it's unrecognizable. Norrell is doing a preliminary examination. It's better you don't see, Dave. She has extensive head trauma."

"Jenna? She can swim like a fish." Kane dropped Carter and rubbed a hand down his face. "I know my wife. Let me see the body." He looked at Wolfe. "You have dental records and DNA, right?"

Wolfe shook his head. "Nope, it's not something I'd keep on record for obvious reasons."

"How did she fall into the river? Who was with her watching her back?" Kane shot a glance at Carter. "What's your involvement in this?"

"I've been searching day and night, Dave. Like everyone else." Carter stood toe to toe with him. "She was with Norrell on a grave excavation. Blackhawk was there as a guide. A dry storm hit. Duke ran off with the thunder. Lightning cut a tree in half and it knocked Jenna into the river. We found her weapon and phone but no blood at the scene. We've searched all the places a body would show if she'd gone over the falls. This body washed up at Cottonwood Creek. It's female, same hair color and build. Blackhawk insists it's not Jenna. No wedding ring and he said Jenna was wearing her leather gloves when she went into the river." He rubbed his neck. "That's all I know."

"Get out of my way." Kane pushed past them. "I want to see her—now."

"Please, Dave." Emily barred the door. "For pity's sake, don't go in there. She hasn't got a face. You don't need to remember her like this."

Watching Kane's anger rise to the surface, Wolfe stepped in front of him. "Will you at least allow me to examine her first? I know she has a few scars." He looked at Emily. "Take her belongings to my office." He turned back to Kane. "First look at her things. If you don't recognize any of them, then look at the body. Deal?"

"Okay." Kane dragged off his mask and nodded slowly and then turned to Emily. "Is Tauri okay, and Duke?"

"Yeah, They're fine. Tauri doesn't know she's missing." Emily squeezed his arm. "Be strong. Dad will know if it's her. Give him a little time, okay?"

"Okay." Kane walked a few paces away and then, in a sound like a gunshot, punched a hole in the wall, straightened, and walked into Wolfe's office.

Stomach in knots, Wolfe followed the others back into the examination room. He shook his head in despair at the body before him. She was approximately the same height and weight as Jenna but had so many injuries. Bruising old and recent covered the body. Someone had beaten this woman repeatedly. He lifted her hands and examined both arms. It was evident both forearms were shattered, likely defensive wounds. He rolled the body over and searched for the scar he'd stitched where Jenna had caught herself climbing through wire, only six months previously. It wasn't there. The hair was matted but appeared lighter than Jenna's dark brown. He turned the body back over. "I don't think it's her either. The hair is a different color, and although she's badly bruised, I can't find a recent scar."

He pulled off his gloves and headed for the door. In his office, Kane sat in his office chair, head down staring at an elastic hair tie. Wolfe moved around the desk. "I don't figure it's her. Her hair is a different color and that cut I stitched is missing. The woman in there was beaten over a time. She has old bruising."

"We don't know what happened to her since we left, do we? This clothing is similar to hers. It's hard to tell, seeing as they're soaking wet, but this is Jenna's." Kane lifted his head and held up the hair tie. "See the yellow paint, the stripes? Tauri painted them on a few of her hair ties to make them special. Jenna wore them around her wrist like bracelets." He stood wearily and slid the band onto his wrist. "I need to see the body. Don't try and stop me, Shane. I'm not in full control right now." He stared at him, and his eyes emptied of emotion. "If it is her, someone is going to pay."

Wolfe straightened. "Okay. If it's not, then she is still out there and we need to find her."

NINETEEN

The zone was a place where the outside world vanished. Emotion, fear, and all concern slid away. Kane slid into the zone, his mind concentrating solely on the job at hand. He slowed his racing heartbeat, forbidding his emotions to take control as he followed Wolfe into the examination room. The conversation died and he caught Norrell's concerned expression. Her eyes held a message of compassion he didn't want to hear right now. He straightened and, pulling on a face mask, approached the body. It was naked, the sheet pulled down for the examination. His gaze moved over the bruised and battered woman, her limbs swollen from being submerged in water. The ligature marks on her wrists and ankles were old. He'd known at once it wasn't Jenna, but needed proof for Wolfe and moved to the shattered face. A crime of passion. This killer believed this woman had betrayed him and he'd not wanted anyone else to have her. One ear untouched and perfect stood out stark white against the bloody mess. He looked at Wolfe. "Jenna has pierced ears. This isn't her..." His gaze fell on the hair tie on his wrist and he looked at Norrell. "Was she wearing the hair tie?"

"Yeah. Do you recognize it?" Norrell frowned.

A jolt of emergency hit Kane hard. "Yeah, which means she met Jenna." His gaze moved over the battered body. "She's already been out there alone overnight and with the man who did this. He could be hunting her down or has made her his second victim."

"Cottonwood Lake is where the body was located." Carter walked to his side. "Blackhawk pointed out an arterial river, Cottonwood Creek, which branches away from Black Rock Falls before the falls. You said Jenna is a strong swimmer. She'd know about the falls and this is proof she made it to Cottonwood Creek." He removed his gloves and balled them up. "I searched the riverbank. It is miles long and heads west, winding through Stanton Forest. I figured she'd leave a sign if she was okay."

Ripping off mask and gloves, Kane headed for the door. "Yeah, unless some lunatic was trying to kill her. She'd follow the river downstream. I need to get out there. What's the terrain like?"

"You'd need a horse to head upstream from the lake." Carter was at his side in seconds. "It's remote, dense forest. I didn't see many signs of habitation. I went back and forth many times, Dave. Everyone has been searching, all the townsfolk. The river system here is vast."

Working out a plan, Kane headed for Wolfe's office with Carter and Wolfe at his heels. He looked at Carter. "I'll need you and Blackhawk. Atohi is the best tracker I know, and we'll need Duke. Where is he?"

"Atohi has him." Wolfe frowned and looked at his watch. "It's going to take two hours to organize everything. I'll need to refuel the chopper and Atohi is out somewhere searching. He'll need to get horses to Cottonwood Lake and you'll need to get yours and your gear from the ranch. Think this through. Don't run off half-cocked or you'll be no good to Jenna." He squeezed Kane's shoulder. "Carter has been flying since daybreak, and you've been on your feet for twenty-four hours straight. Head down to Aunt Betty's to make your plans. I'll organize everything y'all need and ask Atohi to meet you at Cottonwood Lake." He took a breath. "Carter can fly you back to the ranch so you can grab your gear and collect the horses and the Beast. Once you're in the forest, I'll get airborne and search the riverbank. If Jenna sees my chopper she'll come out and wave."

Shaking his head, Kane stared at him. "You figure I can just go and eat while Jenna is alone out there in the wilderness with a madman? Think again. I'll walk if I have to, but I'm leaving now."

"You'll be no good to anyone, either of you, if you haven't eaten or prepared for a search that might last days." Wolfe shook his head. "You're not giving Jenna any credit for her survival skills. I know she took a backpack. She was chatting to Blackhawk about having enough brownies and energy bars to feed an army with her and she had water."

Calming his racing heart, Kane nodded. Wolfe was correct and an unplanned mission was suicide. "If she gave assistance to the other woman, maybe she's not injured. She knows how to hide in the forest and how to follow the river downstream. Atohi told us what berries to eat if we ever got turned around." Weariness dragged at him, but he shook it off and looked at the dark rings under Carter's eyes. His friend looked exhausted. "Okay, we'll eat and then head back to the ranch."

"Okay." Wolfe smiled. "I'll have everything you need loaded into Carter's chopper by the time you return." He looked at Kane. "We'll find her."

Glad he wasn't alone on this seemingly impossible mission, Kane nodded. "Yeah, then we'll hunt down the man who butchered that poor woman. I'm sure looking forward to meeting him."

TWENTY

Stanton Forest

Anger shivered through him as he watched the woman bob away on a rush of water. She could identify him but the chances of her making it through the rapids downstream would be remote. Although with two women's bodies showing up in the lake in the same week, he'd likely have the sheriff nosing around. He wiped sweat-soaked hands on his denim jacket and stared at the sky. Maybe it was time for him to move on, but he didn't want to leave his cabin. It was a safe place and nobody bothered him. Anyone wandering by would assume it was deserted. He liked it that way and kept only the essentials inside so he could pack a bag and disappear whenever the fancy took him.

He'd often left for a week or so, leaving Wanda behind. He taken the odd job while he hunted for someone suitable to bring home. She'd had food and water and her chain allowed her to move around the cabin but not leave it. He'd come back once or twice to find she'd tried to escape. That was against the rules and he'd punish her but then she'd try the next time he'd leave and he'd punish her again. She'd cry and forget to do her chores and he'd slap her around some. He figured she enjoyed being punished as much as he enjoyed hitting her because she was always doing something stupid.

It had become worse than having a wife and he'd grown tired of Wanda. In the last three months or so, he'd found other women to bring to the cabin. Wanda didn't like the other women sharing his bed, but he'd never intended on keeping them for long. Maybe it was because he made her sleep on the floor? She'd look at him with her disgusted expression as if he'd made her jealous, and then mutter under her breath, so he'd killed them in front of her. He found it highly amusing to watch the expression on her face as he squeezed the life out of them, or caved in their heads with the baseball bat, all the while telling her it was her fault for being jealous.

He'd tried keeping two women long term, but he liked them young, and the young ones didn't last long, or they became mindless robots. When that happened, he dug a new grave and went out to buy another girl. For those first few years, Wanda had been perfect. She'd been hard to tame but a few knocks to the head soon put that right. He smiled to himself. He'd had her for years, but once he'd seen Naomi, Wanda looked old and unattractive. He'd decided Wanda had reached her sell-by date and dug the grave. He'd given her what he'd thought was a quick death, one swing with the shovel and she'd stopped breathing. He'd covered her staring eyes with a box and then buried her. No one was more surprised than him to see the grave sunken when he returned. Finding it empty, he'd panicked. Wanda knew everything about him. He smiled at the memory of pushing her bloody body into the river. There could be no doubt she was dead this time.

He'd go get Naomi. Being away from the forest now would

be for the best and by the time he returned, the investigation would be over. So what if two women fell into the river? It wouldn't even make the news. He'd already tossed the dog into the river and finished cleaning out the cabin. The canned goods he'd moved to the root cellar. Anything else he needed he'd collect later from town. He smiled to himself as he mounted his horse. The time he'd spent selecting Naomi had been well spent. She was young and would last him a few years. It would take him less than an hour to be packed and be on his way, leaving no trace behind. He turned the horse back in the direction of the cabin, moving west away from the river. He rode deeper and deeper into the forest where not a soul would find him.

TWENTY-ONE

Ice-cold water ran up her nose and chilled her burning flesh with a shock that made her gasp. Jenna wrapped her arms around her backpack as the strong current pulled her into the middle of the fast-flowing river. It would have been exhilarating if she didn't have to fight for each breath. The white water breached over her head, sending her into a blinding rush of white bubbles. Lungs bursting, she popped up like a cork bobbing along out of control. It was like being on a gigantic slide and slipping down at a reckless speed without being able to see the end. Faster and faster the banks flashed by as the river carried her, twisting its way through the forest. Logs and other debris smashed into her as they dashed past. Panic gripped her as large boulders loomed up ahead. At this speed, hitting one of them would knock her senseless. She tried to judge the direction of the waterflow around them and swam right, kicking and trying to reach the slipstream. The boulder came up so fast her shoulder brushed it as the flow rocketed her through a narrow gap. Boulders meant white water ahead. A place where people loved to go white-water rafting, but they had a raft. She'd be shredded against the rocks.

A left-hand turn was ahead. If she could make it to the bank, she'd be on the sandy side of the river. The opposite side was sheer rock. She'd traveled at least a mile, maybe two, and would be far away from the man hunting her down. Time to make a decision was running out. She kicked hard and then let out a shriek as the water swept her around the bend and down a short narrow section of rapids. Standing in the white water was a grizzly and she was heading straight for it. Unable to stop her momentum, panic gripped her as she rushed toward it, but its attention was thankfully centered on the river. It calmly scooped up a fish, and a second later, it turned its back to carry it in its teeth to a cub on the riverbank. A moment later, the river rushed Jenna past. As her knees and hips bashed against rocks, she cried out in pain and then choked as she dropped suddenly and water filled her mouth.

Caught again in the swirling river as it became deeper and faster, she traveled another half mile. Numb from cold, Jenna picked out another bend ahead. This time, she'd make it or die. Pushing away the pain, she kicked her legs and swam as hard as possible. She made it out of the main tugging current but pushed on to reach the edge. Exhausted, she gave it one last effort and cried out with joy as her feet hit the sandy bottom of the river. "Come on, Jenna. You can do this. Never give up."

Two more steps and she rose out of the water. The backpack and her sodden clothes had become like lead weights as she took one unsteady step and then another toward the bank. Water poured from her clothes as she stepped onto the sand. Totally spent, she fell to her knees and rolled onto her back gasping for breath. The sky above her seemed incredibly blue, but it blurred in and out of focus. So cold, she'd stopped shivering and her numb limbs refused to respond. She just wanted to sleep and lie on the sand with the water lapping at her ankles for some time. *I'm going into shock. Move or die, Jenna.*

Pain and cold hit her with intensity as she lifted her feet

from the water. Hips and knees, bruised from hitting the rocks, screamed with the slightest movement. No longer immersed in freezing water, the numbing effect was wearing off. Common sense told her to move, but her body refused to cooperate. She closed her eyes and Kane's face drifted across her mind. She'd seen his expression when she'd come close to dying. He'd never recover from another tragedy, and then there was Tauri. She'd taken him into her heart with a promise to protect and love him forever. She had to get up.

Rolling onto bruised knees, she unbuckled the backpack. It had saved her life again and she praised God that Kane had insisted on buying waterproof survival kits. She pulled it open and dragged out a silver blanket. Moving stiffly, she spread it out on the riverbank and secured it with rocks. Someone might see it from a chopper and send a rescue party. Getting mobile had been difficult and her teeth chattered incessantly. She scanned the riverbank. It was wide and set away from the perimeter of the forest. The sand was dry and a horseshoe ring of boulders like an ancient artifact in the sand would offer a welcome windbreak. She staggered toward them and dropped her backpack. Weariness dragged at her, but she needed to build a fire and willed her cold legs to move. It took every last ounce of strength to collect driftwood from the shoreline. It was dry and in good-sized pieces. She had found enough to make a fire that would burn all night. After digging a fire hole in the sand, she used some of the toilet paper from her backpack as kindling to start a fire.

The shivering had become so bad she clenched her jaw. She needed to get warm before she died of exposure, and once the wood was well ablaze, she stripped off. After wringing out her clothes, she hung them around the fire on the boulders. Cold wind whipped her damp flesh and she pulled out her woolen sweater from her backpack and, shivering, pulled it over her head. At least she had one dry piece of clothing. She placed one silver blanket on the sand and wrapped herself in another and then hugged the fire. Right now, everything else could wait, she needed to get warm. Exhausted, she added more wood to the fire. It was well alight now. The bigger logs glowed and gave out a ton of welcome heat. Her hair dripped over the outside of the silver blanket, but she didn't care. Totally drained, she rested her head against the rock and closed her eyes. *I'll move again in five minutes.*

TWENTY-TWO

Black Rock Falls

Kane had to admit Wolfe was right. After eating and downing three cups of coffee each, he and Carter both felt human again. The comforting grandma's-kitchen aromas and atmosphere of Aunt Betty's Café soothed his shattered nerves. It was the normal he needed to center his thoughts, and he tempered the raging need to find Jenna urging him to move faster. Organizing a successful mission took time and he couldn't abandon a life-time of training and act like a fool. He'd be no good to her on foot without the necessities to survive. While Wolfe was orga-nizing everything, he walked to the kindergarten. The need to see his little boy was overwhelming. When he walked inside and Tauri noticed him, the little boy's smile warmed his heart. He took him to a quiet corner and crouched down to look at him. "I'm back but Mommy is in the forest. I need to go and find her."

"Okay." Tauri frowned. "Uncle Atohi will go with you. He knows the forest. He told me the spirits guide him."

Nodding, Kane smiled. "He will be with me and Uncle Ty as well. Will you be okay with Nanny Raya if it takes a day or so?"

"I missed Mommy when she didn't come get me last night." Tauri's face crumpled and he leaned into him. "And I missed you too, but Mommy said she'd come get me. Uncle Atohi said she was stuck in the forest and couldn't get home."

Heart aching, Kane held him close. "I'm going to find her now. It might take some time. She lost her phone and we don't know where she is right now, but don't worry. I'll be back as soon as I can."

"I'll be okay. When I'm sad, Nanny Raya tells me stories. When you're away, I feel you in here." Tauri touched his chest. "Last night I had bad dreams about Mommy, and Nanny Raya sang to me. She's nice to me but I want to go home." His bottom lip quivered. "Duke was sad too. Uncle Atohi took him."

Inside Kane's heart was breaking. If something had happened to Jenna, how could he tell Tauri? What would happen with the adoption? Would he lose both of them in the same week? The agony of not knowing was a physical pain and he wanted so much to make it better for Tauri. He stood and swung his little boy into his arms. "You will, very soon, I promise. What happened last night with both of us missing shouldn't happen again. You know we're cops and have to hunt down the bad men. Sometimes, I have to go and help Mommy, but we'll be back soon and I'll come and get you and we'll go home."

"Okay." Tauri rested his head on Kane's shoulder.

Wanting to give Tauri reassurance, Kane set him on his feet and removed the brown Stetson, he'd been wearing for the mission. "Can you take care of my hat?" He dropped it on the little boy's head and grinned when it covered his face.

"Silly Daddy." Tauri lifted it off laughing. "I'll keep it safe."

Kane bent and hugged him and pressed a kiss to his cheek. "We'll be back soon and we'll come get you and take you home, even if it's in the middle of the night." He ruffled the little boy's black and gold hair and sighed. He needed to leave on a positive note. "Atohi has been talking about getting you a pony. Do you figure you're big enough to ride alone?"

"Yes, I'm big and strong just like you." Tauri beamed at him, his eyes dancing.

Nodding, Kane dragged himself away. "You are indeed. I need to go find Mommy now. I'll see you soon." He watched Tauri go back to his group, showing everyone the hat and then headed for the door.

He went back to the ME's office to help Carter pack the chopper and they headed to the ranch. Kane had showered in four minutes and dressed for a long hike in the forest. With camping gear, changes of clothes, and one set for Jenna, they had all the necessities for a prolonged trek, including the water-purification tablets Wolfe had insisted they take. They'd pack everything on the back of Wolfe's daughter's pony, who lived at the ranch with Jenna's mare, Seagull, and Kane's stallion, Warrior. After they loaded the horses into the trailer and climbed into the Beast, Kane looked at Carter. "Okay, where exactly is Cottonwood Lake? I don't ever recall visiting there in all the time I've lived in Black Rock Falls."

"Western end of Stanton Forest. I have the coordinates." Carter tossed a toothpick into his mouth and then indicated over one shoulder with his thumb. "We have enough equipment with us to go off the grid for a month. Why so much gear?"

Kane shrugged. He figured it was obvious. "I'm planning on staying out until I find Jenna. You can leave at any time."

"Nope. I'm with you all the way." Carter shrugged. "If she's out there, we'll find her."

Half an hour later, they arrived at Cottonwood Lake and on the edge of the forest Atohi waited in his truck, with his horse trailer attached. Kane pulled up beside him and climbed out, turning to Carter. "Is this where they found the body?"

"Yeah." Carter indicated with his chin toward the river. "Washed down from the creek. It's a long creek, meanders throughout the forest and must be over one hundred miles long. It won't be easy locating Jenna, when we know she fell into the river at Bear Peak."

Barking broke the silence as Blackhawk climbed from his truck and Duke burst out of the door. Kane bent to greet the wiggling dancing dog intent on licking him all over. "So, you missed me then? Where's Jenna? Seek Jenna, Duke."

The dog moved around in circles and then sat down. Kane rubbed his ears. "When we're close, you'll find her."

"I spoke to Rio just before." Blackhawk moved to Kane's side. "Rowley and a team are heading out from the other end of the river. There is access higher up the mountain, but the deeper west the river travels the denser it becomes. There are a few fire roads but not many. That area is isolated. He has six men with him and supplies for a week or so." He glanced at Carter. "I have a fine mount for you to ride. His name is Moon Dancer." He grinned. "Dave said you rode well."

"I was born in the saddle." Carter gave him a long considering stare. "I appreciate you trusting me with him."

Kane walked to the back of the trailer to unload the horses. Within minutes they were on their way, setting out through a mess of cottonwood trees and deeper into the pine forest. Blackhawk led the way, keeping as close as possible to the water's edge. When Carter came up beside him, he turned to him. "What's puzzling me is, apart from what Jenna dropped at the scene when she fell, nothing else belonging to her has surfaced. This seems strange to me." He raised his voice so Blackhawk could hear him. "Do you recall what Jenna was wearing?"

"Yeah, jeans, boots, and a sweater under a brown puffy jack-et." Blackhawk turned in his saddle to look at him. "She'd left her hat in the truck, and she was carrying a backpack. One of those survival ones you purchased last year. It looked full. She had it on her back when she went into the water."

Suddenly positive, Kane nodded. "Good, they can be used as flotation devices and they're waterproof. They have a double interior to keep everything dry. She'd at least have Zippo lighters, survival blankets, and a first aid kit. Knowing Jenna, she'd pack the kitchen sink, especially as she was out with Norrell and her team."

"She hasn't left a sign along the riverbank. We've all been looking for smoke. She knows to light a fire alongside the river." Carter frowned. "That would tell me she can't for some reason. If she did meet that woman and encounter the man who murdered her, she wouldn't want to advertise the fact she was around, would she?" He cleared his throat. "How is she at stealth?"

The idea Jenna was in danger hadn't left Kane since recognizing the hair tie. "The one thing about Jenna is she's smart. She knows how to hide and survive. If the woman's killer took on both of them, we'd have found two bodies. From the damage to the body, we have to assume this guy is strong. To survive out here he'd need to be self-sufficient. This makes me believe Jenna found the woman and helped her. She discovered her story, and if the man was hunting down the Jane Doe, he wouldn't know about Jenna. In danger and unarmed, she'd hide. She'd move down river, and when she believed she was safe, then she'd leave a marker on the edge of the river."

They'd ridden at least three miles when Kane's satellite phone buzzed. It was Rio. "Kane, what have you got for me?"

"Wolfe sent coordinates. He's spotted what looks like a silver survival blanket on the side of the river." Rio sounded optimistic. *"About fifteen miles from Cottonwood Lake. I'll send you the coordinates. There was no sign of Jenna. The wind gusts are strong in that area. If she'd started a fire, he doubts he'd have seen*

the smoke. The light is fading, so he's returning to base. I've contacted Rowley. They're on their way back. Like you said, she'd be traveling in your direction."

Heart thundering, Kane cleared his throat. "Okay, we'll check it out. I'll report in when we get there." He disconnected and informed the others. "Go, we have a positive sighting. She can't be far away." He urged Warrior forward along a narrow track with Duke bounding out in front. "We'll keep to the riverbank. We must find her before nightfall."

TWENTY-THREE

After riding for another hour and finding nothing, Kane pulled Warrior to a halt beside the river and dismounted. He paced up and down as Warrior drank his fill from the river with Duke at his side. He didn't want to exhaust Duke or he'd be carrying him across his saddle. He stared into the forest, but there was no sign of life, just endless pine trees growing so close together there was no room to pass by. The cottonwoods, the only trees along the riverbank, seemed unusual and out of place against the pine forest behind them. Tiredness dragged at him. He'd been awake for over twenty-four hours and needed to conserve his energy. He sat down on a boulder and removed his backpack. "I want to keep going but it's getting dark, and the horses need a rest. Duke is dead on his feet."

"I figure we have two hours before dark." Blackhawk looked at the sky. "It will be a full moon tonight and we have flashlights. We can travel a good distance in that time, even if you need to carry Duke." He pulled a huge Thermos from his saddlebags and handed it to Kane with cups. "My mother insisted we bring coffee. She knows you well."

Setting down the cups and pouring the coffee, Kane smiled.

"She does indeed. Wolfe has packed military-type rations and I've a ton of cookies and energy bars, so we won't go hungry."

"I brought energy bars, as well as chocolate and dog food." Carter shrugged out of his backpack. "I know I left Zorro at the ranch, but he'd never keep up with the horses in the forest. I figured Duke would appreciate it." He tossed Kane a small bag of dog food. "I have six of those packs."

Glad of the company and thoughtfulness of his friends, Kane nodded. "Thanks. I'm glad you both came along. It's good to have company out here. I haven't seen a hiking trail or a cabin since we walked into the forest. It's like going back in time. I'm waiting for a dinosaur to come crashing through the trees at any minute." He tore open the bag of dog food and set it down for Duke. "We'll take a fifteen-minute break and then push on until nightfall." He rubbed his chin. "This winding river is so frustrating. She could be just around the next bend and we wouldn't be able to see her."

"Duke would know she was there." Blackhawk opened an energy bar. "He'll find her." He took a bite, chewed, and then sipped his coffee.

Kane leaned back against a boulder. "When we get closer to the coordinates, I'll call out. If she's being hunted down by the killer, she'll be hiding somewhere." He sipped his coffee and sighed. "I know her so well. She'll be able to hide and can remain motionless for a long time. I just hope she still has her backpack."

"I'm sure she wouldn't risk taking it off." Blackhawk shrugged. "If she used one of the silver blankets as a signal, she must have it with her. I figure for now she's safe or she wouldn't have risked giving away her position."

Shaking his head, Kane slowly unwrapped an energy bar. "She is in trouble just being here but she knows the team would put choppers in the air to search for her, so laid that foil blanket out regardless. I know her. Then she'd hightail it downstream.

We've discussed getting turned around in the forest. Leave a marker and head downstream. If she can move safely, she'll be heading toward us."

"I figure when we've found Jenna, we'll need to hunt down the killer of Jane Doe without delay." Carter leaned back against a rock and stared at the darkening sky. "If Jenna witnessed a murder, she'll be in danger until we catch him. He could be anywhere in this wilderness. From what I could see from the victim, that girl was restrained and for a long time. He might have taken her as a kid. You know what those guys are like, right?"

Flashes of past cases filled Kane's mind. "Vividly. It's happening all over. Wolfe was telling me about a case over in Rattlesnake Creek. One of the missing girls ended up in San Francisco. They found others in a brothel. They didn't find out who was involved. The girl was murdered and tossed in the bay."

"There are many ways to track a man, Dave." Blackhawk's brow furrowed. "If he was anywhere near Jenna, we can use that as a starting point. Rest assured, we'll find him sooner or later."

"That's one weird place." Carter met Kane's gaze with a frown. "Rattlesnake Creek. I recently met the FBI team there. Dax Styles has been there for a time and he has a new partner, Beth Katz from DC. Man, they are complete opposites. He is a hands-on justice kind of guy and she is used to working alone. Good agent and she gets the job done, although by looking at her you'd never think it."

Raising both eyebrows at the locker talk, Kane shook his head. "What do you mean by that? Has your filter slipped again?"

"Ha, no, I wasn't being derogatory or sexist." Carter tossed a toothpick into his mouth. "She's a babe and is city slick, not country, if you get my meaning. That's not sexist, it's the truth.

It's like placing a piece of fine china in the Triple Z Bar." He chuckled. "The thing is, Styles tells me she excels at just about everything and doesn't need him around for protection, that's for darn sure."

"Don't tell me you've finally found someone you like?" Blackhawk grinned at him.

"Okay, yeah, I find her attractive but she's way out of my league. Beth Katz is someone to admire but I can't figure for the life of me why she ended up working with Dax Styles." Carter shrugged.

Groaning, Kane shook his head. "You always want what you can't have, Ty. How did you meet her?"

"They've been having the wildest cases and called us in for Jo's appraisal on a serial killer's profile." Carter drained his cup and stood. He sniffed the air. "I smell smoke. The wind is coming from the north."

It was the first positive sign since they'd stepped into the forest. Kane leapt to his feet and stuffed things back into his backpack. "Let's go."

TWENTY-FOUR

Something touched Jenna's face and she woke in panic slapping at her cheek but found nothing. She stared at the fire. It was almost out and she scrabbled around, grabbing up pieces of dried wood and poking them in to the smoldering embers. How long had she slept? She looked at the darkening sky and shivered. The sun had slid down and sat under the horizon. The north wind was cold at night and her feet were turning blue. Why hadn't she heard a chopper? Had everyone given up on her already? Kane would never give up. Was he home yet? Was he even alive? If he was still on a mission, no one could contact him. She'd just have to survive until he found her or she walked out of the forest. Trying to be optimistic, she grabbed her clothes. The heat from the fire had done its job, and apart from a few damp patches on her jeans and puffy jacket, the rest had dried. She'd placed her boots upside down on sticks beside the fire and the leather was stiff and misshapen. Dragging them on she wiggled her toes. They'd be the first things she'd replace when she found her way out of here.

Keeping positive, she dressed fully aware of her bruised and battered body. Her stiffened joints ached and just sitting hurt.

She tried stretching and gasped in pain. Her hip was bruised black and she had grazes all over. One kneecap was swollen to twice its size and she could hardly get her jeans on over it. She rummaged through her backpack for the first aid box and found some Tylenol. Next, she'd need something to eat and drink. Kane's voice drifted into her thoughts, almost as if he were standing right beside her. *If ever you're in trouble, eat when you can to keep up your strength. You never know what might happen next.*

"What is happening next? I'm lost. No one seems to give a darn. You're AWOL." Jenna ground her teeth. "I don't want to die out here."

There was his voice again. Had she lost her mind? *Keep moving downstream. Towns are built on rivers. Look for roads.*

It was too late to continue her trip along the riverbank and after seeing the grizzly she had no idea if there were more in the area. The place was so remote they could be anywhere. She'd rarely seen one in Stanton but had seen the evidence they'd been around, and carrying food would attract them. Although she'd packed everything inside containers, it wasn't worth the risk. She ate the brownies and sipped water. Mindful the water wouldn't last long, she pushed painfully to her feet and went to the riverbank, filled the aluminum container with water, and set it to boil on the hot embers on the edge of the firepit. Once boiled, it would soon cool down and she'd store it in the empty water bottles. Mind racing to find a solution to her problems, she sat watching the water boil, and then using a long stick, eased it from the embers. The sounds of the forest became louder as if making ready for nightfall. If she hadn't been alone, it would have been relaxing, but the strange sounds sent her heart racing.

Dark shadows crossed the firepit as if the trees were closing in around her, almost sneaking up to swallow her alive. In a rush of desperation, fear gripped Jenna. The approaching darkness was suffocating. Memories flooded in, making her relive the last few hours in such clarity she trembled. A young woman had died almost in front of her and she hadn't been able to save her. She hadn't seen what had happened, but she'd heard it and seen the aftermath. A sob escaped her lips and she swallowed it down. She wanted to run and find a way out of this maze, but the idea of encountering the maniac again terrified her. What if he'd seen the smoke from her fire? It wouldn't take a man on horseback long to travel a few miles.

Just how far had the river swept her along? Two miles? Five miles? It was impossible to judge. The river flowed so fast and wound around so many bends she had no idea how far she'd traveled since jumping into the river. She'd gone under the water when she jumped and not surfaced until her lungs had hurt. Swept along in the bubbling firmament, there had been no up or down. When she'd surfaced, the river had snaked its way through the forest. Maybe the killer had figured she'd drowned? If not, surely with the smell of the fire, he'd have found her asleep and caved in her head just like Wanda? So many questions spun around inside her head, Jenna rubbed her temples, unsure of her next move.

The hairs on the back of her neck prickled at the sound of horses moving through the forest. She pushed the precious tin of water toward the bushes and covered it with the lid, hiding it under dried leaves, next she pushed sand over the fire using the mound she'd dug out earlier. She strapped on her backpack and disappeared into the bushes alongside the riverbank. Crawling into the dense vegetation, she wrapped her arms around her knees and, teeth chattering with fear, waited. Had the maniac returned with his friends? Heart thumping, she peered through the bushes into the shadows as two riders went by. She could hear them clearly and they were two Native Americans speaking in their own language. Part of her wanted to call out for help but what if these men were friends of the murderer?

Paralyzed with indecision and fear, she waited for them to pass. Sitting until ants decided on her as their next meal, she crawled back to her camp and using a stick uncovered the fire and added more wood. The one thing about being in a forest, there was no lack of fuel for the fire, and keeping the firepit alongside the river meant she wouldn't start a wildfire if the wind changed direction. Suddenly cold, she untied the puffy jacket from around her waist and pulled it on. Looking around, she found her leather gloves pushed into a pocket on her backpack and, although stiff, they'd protected her hands and would again. She stared into the approaching darkness and watched the full moon climb into the sky. "Where are you, Dave?"

TWENTY-FIVE

Moving at a steady pace toward the smell of fire, Kane had carried Duke for a time, but from the constant wiggling, it was obvious the dog had had enough. He pulled to a halt and dismounted, placing Duke on the ground. Without warning Warrior whinnied and the horses in front of him danced sideways and snorted. Seagull, Jenna's mount, was rearing and twisting in the air. Her reins were looped over the front of Kane's saddle and only snatching hold of Warrior's bridle prevented him taking off. "What the heck is wrong with you?" He looked around. "Is it a bear or a wildcat?"

"Someone is coming." Blackhawk stood in his stirrups and stared ahead. "Two men on horseback. They're riding mustangs. One is likely a stallion. Warrior has his mares around him, he is defending his territory."

Mounting, Kane patted Warrior's neck. "Settle down, good boy." He looked at Blackhawk. "Maybe I should go first. This looks like the only trail along the riverbank." He looked at Carter. "All good?"

"Yeah, I'm riding a mare." Carter smiled at him. "That

horse of yours is well named. He's ready to fight all the darn time."

Hearing the approaching men's conversation, Kane understood it fine. He'd picked up seven or so languages in his lifetime and the local Native American tongue was one of them. He held up a hand in greeting. "It is good to see others in the forest. You are the first people we've seen all day."

"Same. Not many come here to fish and hunt, but everything is plentiful at this time of the year." One of the men smiled. "Are you lost?"

"No, not lost." Blackhawk moved up beside Kane. "We're searching for a woman who fell into the creek. Have you seen anyone?"

"A man on horseback riding west about five miles back." The man shrugged. "No woman but someone lit a fire about one mile back and there was a silver blanket spread out on the riverbank. We assumed it belonged to the man." He edged his horse past. "I hope you find her."

Under him, Warrior snorted and danced sideways, tossing his head. Kane reined him in and waited for the men to pass. He stared after them. "Jenna must be close by, maybe only another mile away. We must keep going."

"The way is clear along the riverbank in the moonlight." Carter shrugged. "We search for the foil blanket and if she's not around, then we rest up for the night. She must be here somewhere. If she laid it out, she must be mobile."

Urging Warrior along the moonlit trail, Kane scanned ahead, hoping for one small sign. He cupped his hands. "Jenna, call out. It's Dave. Jenna."

He kept calling every five minutes as they moved through the forest. They rounded the bend and ahead the moonlight reflected on a silver strip on the sandy shore. "Jenna, where are you? It's Dave. Call out."

"I'm here, Dave." Jenna's voice came on the wind. "I'm here."

Duke barked and took off faster than Kane had ever seen him move. He tossed Seagull's reins to Carter and urged Warrior forward and then he saw her, standing in the moonlight waving. Duke got to her first and almost knocked her over in his enthusiasm at seeing her. Kane jumped from his horse and ran to her, scooping her up in his arms and holding her close. "Oh, thank God. I've found you."

"There's a man. He wants to kill me." Jenna was sobbing into his shoulder and holding him so tightly, as if she never wanted to let go. "I knew you'd come find me. I was so scared."

Overwhelmed by emotion, Kane buried his face in her hair. "Did he kill a woman and toss her into the river? We found a body in Cottonwood Lake."

"Yeah. Her name was Wanda." Jenna's tears glistened in the moonlight. "She's been his prisoner for four years. He buried her alive, and when she escaped, he hunted her down and murdered her. I couldn't do a thing to stop him." She trembled in his arms. "Then he came after. I saw him, Dave, and he knows it. I couldn't pick him out in a lineup, but I have a general description to go on. I'm going to find that monster and put him away forever."

Anger rippled through him when Jenna winced at his touch. She'd been injured but hadn't said a word. He smoothed her hair. "We'll find him together. Did he hurt you?"

"No but he chased me down and I had to jump into the river to get away from him. I went down the rapids and got banged up. I'm stiff, is all, and thirsty. I boiled water but it's too hot to drink right now." Jenna looked over his shoulder. "Oh, there's Carter and Atohi. Thank goodness. I don't want to get lost again. This forest is terrifying enough without a killer on the loose."

As Carter and Blackhawk kept a discreet distance away and unsaddled the horses, Kane soothed Jenna with soft words. Holding her close until she stopped trembling and then reluctantly he let go and led her to a boulder beside the fire. "Sit down and keep warm. It's too late to return tonight and the horses need to rest. We'll set up a camp. We have tents and I've brought a change of clothes for you. I'll take a look at your injuries and then we'll eat." He removed his backpack, took off his jacket, and wrapped it around her legs. "It's going to be okay. We'll catch the killer. You're safe now. I won't let him near you."

"Tauri will be so worried." Jenna burst into tears. "I promised him I'd always be there for him."

Concerned, Kane crouched down in front of her and took her hands. "Tauri is fine. I spoke to him before I left and explained everything. You'll see him first thing in the morning. He can miss kindergarten for one day." He pulled a pack of tissues from his backpack and handed them to her. "We need a day to recover. The team can cope for one day without you and start hunting down the killer.

"Okay, no arguments from me. How did the trip go?" Jenna gave him a meaningful glance.

"It went well but I've been awake for a long time." Kane smiled at her. "So, one hundred pushups right now might be a problem."

"Hey, Jenna." Carter dropped saddlebags close by. "Good to see you. You had us worried there for a while. It's just as well Wolfe spotted the foil blanket on the riverbank, or we'd never have found you. Good thinking." He headed back to the horses.

"Ah there you are, Jenna." Blackhawk dropped bags beside the fire and in seconds was filling a cup with coffee and adding the fixings. "My mother insisted she send along two Thermoses of coffee. I even have a jar of instant in case we need it." He handed her a cup. "Tauri sends his love. He feels you in his heart as do I. We are family."

"Thank you." Jenna squeezed his arm. "Did anyone find my phone or my weapon?"

"Yeah." Carter dropped tents onto the ground. "They're back at the office. We'll set up the camp and get the food cooking." He glanced at Kane. "Maybe someone should call it in? People are still out searching."

Reluctant to leave Jenna, Kane sat on the boulder beside her. "I'll do it." Bone weary, he pulled out his phone and called Wolfe. "We found her. She's okay but a bit banged up. We'll camp out tonight and come back at daybreak." He hadn't placed the phone on speaker just in case Wolfe needed to speak to him privately. "I'll call Rio next and tell him to call off the search and get some rest."

"How bad is she?" Wolfe's footsteps sounded on a tiled floor.

Kane chuckled. "Yeah, she went into the river twice to avoid the killer. She's right beside me in front of a fire."

"She's probably in shock and it might not set in immediately. Y'all need to watch her closely. Any major injuries? Is she lucid, crying, or rambling?"

Trying to keep the conversation light and not cause Jenna any more concern, Kane cleared his throat. "Nothing is evident as yet. I'd say, yes, yes, and a little. It's all been very confusing. The forest is very dense here. She witnessed the murder, so we have some idea what the suspect looks like at least, but we'll leave that to the team for now. I want her to rest up tomorrow."

"Okay. I'll drop by around noon. If she gets worse or you suspect internal bleeding, take her to the hospital. Get some sleep." Wolfe disconnected.

It surprised Kane to find Rio and Rowley still at the office when he called. This time he placed the call on speaker. "We found her. She's okay. There's a killer roaming the forest. I'll get a description over to you first thing in the morning. Rio, call off the search and send out a press release. Go and get some rest.

We'll be at home tomorrow, so I'll need you to start an investigation. First up, visit the stores in Cottonwood Creek and ask them if they have any regulars. Men who live off the grid in the forest. See what you can find out about them."

"He's about six foot, forty-five to sixty, long beard with white in it, long dark hair over his collar. He rides a bay gelding with one white sock." Jenna leaned in closer. "This man is dangerous. Don't chase him down without backup. That's an order." She looked at Kane and tears filled her eyes. "Thank you for searching for me."

"We wouldn't have given up." Rowley's voice came through the speaker.

"The town was all out searching. I've never seen anything like it." Rio chuckled. *"They'll be so pleased you're okay."*

Kane smiled at Jenna. "Be sure to thank everyone in that press release. I need to make camp. We'll rest up for a few hours and then head home at daybreak. Catch you later." He disconnected.

"The townsfolk are all good people." Jenna smiled through the tears. "I thought you'd given up on me. Time goes so slow here and the first night was terrifying. I saw a grizzly fishing in the river yesterday. I was in the river at the time. You know, she caught a fish and when I went by, she didn't give me a second glance."

"It probably thought it was too much trouble unwrapping you." Carter grinned around a toothpick. "Tents are up. You really should allow Kane to check your injuries. Atohi's mom has sent along a meal we can heat over the fire. It will be ready soon, so don't take too long."

"Okay." Jenna smiled at him. "Thanks. I appreciate you."

"My pleasure, ma'am." Carter touched his hat.

TWENTY-SIX

Waking up at night gave Naomi King the creeps. She peered into the shadows expecting someone to jump out and murder her. Unable to sleep, she'd lain awake for hours. She hated the foster home. The man they expected her to call Daddy kept looking at her. He followed her around with his phone taking her picture. She'd asked the other kids about him, but the two girls younger than her just shrugged. One of them sucked her thumb. Nobody liked it there. When she'd asked for the key to her bedroom door, "Daddy" told her the lock was there so she didn't run away, not to stop people from going inside. Footsteps creaked the floorboards and the door handle turned. Terrified, she lay very still. Someone was there, close by. The smell of sweat crawled across the room and the sound of heavy breathing reached her. Had "Daddy" come in to stare at her again? If she didn't move, he'd leave soon.

The sheet twitched and the hairs on Naomi's body stood to attention. Her heart pounded in her chest as the tatty sheet covering her slid from her body. A hot hand touched her leg and horrified she opened her mouth to scream. Tape slammed down on her lips crushing them against her teeth and dragged up by the hair, she stared into the shadowed outline of a man. She tried to scream as he wrapped the tape around her head but only a gurgle left her throat. Fighting back was impossible. He was so strong and tossed her around as if she weighed nothing.

Naomi kicked and punched his head but in seconds the tape was around both hands and then both ankles. She couldn't fight back when he wrapped her in a sheet, and as he tossed her over one shoulder, the breath rushed from her lungs. Sobbing with fear, she bucked trying desperately to get free when she heard the sound of "Daddy's" voice.

"This man here is your husband. He owns you now." He chuckled. "You always said you wanted to be married and out of foster care, so now you have your wish." He slapped her on the rear like a horse. "Don't think about trying to escape and going to the cops. They'll just take you back. You belong to him now. Do what he says and you'll be just fine. Disobey him and you'll get a whipping."

Trembling as she caught his amused expression, as he followed the man holding her to his vehicle, she blinked as her old backpack was tossed into the back seat. Dumped in after it and covered by a rough blanket, Naomi smelled the stink of dog and mold. The two men walked away and talked for a time before the door opened and closed. The vehicle was old and creaked and groaned as it started. Where was he taking her? What was happening? The truck rumbled along, weaving through streets and then along a straight highway for an hour or so. It was dark inside the cab and the driver had the tunes on the radio turned up to full volume. The next moment they took a sharp left and bounced along what could only be a dirt road. The music stopped and after a time the truck slowed and the engine died with a hiss of steam. She peered at the dark windows, seeing a forest lit by a waning moon. The man hadn't said a word to her the entire time. Had he gone to so much trouble just to take her into the forest to kill her?

The door opened and the man got out. He was gone for some time and the cold evening air seeped through the sheet, raising goosebumps on her flesh. She rolled onto her back and lifted her legs to unwrap the sheet. Then she kicked at the door willing it to open. The next moment it flung open and he stood there staring at her. She gurgled through the gag and shook her head but he only laughed at her.

"Your daddy said you had a brain." The man stared at her. "You do chores and cook. Is that right?"

Too afraid to move, Naomi nodded. At twelve-years-old, she'd learned to survive long ago. It had been four years since she first went into foster care, knowing no one would ever come for her. This wasn't foster care. This was different.

"I had a few girls to choose from and I took you." The man pulled her toward him by her feet and then stood her up. "I'd hoped to have someone to help train you to be a good wife, but she's gone now. She went into the forest and the grizzlies ate her. You don't want that now, do you?"

Shaking her head, Naomi trembled. She couldn't escape, she could hardly move. He wanted her to be his wife? She wasn't old enough to be married and she wouldn't marry someone like him—not ever.

"Good and you get a new name today too." He bent and stared into her eyes. "Your name is Grace and you'll call me 'husband.'" He picked her up and tossed her over one shoulder.

She heard a horse and tried to cry out in protest when he threw her over the rump and tied her securely before mounting and riding into the forest. The blood rushed to her head and after some time winding through the forest, nausea gripped Naomi. She swallowed hard. If she spewed now, she'd choke to death. The smell of smoke drifted toward her as they came to a clearing. Not far away she made out light pouring from the window of a cabin. The horse stopped walking and the man dismounted. He cut the tape from her ankles, dragged her from the horse, and dropped her to her feet. She staggered and then cried out as the tape was ripped from her mouth and hair. He took her to a line of disturbed ground, and horror gripped her as she realized the mounds were graves.

"See these graves, Grace?" Husband's hand went around the back of her neck and he pushed her head down to look at them. "This is where I buried all my wives. Do everything I say or I'll beat you, and if you ever try to run away, I'll dig one for you."

TWENTY-SEVEN

THURSDAY

Walking back from the stables in the brilliant sunshine, Deputy Jake Rowley smiled as he headed inside his ranch house. His twins ran to greet him as if he'd been away for a month instead of half an hour. He scooped one onto each hip and carried them to the kitchen. "I figure it's time for breakfast."

He dropped them into booster chairs at the table and turned to kiss his wife, Sandy, on the cheek. "I'm so glad they found Jenna. I was starting to believe she was gone forever. How she survived in that river after the rain we've had is a miracle. Not once but twice. When Dave called last night, he said she jumped back into the river to avoid the killer. It was just as well she had her backpack. Those new survival packs are essential."

"I hope she's staying home today to recover. Emily called me last night and mentioned Jenna had gotten banged up going down the rapids. She said her hip was black and her knee really bad. It will be worse this morning. Although they do have a hot tub. That would help some." Sandy looked over one shoulder. "Wash up. Breakfast will be in five. Will you be hunting down the killer of that poor woman you found in Cottonwood Lake today?"

Nodding, Rowley went to the sink to wash his hands. He'd fed the dog and checked out the water level in the horse trough in the corral. His two horses were just fine grazing on the lush green summer grass. "Yeah, we'll be looking for suspects. Jenna will be back tomorrow. Nothing will keep her away from the office for long. I figure they both want to spend some time with Tauri today." He rubbed his chin. "The court date for the adoption is coming up soon. I don't figure there'll be a problem. Jenna and Dave impressed the judge when they asked to adopt Tauri."

"Tauri is very happy with them. It's as if he belongs to them." Sandy smiled. "I'm so pleased for them. They deserve to be happy." She placed loaded plates on the table and looked at the twins. "There you go. No throwing food all over, okay?"

Rowley buttered his toast. "Where do you think Kane and Wolfe disappeared to? Have you ever seen Kane unshaven? He looked like they'd been on a two-day bender when we met up with them last night." He sighed. "He was different and snapped out orders. Something happened they're not telling us about."

"Jenna said they were going to a conference in Helena." Sandy bit into a slice of toast. "Probably forensics or something. You know Dave is into that kind of thing."

Sipping his cup of coffee, Rowley shook his head slowly. "Don't say anything, but some time ago I overheard Kane talking to Wolfe about someone called Annie. He was talking about Tauri. He said that Tauri was his only connection to Annie left on this earth."

"What did Wolfe say?" Sandy leaned forward with an interested expression.

Not wanting to gossip, but Rowley knew his wife would never repeat anything they discussed, he met her gaze. "Wolfe said it was time he put Annie to rest and that Jenna was his wife now."

"What?" Sandy stared at him, her mouth open and eyes wide with surprise. "You think that Tauri is really his son from an ex-wife?"

Shrugging, Rowley stared at her. "Tauri is big like Kane. He's four, and it's five years since Kane arrived here. We always wondered why he took so long to get involved with Jenna. If he already had a wife, it would complicate matters." He sighed. "Perhaps Annie was a Native American. Kane speaks Black-hawk's language fluently and I've lived here all my life and I'm ashamed to say I know only a few phrases. There are so many different Native American languages in Montana."

"Well, it's none of our business, is it?" Sandy stood and collected the plates. "I just hope Jenna knows, especially if Tauri is Kane's blood. I'm just surprised they haven't told us about Annie. I mean, who really cares if Dave was married before?" She pressed both hands on the table and stared at him. "Forget what you heard. If Jenna is ignorant of the facts, it could break up their marriage. It's not our place to tell her. I'm sure Dave will in his own good time."

Rowley drained his cup and stood. "My lips are sealed." He kissed the twins on the head, avoiding the egg-covered cheeks, and grabbed his hat. "I have no idea when I'll be home." He swung Sandy around and kissed her. "I'll call you later." He headed for the door.

After Rowley dropped by the office to collect Rio, they headed to Cottonwood Lake. It was a spectacular lake, set in the lowlands with views to the mountains. The wide expanse of water reflected the brilliant blue sky. A few boats sat lazily in the water, way out in the middle with men fishing. It called to Rowley and he sighed, wishing he could bring his boat down to the boat ramp and spend the day thinking in peace and quiet. That's what he aimed for and any fish he caught were a bonus, but it was the time alone he enjoyed the most. As he drove along the access road, he noticed a few fishing huts beneath the cottonwood trees. They looked deserted and were likely used for weekends and maybe vacations. The town consisted of a few stores, a fish bait and tackle store, a diner, a general store with gas pumps outside, and a saloon with rooms to rent. Ranch houses dotted the lowlands and only six or so were lakeside. He glanced at Rio. "Well, we'll get this done in under an hour."

"It's a close-knit town, tread easy." Rio yawned and blinked as if warding off tiredness. "Don't mention the body in the lake unless they bring it up, then say nothing. Maybe say it was an accident, something like that. I don't want to spook them."

Shaking his head, Rowley grinned. "I have done this before, like a million times. I have an advantage because I was born and raised here. You still sound like an outsider." He pulled up outside the general store. "Anyone living off the grid would drop by here. They'd need ammo and basic supplies. They might trade for goods as well."

"Trade what?" Rio shrugged. "They can't trade meat or skins. What else is out there in the forest?"

Rowley indicated to a display of "forest fresh gooseberries." "Those for instance, mushrooms, other berries. Firewood, pine cones. Some make things they can sell. Furniture comes to mind. It is a pine forest and anyone can remove the dead trees." He walked up to the counter. "Morning."

"What can I do for you, Deputies?" A gray-haired middle-age man wearing a brown leather apron peered at him over the top of his glasses.

"We're looking for a man, maybe forty-five to sixty, long beard, messy dark hair who rides a bay horse with one white sock." Rio leaned casually against the counter. "He lives in the forest and we need to locate him."

"I don't take much notice of horses, Deputy." The man grinned. "They don't usually come inside my store." He scratched his substantial belly. "Hmm, the man you're describing could be any one of the three men who come by once in a while. They all have tabs with me. I sell some of the things they bring in and we trade goods." He smiled. "We do get tourists, believe it or not."

Rowley nodded. Had they found three suspects in one hit? "When did you see any of them last?"

"Recently." The man indicated to the gooseberries. "They came in yesterday and I have a ton of firewood out back. They come by in summer. It's the best time to sell. I don't see them in winter at all. They must hole up in their cabins or caves, wherever they live out there." He waved toward the forest. "If you're asking for an address, I don't know, apart from a general idea of the direction they live."

"That's very helpful." Rio looked ready to leave. "So anywhere in the forest?"

"Like I said, they don't have an address." The man frowned at him.

Rowley exchanged a glance with Rio. "Ah, are any of them married, or live with a woman do you know? I mean do they ever come in with a woman or buy feminine products?"

"Maybe they do and maybe they don't." The man frowned. "It's none of my business what they do in their own homes. None of my business or yours."

Rowley cleared his throat and tried again. "I know but we have a young woman's safety in mind. Her family is concerned about her. Can you at least give us the names of the three men you've mentioned?"

"Well, if a young woman is in trouble, I guess it's my civic duty." The man pulled a book from under the counter. "I don't hold with computers. Everything is in this book." He flipped through the pages. "Here you go: Elias Miller, Josiah Washington, and Christopher Grant. One thing I can tell you, Josiah likes to take a drink. I don't figure I've ever seen him sober. Maybe he's up in the hills making moonshine."

After making a note of the information, Rowley smiled at the man. "This is a great place. Is the fishing good?"

"The best." The man smiled at him. "Maybe we'll see you back. This lake is addictive. Real fishermen can't get enough of it. Come back and bring your friends."

Rowley chuckled. "I sure will." He headed for the door.

"Where to now?" Rio stared along the sidewalk.

Considering the possibilities, Rowley stopped walking and turned to him. "It's a safe haven. We never come here, and if the body hadn't been found in the lake, we'd have never given the place a second thought. It's perfect for anyone living off the grid. I don't believe they'd earn enough trading for essentials. Living off the land is one thing, but people need things, like coffee, and maybe bread or flour and sugar. They'd need food to see them over winter. They must have an income of some type." He looked at the bait store.

In the window was a sign advertising fishing trips and boats for charter. Rowley pointed to the sign. "Look at that, these businesses wouldn't have that many staff, so they must use outsiders to run fishing charters for the tourists."

"It's a long shot but we can ask." Rio headed inside and went straight to the counter.

The bait store sold everything from fishing rods, hooks and flies to rifles and ammunition. Items of every description littered the shelves. Mounted antlers sat in a row in graduated sizes. A brown bear's head, mouth wide open and eyes glowing, stared down at them from above the counter. The store had a strange smell, musky with a hint of fish. The floor was scrubbed clean, the wooden floorboards worn down from many years of boots. It was like stepping back in time and Rowley shook his head in wonder. It was just like the stores his grandpa used to tell him about when he was a kid. He followed Rio to the counter, surprised to see a man of his own age come out from the back. He was fair haired with a bright smile. "Morning. Your boat charter for fishing trips—do you do that yourself or does someone in town run that side of things?"

"I don't have the time to run the charters, but we do own the boats." The man scratched his cheek. "It was my pa's business. My mom used to run the store and he'd take out the tourists, but he's retired now and I don't have anyone to run the store. It's not overly busy. We have three boats out now. Two of them are locals and go out alone. One is a man who comes down regular once or twice a month in the warmer weather. He takes the fishing tour package. He has someone to take out the boat and we supply all the gear. They get lunch and drinks supplied. We have a few regulars from Black Rock Falls, especially at this time of the year."

"So would Elias Miller, Josiah Washington, or Christopher Grant be involved?" Rio stared at the man.

"Elias takes out the boats sometimes for me. Grant too on occasion, but he's hard to contact." The man frowned. "Why, is there a problem with their permits or something?"

Rowley smiled. He couldn't believe his luck. "Is one of them out on the lake now?"

"Nope." The man frowned. "I couldn't contact Elias and got one of the local fishermen to take the job. It pays well. Tourists usually have money to burn."

"How do you contact Elias and Grant?" Rio rested one hand on his pistol and stood shoulders back and feet apart.

"CB radio." The man shrugged. "They're off the grid. No phones. They must have generators because they come into town for fuel. They buy a ton of batteries as well and water purifying filters."

"Do many people this way have CB radios?" Rio's gaze moved to the back room.

"Oh, yeah." The man indicated behind him. "We have one

CB out back and I have one in my truck. Many of the townsfolk have them in these parts. It's faster to get help if needed."

"Can you give us their call signs?" Rio smiled. "We need to contact them. Do you know where they live?"

"West of Cottonwood Creek is what they told me. There are a few small creeks that run through the backcountry and they'd need a water supply." The man shrugged and gave them the information. "I figure they've built cabins out there somewhere. I'm not aware if they know each other. They don't say much when they drop by. I guess, being alone out there, they lose the art of conversation."

Rowley nodded. "Okay, thanks for your help." He led the way out of the door and headed for the cruiser. "I figure these three are prime suspects. Let's get back to the office and run their names and see what we come up with."

"Let's hope they're using their real names." Rio climbed into Rowley's cruiser.

Starting the engine, Rowley sighed. "Yeah, but they'd need ID to get a fishing permit. Finding them is going to be the problem. They could be living in cabins but might be underground. There are plenty of survivalists out this way who live in bunkers."

"It just gets better by the second, but I'm just glad we'll have something to give Jenna in the morning. Kane was very specific with his orders." Rio buckled up. "He was acting strange. Most of the time, he's so in control he's almost emotionless but when it comes to Jenna's safety, he changes. Emily said he tossed Carter against a wall at the morgue as if he weighed nothing and held him there by his throat. When he's like that, I'd rather face a grizzly."

TWENTY-EIGHT

"Mommy." Tauri's voice came through Jenna's dream and when he pushed open one of her eyelids, the little boy's face came into blurry view. "Are you in there?"

"Yeah, sweetheart, I'm here." Jenna slipped one arm around the sturdy body and hugged him. "What's wrong?"

"Where's Daddy and how come I'm here?" Tauri's brow wrinkled and his eagle-colored eyes drifted to the other side of the bed. "Duke's gone too. I looked everywhere for him. Has Daddy gone away again?"

Muscles stiff and sore, Jenna sat up slowly and pulled him onto the bed beside her. "No. Daddy is probably doing his chores and we dropped by Nanny Raya's to get you. Daddy carried you out to the truck. You were sound asleep. We thought you'd like to wake up in your own bed. It was very early when we came home, so we all decided to get some more sleep."

"What happened to you?" Tauri pointed to her grazed and bruised arms. "Did you fall over?"

Smiling Jenna shook her head. She'd give him the edited version of the truth. "Well, not exactly. I was in the forest by the river. Lightning struck a tree and it fell down. One of the branches pushed me into the river. I hurt myself on the rocks but I'm fine. I'm a great swimmer." Suddenly realizing how little she actually knew about Tauri's life, she looked at him. "Can you swim?"

"Not in the river, it moves too fast." Uncle Atohi said that I need to swim like a fish before I go into the river. You must swim like a fish."

Footsteps on the polished floor and the sound of Duke's unmistakable bounding came from the hallway. "There's Daddy and Duke."

"Daddy." Tauri jumped from the bed and ran at Kane wrapping his arms around his legs. He looked up at him. "Mommy fell in the river. Will you teach me how to swim like a fish?"

"Yeah, and ride a horse." Kane grinned down at him. "When you're bigger, I'll teach you how to shoot straight." He rubbed his chin. "You'll be helping me and Uncle Shane build the Harley for Uncle Ty, won't you?"

"I want to ride one too." Tauri followed Kane into the bathroom. "Will you build me one for when I'm big like you?"

"We'll build it together." Kane chuckled. "I'll wash my hands and you go and get dressed. We're staying home today."

"Good." Tauri said something in his own language and then grinned before scampering away.

"Okay." Kane grinned after him as he came out of the bathroom.

Jenna stared at him. "Are you teaching him his native language? Atohi said he doesn't understand it." She pushed hair from her eyes. "They all speak English as well. Is there a point to it?"

"Yeah, I'm teaching him and so is Nanny Raya." Kane bent to kiss her. "I know they all speak English on the res, but they speak their own tongue as well. When he visits there, I want him to fit in. It's part of his culture. He shouldn't be denied the chance to learn it because we're raising him." He pushed Jenna's hair behind one ear. "You should learn as much as you can as well."

Sighing Jenna nodded. "I know a few words but I'm not like you. When you hear a different language, you pick it up in days; for me, three years of Spanish and I still have difficulty getting out a sentence. My brain is set on English. What did he say to you before?"

"Hotcakes." Kane grinned. "That's what he wants for breakfast." He looked her over and sighed. "You look like you came off a bicycle at the Trans Am Bike Race and slid along the blacktop."

Staring at him and shaking her head, Jenna smiled. "You say the nicest things, Dave. You are sooooo romantic." She glanced at the clock and gasped. "It's eleven and we haven't fed Tauri yet. I figured it was eight at the latest. Why didn't you wake me?"

"Both of you were tuckered out, and letting you sleep was the best thing to do." Kane chuckled. "You need to be flexible with kids. They don't cope well when they're tired. A routine is fine, but I listen to Wolfe. He gives very sound advice."

Jenna slid out of bed and headed for the shower. "So what have you been doing?"

"I checked the horses. It was a hard ride yesterday, but they all look fine." He leaned on the bathroom door. "I cleaned the tack, and then restocked the emergency packs."

Jenna showered fast. The water stung her cuts and bruises. The hot tub the previous night had helped some, but she was black and blue. She stepped out, wrapping a towel around her. "Rio and Rowley should be out at Cottonwood Creek. I hope they find a few leads."

"I'm sure they're hunting down names at least." Kane took the first aid kit from the bathroom shelf. "You'll need the grazes on your back tended. I'll fix them up and then go and get breakfast. It's going to be more like brunch. I'll make extra bacon." He sighed and went to work, dabbing antiseptic on her back. "We'll all be hungry again by two. Maybe we'll have dinner at seven. That should work out just fine."

Jenna stared at him over one shoulder, trying not to wince at the discomfort. "We should go into the office. I can't find Wanda's killer by sitting at home."

"We have nothing to go on, Jenna, and what we do have is being handled by some very competent people." Kane met her gaze in the mirror's reflection. "Carter was gone when I went out this morning, so he's on the job as well. We both need to rest and Tauri needs us right now. He's been the one most affected by both of us missing, so let's make it a nice day and worry about how the team is doing in the morning."

Thinking about Wanda and what she knew about her, Jenna nodded. "Okay, fine, but I need to make one call to Carter. I know Wanda's name, her age, and where she came from. Someone must have reported her missing. Carter can follow up on that for us."

"Okay, one call." Kane looked down at Jenna's bruised hip and winced. "Wolfe is dropping by today to take a look at you. I'm surprised you can walk. Your hip, knees, elbows, and back are all bruised and grazed. Take the day, Jenna. You're not superhuman."

Raising both eyebrows, Jenna looked at him. "Oh, darn, and I figured I was someone special."

TWENTY-NINE

FRIDAY

"You should take Wolfe's advice and stay home for another day." Kane turned the Beast onto Main. "You're not okay and I'm capable of handling the office, Jenna."

The last thing Jenna had wanted was to get out of bed, but she had responsibilities and all of her deputies had made it to work injured at one time or another. Rowley still hadn't fully recovered some six months after being shot by a crossbow bolt. He never said a word and did his job, but she'd seen him rubbing his arm to ease the discomfort. Being the sheriff meant she had to be titanium. She glanced at Kane and sighed. "I know you're concerned about me, but everything is manageable with a couple of Tylenol. You work with your headaches, right? I'm needed in the office right now. I'm also the only person who can identify Wanda."

"No, you can't." Kane's face was grim. "Trust me, her own mother wouldn't recognize her. I doubt Wolfe will allow you to see the body."

Annoyed, Jenna shook her head. "You both need to stop protecting me. I'm the sheriff and I need to see the victim. It's protocol. I'm the last person to have seen her alive, Dave. I owe it to her to at least give her a name."

"She hasn't got a face, okay?" Kane shot her a glance. "They figured it was you. I had to identify your body. Yeah, that bad. If you can recall what she was wearing, you can ID her clothes."

Glad that they'd already dropped by the kindergarten with Tauri, Jenna turned in her seat to stare at him. "I gathered that but, yes, I'd recognize her clothes and boots. I also would recognize the restraint marks on her wrists. I figure she was chained up, but when I spoke to her she couldn't recall anything more than four years previously. She had a nasty cut on her forehead, and I believe he hit her so hard he figured she was dead and buried her alive." She chewed on her fingers recalling the blood-drenched filthy woman. "She was suffering memory loss and believed she was fourteen. The recent head injury must have caused the amnesia. We worked out she'd been chained up in his cabin for four years." She punched the seat. "In my county. This happened under my watch, Dave. We didn't even know Wanda was missing. I need to put this right and catch this monster."

"Okay, okay." Kane stopped outside the sheriff's office and squeezed her arm. "We'll find him. This time, we at least have a description and a general area of where he lives. It's sketchy but it's a start." He unclenched her fist and kissed her knuckles. "We've had less to go on and solved the case. The other thing, Jenna: Crimes that happen in this county are never your fault. You can't beat yourself up every time something happens to a kid. We have no control over other people's behavior."

Nodding, Jenna straightened her shoulders, ready to start another day. "I'm not going into the office yet. Take me to the morgue. I'm the only person who can say if this is the woman I met in the forest. I need to see the body and the personal effects. Tell Wolfe to cover the head if needs be, but this is my job and I intend to do it."

"Okay." Kane backed out the Beast onto Main and headed to the medical examiner's office. "I'll ask him to cover the head. It would be for the best."

Calming her churning stomach, Jenna stood in the sunshine outside the ME's office for a few seconds, inhaling deep breaths. The summer day was crisp but promised sunshine and blue skies. She turned to look at the mountains. The view was a perpetual beauty and just looking at the vast forest and snow-capped peaks calmed her. Apart from the seasonal changes, it remained the same. Absorbing its wild untamed beauty, she closed her eyes. Serenity surrounded her as the ancient rock formations and the endless forests shared their peace with her, as if she'd always meant to live there and become part of it. She opened her eyes and turned to Kane. "I so love the forest and the mountains, but I was scared out there alone. It seemed so surreal, but now, looking at the view, I feel so peaceful, regenerated. Do you know what I mean?"

"I do." Kane tucked her under one arm and pulled her against his side. He stared into the distance. "It's not the forest that will harm you, Jenna. Atohi's people have lived in harmony with the land for thousands of years." He sighed. "Unfortunately, it's also a great place to hide from the law. It seems there's always someone wanting to spoil the peace but that's why we're here." He squeezed her. "I figure everything has a reason for being here." He looked at her. "Ready to go now? Duke is waiting outside the door. He knows Wolfe will have a bowl of doggy treats in his office."

Jenna smiled. "He spoils him. Why doesn't he get a dog?"

"He figures he doesn't have the time to care for one." Kane pushed open the door and walked through the foyer. He swiped his card to gain access to the morgue. "We didn't call ahead. I guess we try the office first."

Following Kane and Duke along the hallway, Jenna shivered at the sudden drop in temperature. The smell of the morgue crawled up her nostrils. It was as if the smell of death had seeped into the white tiles and oozed out with every step closer to the examination rooms. Wolfe kept the building spotlessly clean, with air filtration systems, endless amounts of disinfectants, but nothing would stop the rancid stink of decaying flesh. Wolfe was very particular about not taking the smell of his work home with him. When he came to visit the ranch, he took great care with his appearance and never once had she smelled the morgue on him, and yet she could pick out the local workers from the meat-processing plant by their odor at five yards. The door to Wolfe's office opened and he poked his head out. Jenna smiled at him. "You're a hard man to sneak up on, Shane."

"You'd need to be a ghost to get by the buzzer on the door and the CCTV camera." Wolfe waved them into his office. "What are y'all doing here at this time of the morning? You feeling poorly, Jenna?"

Jenna shook her head. "I'm doing okay. I came to see the personal effects and the body of the Jane Doe. If I recognize her, she'll have a name and we can start hunting down her relatives." She gave him a direct stare. "I know about the head injuries, but I'll be able to tell if the restraint marks are the same. I did spend a few hours with her." She drew a deep breath. "One thing, during the autopsy please look for any other head trauma, or broken bones and injuries that she might have sustained over a four-year period. From what she told me, I believe she's been a prisoner for four years but has no memory of how she got there."

"She's dead, Jenna." Wolfe exchanged a concerned look with Kane. "If she was a prisoner and beaten, I'll know. The head trauma was the cause of death, and it would most certainly account for her memory loss."

Jenna shook her head trying to dislodge the frightened woman's face from her mind, realizing she'd been speaking as if the woman were still alive and she'd seen her murdered. "It's okay, I'm not losing my mind. I know she's dead. I watched her killer toss her into the river." She stared at him. "Can we get this over with, Shane? I really need to get the investigation under way."

"Sure, sure. Give me five minutes. I'll ask Emily to get the personal effects for you." Wolfe headed for the door. "Maybe you should sit down. Take your time looking over her things and help yourself to coffee."

THIRTY

Jenna stared after Wolfe and sighed. The thought of seeing Wanda's practically headless body made her anxious but identifying her was a crucial part of the investigation. Only she could identify her right now, and until she could find a relative to collect DNA she had no choice. She needed to move on with the case.

"Hey." Kane pulled her close. "You're acting a little stressed. Are you sure you don't need more time? There's nothing wrong with taking a couple of personal days after going through such an ordeal."

Defiant, Jenna shook her head. "I'm fine. It's just everything seems to be moving so slowly. Not doing anything yesterday was like pulling teeth. All I could think about was if that terrible man was torturing another young woman." She sat down and blew out a sigh. "Did I insist you rest after spending the last few days killing people and then heading out to search for me? How long had it been since you'd slept?"

"It's different." Kane shook his head. "I wasn't injured, just tired. Okay, I admit I went a little crazy when they told me they thought you were in the morgue, but I can function on very little sleep. You went through a traumatic near-death experience twice, witnessed a murder, and then were in fear of your life."

Jenna watched him go to the coffee machine. "How many people did you kill and how dangerous was your mission?"

"That's classified and you should know not to ask, Jenna." Kane's shoulders dropped.

Recalling a news bulletin, Jenna stared at his back. "Oh, I've figured it out. You were involved with taking down the people who attempted to assassinate POTUS. It was you who took out the shooters. It wasn't the Secret Service like they said on the news, was it?" She jumped to her feet. "It was a dirty job, life-threatening, but someone had to do it, right? You took down the three of them singlehanded, didn't you?"

Kane said nothing, just added the fixings to two cups of coffee and turned and placed them on the table.

Unable to believe he wouldn't confide in her, she glared at him. "Dave, I have clearance and you know I would never compromise you."

"You have already by suggesting I was involved. It's just as well this office is bug free, Jenna. All you need to know is any missions I go on are classified." Kane met her eyes over the rim of his cup. "I keep you safe by not telling you details, Jenna. You knew when we married that I could be called into action at any time. If I was in black ops, it would be the same. We don't discuss our missions. Apart from the fact that phones and other devices could be listening in, the idea of you being captured and tortured for what you know isn't gonna happen."

Nerves on edge, Jenna met his gaze. "Did you tell Annie everything? Your real name, for instance, and what you did for POTUS?"

"No, she understood the term *classified* just fine." He stood and walked out the door with Duke on his heels.

Biting her bottom lip, Jenna took some deep breaths. The

last few days had been terrifying and she shouldn't have taken it out on Kane. A few moments later, Emily walked into the office carrying a pile of evidence bags and dropped them on the desk. "Thanks, Em."

"What's up with Dave?" Emily glanced over her shoulder. "Is he still angry?"

Confused, Jenna stood and peered at the bags. "What do you mean by 'still angry'?"

"Oh, he was scary angry when he came in to see the body of Jane Doe." Emily looked at her. "The body from the lake?"

Jenna nodded. "Yeah, I know who she is, but why was he angry? He never gets angry."

"Well, he sure does now." Emily spread out the evidence bags and then looked up at her. "The body is a mess. The head trauma is extensive, leaving the features unrecognizable. She's your size and build and she'd been in the water for a time. We figured it might be you. Carter tried to stop Dave from looking at the body and he..." Her cheeks pinked. "Dave picked him up by the throat and tossed him into the wall. Dad had to get between them, but Carter didn't try and fight back. He just ignored him. It was surreal. The next minute, Dave went... like cold. He kinda shut off from the world. The moment he walked into the examination room and looked at the body, he said it wasn't you. He knew in a second. The next minute, Dad had to stop him from driving off to hunt for you. He was going on foot without even a backpack. I've never seen him like that. He was like a different person. Is he okay? He seems upset."

Realizing the extent of the stress Kane had suffered, tightened Jenna's stomach. He must have been devastated to act like that. Somehow, she managed a shrug. "He doesn't want me to see the body. I met Wanda in the forest and was there when she was murdered. It's been a terrible few days, and we're both on edge. I want to get out and find the killer, and Kane figures I should rest." She scanned the items on the table. "I recognize these as what Wanda was wearing when I last saw her. I'll see the body now, if that's okay?"

"Sure." Emily collected up the bags. "I'll put these back into the evidence locker. She's in examination room two. Go right in." She smiled. "You'll need a mask."

Readying herself, Jenna went into the hallway and grabbed a mask and gloves from the alcove outside the examination rooms. She left her hat on the counter with her gloves and jacket. Taking a deep breath, she swiped her card and went inside, surprised to see that Kane wasn't there. She took a quick look at the body, recognizing the ligature marks on her wrists and ankles. The head was covered and Wolfe stood beside the gurney. "That's the woman I know as Wanda. I'll write a statement for you and email it when I get back to the office."

"Thanks." Wolfe covered the body and slid in into the mortuary refrigerator. "I've already taken X-rays. As you suspected, she has long-standing injuries, many broken bones going back about four years or so. From the look of them, they were crudely treated and she'd suffered ill treatment over a long period of time." He glanced at the door. "Where's Dave?"

Jenna shrugged. "I have no idea. He went charging out of here when I asked him about his time away. I asked him if he'd told Annie about himself or was it just me?"

"No, it was classified, but she knew he was in black ops. He met her on a mission. She was his mission. She'd been kidnapped and taken to Syria. He married her under an assumed name to keep her safe. He actually took her name after they married." Wolfe removed his gloves and leaned against the counter. "I don't know his real name either. He used the name Dave for Annie rather than his codename. When she died, he kept it."

Knowing she could speak to Wolfe, she lifted her chin. "Do you know about the connection Tauri has to Annie?"

"Yeah, Dave mentioned it." He gave her a long look. "He

wanted me to hunt down any other blood relatives. We found no one alive but we did confirm his father's ancestors went back to Blackhawk's tribe by testing the elders' DNA. They were very helpful and offered samples. If his father is alive, he's never been DNA tested." He sighed. "Tauri does have one of Annie's ancestors in his background, is all. She wasn't a close relative, and if it makes you feel any better, Dave didn't take that into consideration when he first met the boy. He told me that he felt a connection to Tauri the moment he laid eyes on him, and when Blackhawk revealed the DNA results, he figured Tauri should be with y'all."

Thinking it through, Jenna had the same instant connection. "I admit I was shocked at first. I've always understood Dave's great love for Annie, and I don't blame him for wanting a small part of her in his life. I don't believe for a second that was his only reason for wanting to adopt Tauri. You've seen how he dotes on him."

"You do too." Wolfe smiled. "Or is something else worrying you?" He raised both eyebrows. "Don't for one second believe if you have a baby that he won't love it as much as Tauri. He loves you, Jenna. I was with him when he said goodbye to Annie at her gravesite. He told her he was in love with you and would never return. He'd carried her ghost with him for way too long. Allow him to keep her as a fond memory but never be jealous of her. She told him to remarry if she died. She made him promise to go on with his life. You have a fine son. Sent to you to love and cherish. Don't allow ghosts from the past to spoil the future y'all have together."

Nodding, Jenna straightened. "I guess deep down I figured Annie, even in death, could give him what he most wanted. I love Tauri so much, but I've failed Dave. He wanted a house filled with kids."

"Life hasn't been easy for any of us, but we're here, alive

and healthy." Wolfe smiled. "The future is what we make it. If life throws you a slider, hit it out of the park."

THIRTY-ONE

Thinking things through, Kane waited for Jenna to climb back into the Beast. "Was it her?"

"Yeah." Jenna looked at him. "I'm sorry about before. I just worry about you."

Blowing out a sigh, Kane shrugged. "Don't. I don't do anything I can't handle."

"I hope Rowley and Rio have found some suspects." Jenna leaned back in her seat. "The man I saw was distinctive. I just wish I'd gotten a closer look at his face."

Nodding, Kane headed for the office. "If he has a full beard and is untidy, he could shave and get a haircut, and then walk right past you and you wouldn't recognize him. That part of the forest is about as dense as it gets. Locating him will be difficult. Carter and Wolfe flew all over and didn't see a cabin. I figure the forest canopy hides everything."

"He was on horseback." Jenna glanced at him. "Atohi will be able to track him for sure."

Kane pulled into his parking slot outside the sheriff's office. "Maybe, but we met two men on horseback when we were looking for you. So, it might be more difficult tracking him than you imagine."

"I'll head inside and see what the team have discovered." Jenna slipped from the truck and hurried up the steps.

Kane climbed out and opened the back door to unclip Duke's harness. "She's still mad at me. Maybe I'll be sharing your basket tonight." He chuckled imagining him, Duke, and Pumpkin the cat all curled up together.

Inside the office, Kane waved at Maggie on the front counter and hurried up the steps to Jenna's office. Inside Rio, Rowley, and Carter occupied the chairs, and Jenna was at the whiteboard taking down notes. "Morning. What did I miss?"

"We have three suspects, all fitting the general description, and all of them live off the grid in Stanton west of Cottonwood Creek. No actual address." Rowley was staring at his notes. "We do have their CB call signs, so they might respond if we call them."

"Maybe not." Carter stood and went to the coffee machine and poured a cup. "If they're doing anything illegal, they'll only respond to people they know."

Kane nodded and watched Jenna write three names on the whiteboard. He turned to Carter. "You left early. Did you have something you needed to chase down?"

"Yeah, I've been hunting down backgrounds on the possible suspects, and then Jenna called and gave me the potential name of the Jane Doe and where she was living before she ended up in the forest." Carter smiled around a toothpick and dropped back into his chair. "I searched through the databases for missing persons and found her."

"When and where did she go missing?" Jenna turned from the whiteboard to look at him.

"From Bozeman, four years ago." Carter held his coffee cup in both hands and leaned back in his chair. "Did she mention being in foster care?"

"Yeah. She said it was temporary, while her aunt was ill. Her father works in the UK in renewable energy." Jenna made notes on the whiteboard and then turned back to him. "Why?"

"Oh, something came across my desk about a sex slave ring, selling young girls. One missing girl was found dead, one vanished." Carter sipped his brew and raised both eyebrows. "The problem was he liked to take two young girls, rape and murder one of them, and we figure he sold the other. We investigated a foster care link, but nothing came of it."

Hearing about the case, Kane went to the counter and poured a cup of coffee. "As I recall, they got nothing from the killer, did they?"

"Nope." Carter sighed. "I won't go into the details. There are too many cold cases to go through and the bureau is working on it as we speak. Why I mentioned it is we don't know how far this pedophile sex slave ring has spread. There must be a connection between them. I'm wondering how many of the missing kids were in foster care."

Kane dragged the chair from behind his desk to the group and then sat down. He stared at Carter. "You've seen a connection. What is it?"

"The report on Wanda Beauchamp. It's so vague, as if the foster parents didn't care if the cops found her. The report gives basic details of height, weight, a general description, almost generic. They said they believed her to be a runaway, so waited three days before reporting her missing." Carter drained his cup and placed it on the desk. "For me that sounds suspicious. There was no follow-up on the case, no search made apart from the local deputies doing a perimeter search of the house. It had been raining since the girl went missing, so there were no tracks or scents to follow, so they didn't try."

"Did you dig deeper?" Jenna went behind her desk and sat down. "Did you launch FBI whiz kid Bobby Kalo into action?"

"How did you guess?" Carter tossed a toothpick into his

mouth. "When he dug into the cold cases, three more girls in foster care were declared runaways over the past ten years or so."

Knowing the answer but needing confirmation, Kane turned his cup around with the tips of his fingers. "Any of them found?"

"Nope." Carter's brow wrinkled into a frown. "Not a trace. It smacks of organized kidnapping, but here's the problem: This is a current FBI investigation. There's a task force working across states. We can ask for updates if it concerns any of our current victims, but we can't go stepping on toes."

"We can't go to Bozeman and speak to the foster parents either." Jenna chewed on her bottom lip. "It's not in our jurisdiction."

Kane sipped the coffee and sighed. "We can contact Wanda Beauchamp's father. If he works in renewable energy, we should be able to trace him. He might be able to give us the name of a close relative for a DNA sample." He looked at Carter. "Can you ask Kalo to find him? We'll need to contact him to give him information on his daughter's murder and obtain a positive ID."

"I'll call Kalo as soon as we're done here." Carter yawned. "I need to check in with Jo. I'll tell her this will take time."

"Maybe she'll want to join the investigation?" Jenna smiled at him. "I enjoy her company."

"That would mean I'd need to fly home and get her." Carter shrugged. "If there's a chance more women might be in danger, I don't figure I have the time." He grinned around his toothpick. "I could tempt her with the grisly details and maybe she'll get a ride with the local search and rescue. She has before." He chuckled. "The one thing about Jo is that when it comes to dissecting a new psychopath, she's very resourceful."

THIRTY-TWO

Thinking over the little information they had on the case, Kane glanced at the whiteboard. "These three suspects: Elias Miller, Josiah Washington, and Christopher Grant. What have you discovered about them?"

"Well." Rio rubbed the back of his neck. "According to local records, Elias Miller died when he was two, Josiah Washington died in a wreck ten years ago, and Christopher Grant died in combat twelve years ago." He dashed a hand through his hair. "Somehow, these three men all decided to take on the identities of dead people."

"We double-checked for men between the ages of thirty-five and sixty-five living in our county and then ran the names through the state database." Rowley looked at Kane. "The store-keeper figured the men didn't know each other. How come they're all doing the same thing?"

"I've heard of people doing that before, but these days you need more than a birth certificate to prove your identity. Then again you don't need a driver's license to own a horse, do you?" Jenna leaned back in her chair. "The storekeeper hasn't mentioned seeing any of them driving, has he?"

"He didn't mention anything about vehicles." Rio shrugged. "I was hoping using fake names of dead people would link them."

Nodding, Kane looked at Jenna. "Taking names from gravestones isn't unusual for people wanting to vanish off the grid. So don't read too much into it. My guess is if you checked out everyone hiding in the forest, less than five percent would give you their real name. Unfortunately, fake IDs are easy to come by and the local storekeeper isn't going to be looking too hard at them for a fishing license, especially when it's someone he does business with. It's a fact of life, I'm afraid."

"I was hoping we'd have a reason to speak to them." Jenna pushed both hands through her hair. "We've got nothing. As usual we're chasing shadows. How can we possibly search that part of the forest for them. It will take us years."

"There will be signs of habitation, smoke for instance or a clearing where they built their cabins, but you'll be needing the chopper." Carter shrugged. "Searching the forest will be impossible on foot."

"What we need is for the storekeeper at the general store to contact us when he hears from them." Rowley looked up from his iPad.

"Like he's gonna do that." Carter snorted. "Maybe if I go see him and flash my badge and ask him to call them for a charter job, we can hang about and then follow them back to where they live?"

"That's entrapment." Jenna chewed on her pen. "No can do."

An idea sprang into Kane's head. "We could charter a couple of fishing boats." He smiled at Carter. "We'd have a captive audience out on the lake, wouldn't we? Plenty of time to assess them, and maybe get some information. Then we follow them into the forest. We could even tell them we plan on going hunting so we won't arouse suspicion if they see us." He swung around to look at Rowley and Rio. "You in?"

"Sure." Rowley grinned. "I already told the storekeeper I wanted to go fishing."

"I'll go along. I'm fine with boats but I don't have fishing gear." Rio shrugged. "I guess I can rent some."

"I have enough for both of us." Rowley chuckled. "Shoulder holsters and undercover, right?"

Nodding, Kane looked at Jenna. "Yeah, if Jenna approves, we can make plans."

"How exactly are you planning on tracking these guys to their homes after being out in a boat all day?" Jenna stared at Kane. "I'm not tracking them alone or with Blackhawk. There's no way I'm going back into that part of the forest without serious backup." She shook her head and looked at Carter. "You can't possibly believe you can track them in an FBI chopper. They're not stupid, they'll see you following them. If we're doing this, it has to be on horseback. Trail bikes will make too much noise." She thought for a beat. "You're planning on asking them some subtle questions before we follow them? I mean it's just a hunch one of these men is a homicide suspect and we could be way off base."

Aware that Jenna was recovering from a great deal of stress after her ordeal, Kane smiled at her. "We only need to charter a boat for half a day. So, we'd be back by lunchtime. We'll do a catch and release, so we won't have rotting fish to worry about." He thought for a beat. "There's no cell phone coverage in the forest, so we'll take satellite sleeves for our phones, but we do have satellite coms as well. We'll be splitting up into groups to follow the men, so we'll need to keep in touch. I'll call Black-hawk. He'll be able to find us a reliable tracker to go with us."

"Make sure he's aware of the danger." Carter frowned. "Having civilians along is always a problem. There are no rules in the forest. We'll be in their yards. They'll have the advantage."

Kane shook his head. "You worry too much. The forest can work for us too. There's plenty of places to hide. As for being civilians, Jenna can deputize them, so if anything happens, they'll be covered by the department's insurance. You can trust Blackhawk to bring someone competent. If we get into a situation, we'll ask them to drop back."

"Okay, that works for me but what about the horses?" Jenna balled her hands on her hips. "They can't hang around in the trailer while you're all out enjoying yourselves and neither can the dogs."

Exasperated, Kane stared at her. "Being trapped in a boat with a potential serial killer isn't my idea of fun and we won't all be fishing. One of us will be watching the potential suspect and asking him very subtle questions. I'm not planning on any of us ending up victims, Jenna."

"Okay but you can't take the dogs on a boat and Duke is still tuckered out after searching for me." Jenna chewed on her bottom lip. "We can't drag him through the forest again so soon."

"The dogs will be staying at the ranch." Carter shrugged. "They have food and water, a place to sleep. They'll be fine for a few days if necessary. We can fill their feeders and water before we leave. They'll have a ball."

"Fine, so what about the horses?" Jenna looked around. "You know the terrain. They'll need to be fresh."

"Cottonwood Lake is surrounded by ranches." Rowley glanced at her. "I'll call around and see if we can rent a couple of corrals close to town for a few hours."

Kane nodded. "Good thinking. We'll call ahead when we're heading back to shore. Jenna, will you and Atohi be able to load them onto the trailers and bring them back to town?"

"You want me to drive the Beast?" Jenna giggled and wiggled her eyebrows. "Really?"

Clearing his throat, Kane gave her his best attempt at a stern expression. In truth, there wasn't much anyone could do to harm the Beast. "Well, you'll need to drive back to the office while we're out fishing. Unless you're planning on sitting around town for four hours or so?"

"Oh, I'm not waiting around for you guys." Jenna shook her head. "I'll be making breakfast for our son and driving him to kindergarten before heading to the office. You can take Carter and the horses with you. If Atohi and his friend agree to come with us, he can give me a ride to Cottonwood Lake. Nanny Raya will collect Tauri as usual and care for him until we return. I suggest you take something to eat with you, as you won't have time to visit the diner when you return." She smiled at him. "I'm happy to get there ahead of time and drive the Beast to go pick up the horses. They'll be ready for you when you get back." She looked at Rowley. "Are you happy for Atohi to drive your truck?"

"Yeah, sure." Rowley smiled. "I'll be sure to give you the spare key."

Kane smiled at Jenna. "Okay, let's set this plan into action."

THIRTY-THREE

Stanton Forest

Naomi King stared around the cabin and her nose wrinkled in disgust. When they'd arrived in the dead of night, he hadn't said much. He'd told her to wash her feet and then ordered her to his bed. Terrified of what might happen, she shook her head and backed away. He'd slowly removed his strap and beaten her. Shocked and sobbing, he'd said nothing when he thrust her into a closet with brooms and buckets and locked the door. It was so cold and pitch black. Feeling around, she'd located a bucket and sat down, wrapping her arms around herself and shivering. No one had ever beaten her before, and every inch of her back and legs stung. She'd sat in the dark until sunlight crept through the cracks in the door. Outside, she heard him moving around, his boots clattering on the dusty wooden floors.

Footsteps came toward her, and she shrank back feeling around for a weapon. Finding nothing but an old broom, she bit back a sob. Defeated, she sank back down on the bucket. What was the point? He'd only beat her again. The man was a cruel monster and she had no chance of escape. The sunlight blinded her when he eventually opened the door. Afraid, she stumbled to her feet and moved along the wall to get away from him. His hand came out as quick as a snake and grabbed her wrist.

"I give my wives two choices." Husband glared down at her, his fingers digging deep into her flesh. "Do as I say, when I say, or I'll chain you to the bed. If you don't want to be chained and decide to cooperate, your life will be decent. You'll clean and cook. I'll allow you outside to hang the washing on the line and feed the chickens. If you mess up, I'll beat you. If you try and leave, I'll beat you. Your life from then on will be in chains. There are no second chances. Once the chains are on there's no going back. Do you understand, Grace?"

Naomi nodded. "I was just going to the bathroom. I'd like to get dressed. I'm cold."

"Okay, then make the coffee and cook me breakfast." He grinned at her. "I'm glad you decided to cooperate. Your daddy said you were docile and someone who would make me a good wife." He chuckled. "I have plans for you today, so guess I'll soon find out." He looked her over, his gaze traveling from head to foot. "You're as nice as your photo. In the dark last night, I could only hope I hadn't been sold an ugly one."

Sold? I've been sold to this horrible, smelly man? Not wanting to be beaten again, Naomi nodded. She'd escape as soon as she could, but where would she go? She had no idea where he'd taken her. It was deep in the forest, but what forest? She looked around at the small cabin. Skins, smelly but dried, were piled up in one corner with flies buzzing around them. Where did this man get his money from? She needed to try and converse with him, and maybe make him like her. "Was I expensive?"

"Yeah, but you'll be worth it. I'll make sure of that." Husband chuckled. "When you're all settled in, in maybe a month or so, you'll help me in my job. By then you'll be able to train the others. I had planned to have someone here for you, to make you see my way is the only way from now on, but she's gone."

Swallowing the fear, Naomi lifted her chin. "I'll need to know the rules, so I don't break them. I don't like being beaten."

"Rules, huh? You're a brave little girl." He grinned a yellow smile. "Shame you have a short memory. I've already given you the rules. You do as I say and don't run away. You act nice, no matter what I ask you to do." He moved closer and wrapped her hair around his fist. "You no longer exist. Naomi King is already dead. You are Grace now. You have no rights here. You can never make any requests or demands. I own you and will do anything I like to you." He sniffed her hair and then dropped it. "Is that clear enough now?"

A shiver of fear slid down Naomi's back. She nodded. Last night was a respite because he was exhausted, but life was going to become intolerable very soon. She tried to stop her bottom lip from trembling, but every part of her was shaking. He terrified her. "What happened to her? The one who was supposed to help me?"

"You saw the mound of earth, Grace." Husband stretched and dropped his hands with a grunt. "She disobeyed me and now she's dead. I enjoyed killing her. I'll enjoy killing you too one day." He pointed to the kitchen. "Are you gonna stand there all day? Go make the coffee or do I need to take my strap to you again?"

THIRTY-FOUR

SATURDAY

Cottonwood Lake

The previous evening around the dinner table, Carter had discussed tactics with Kane and Jenna. He'd go fishing with Kane, and Rowley with Rio. They'd booked their charters separately and waited for confirmation. It had been hit or miss to see if the storekeeper managed to get two of the suspects living in the forest to captain the boats. When told the cost involved, Jenna had winced, but Kane had insisted the budget would hold up, which meant he'd probably pay the fees himself. Kane was an enigma, and Carter's instincts told him there was something more to his background than he had told him. If it was a secret, well, he had no intentions of prying, but that didn't mean curiosity didn't eat at him, and he had to admit he'd scanned the military files for men of Kane's description. He'd found many but none of them resembled David Kane.

It was fortunate that everyone except him owned a horse. His mount was being supplied by Blackhawk as before, and

Rio's gelding was stabled at Rowley's ranch, so they'd arrive together. Everything had fallen into place without a problem. Kane had insisted on getting there early and they'd gone by the store to pay for the charter and discovered the men left their horses at a local farrier's. It was at the same place where they'd rented a couple of corrals. When he arrived at Cottonwood Lake with Kane, they passed Rio and Rowley as they were leaving the farrier's and heading toward the boat ramp. On their arrival, Carter looked at the farrier. "We're heading out on a fishing charter, but I heard the fishing is also good in Cottonwood Creek. What's the access like to the riverbank?"

"You'd need your horses, a GPS, and a satellite phone to venture in there." The farrier smiled at them. "It's easy to get turned around and a few grizzlies have been seen along the riverbank."

"I'm seeing more horses here than any of the other local towns. What's the deal?" Kane glanced around. "In Black Rock Falls horses are for recreation; here they are a serious mode of transport."

"That would be true. Everyone who lives in this section of the forest rides horses. There are very few roads. A few fire roads were cut through the forest a couple of years ago but most of the men who live there keep themselves hidden." The farrier pointed out two horses. "Those there belong to your charter boat captains. They're owned by Elias Miller and Christopher Grant."

Carter peered into the stalls. Both were bays with white feet. "Dave mentioned one of his old friends who lives out this way. What was his name, Dave?"

"Josiah Washington." Kane pulled bills from a wad and handed them to the farrier. "He went off the grid some years back. I haven't laid eyes on him for a time."

"Josiah? Yeah, he comes by from time to time." The farrier smiled. "The one thing about horses, they need tending. Josiah isn't too worried about himself, but a sound horse is essential in that forest. It's not like Black Rock Falls. This part of the county is wild and dangerous."

"What does he ride?" Kane leaned casually against the wall, arms at his sides in a relaxed pose. "He'd need a decent horse to live out there over winter."

"Most around these parts own mustangs, likely broke them themselves." The farrier shrugged. "They're tough horses."

Carter glanced at his watch. "Thanks. We have to go. We'll be back by noon."

He followed Kane out of the building. They grabbed their fishing gear and lunch, leaving the Beast and trailer parked beside the farrier's barn and then walked down Main to the boat ramp to meet Elias Miller. He and Christopher Grant—Grant, the storekeeper had called him—would have the boats ready by six-thirty sharp. He looked ahead as a boat headed out on the lake. "There goes Rio and Rowley now. Seems to me we hit lucky twice today."

"Yeah, I was prepared to force myself to go on fishing charters until we got to meet both suspects. It's a chore but someone has to do it, right?" Kane smiled. "As much as it pains me to say this, you fish and I'll watch."

Grinning, Carter headed for the boat. "Nice. I'll owe you one."

THIRTY-FIVE

The lake was like a sheet of ice. Although small waves broke along the shoreline, out in the deep water it was calm and so clear that Rio could see the fish swimming in the shafts of sunlight. A light breeze brushed his skin as he waited for Rowley to cast his line and then he moved up to the man dropping the anchor. "This is a beautiful place. Lived here long?"

"Oh, yeah, some years now." The man was tall with a strong build, long untidy hair sticking out from under a ball cap advertising a popular soda, and a beard with white streaks that came down to his chest. His golden skin was from days of being out in the sun. The wrinkles around his eyes made him look older than his years.

Rio moved his attention to Grant's arms as he spun the pulley to drop the anchor. Older men's skin even if they were fit usually had some sagging and he saw no evidence of this, in fact the man's inner arms were toned much like his own, so this guy was around his own age, maybe thirty-five to forty. He needed to engage him in conversation. "Is there much work around these parts?"

"Some." Grant shrugged. "I work the charter boats when they need me, is all. I live off the land."

Seeing a chance to get the conversation flowing, Rio pushed a little more. "I've often wanted to disappear into the forest and never come out. Life today is getting harder. So many people trying to steal your stuff or cause trouble. I prefer a quiet life."

"Same." Grant went to a cooler and pulled out a soda, he popped the top. "I came here, just like you. I went fishing and then decided to explore the forest." He chuckled. "I got myself turned around and couldn't find my way back. Spent the night under a bush. Next morning, I came across an old man collecting berries. He took me to his cabin and taught me how to survive. I stayed with him until he died. The one good thing about knowing him was his horses. He showed me the trail back to town, and if I got lost, I just gave the horse its head and it would walk home. Horses are smart. After a while I came to know the forest. The fishing is good, and there's creeks all through it. There are plenty of non-game animals to shoot if you need meat."

Carter shrugged. "So you live out there all on your lonesome?"

"It's peaceful." Grant shrugged. "I still have my truck and a horse trailer if I need to go somewhere. I have a deal with the farrier. He can use it whenever he wants, as long as he maintains it and keeps it gassed up." He rubbed his chin. "I do need it sometimes, like to go to the dentist or the time I broke my arm."

"I don't figure I could survive without a woman." Rowley slowly turned his fishing reel and looked over his shoulder at them. "I figure getting one to live in the forest would be difficult." He pulled in a fish and went to release it.

"Hey, I'll take the fish, unless you're with fish rights or whatever?" Grant stared at Rowley. "It will save me buying something for dinner tonight."

"Sure." Rowley exchanged a look with Rio and unhooked the fish. "Be my guest." He held the fish out to Grant.

Not wanting to spook him, Rio said nothing for a while, and admired the view. He took a few shots with his phone like a tourist, making sure Grant was in at least one of the photographs. Acting nonchalant, he sat and watched Rowley pull in fish after fish. In the distance, he made out another boat and assumed it was Carter and Kane. He hadn't gotten any useful information apart from the man lived in the forest. Even Rowley's attempt at conversation about women had drawn a blank. He turned to Grant. The man seemed harmless enough, and ready to communicate with them. "Do you know of any empty cabins in the forest. I'd say they're not actually owned by anyone are they?"

"Not that I'm aware and there are cabins if you're prepared to hunt them down. I've come across a few when I'm out hunting." Grant stroked his beard and a yellow smile emerged from the thick hair. "You don't seem the type to go off the grid. You're too neat."

Rio shrugged. "Maybe one day, but I'll be taking a woman with me. I need someone to cook and clean for me, right?" He chuckled. "I'll be out hunting and she'll be nice and warm to come home to."

"You got that right." Grant grinned at him. "But I wouldn't marry one. When one gets too old, I'd swap them out for something younger."

There you go, Suspect number one in the bag. Rio gripped Rowley's shoulder. "Now that would suit you, wouldn't it?"

"Sure, that would work out just fine." Rowley's line twitched and he turned the reel slowly. "Now all we need is a cabin and we can walk away from all the rules and regulations. We'll build another close by and then go find us some women."

Rio chuckled. "Now that sounds like a plan. Maybe Grant here can point us in the right direction."

"It's been a time since I went out that way." Grant sighed.

"Are there any empty cabins near your place?" Rowley glanced at him. "We might need some guidance. You know, on how to survive?"

"Maybe." Grant stroked his beard and looked them over, his eyes sparkled with amusement. "Let me think on it for a time."

A cold warning chill slid down Rio's back. This guy was looking at them like a predator. He must think they were a pair of suckers, ripe for the picking.

THIRTY-SIX

Kane pushed down the rim of his Stetson and slid on his sunglasses as the boat skimmed across the lake. The boat moved swiftly but he could imagine the thrill of a speedboat, tearing down the length of the lake. It was vast and he'd be able to reach a great rate of knots. Slow had never been his style. He needed the fastest horse, vehicle, and Harley. Speed thrilled him and he couldn't wait until the first snow and the chance to fly down the slopes with Jenna. Would Tauri enjoy learning to ski? They'd take a week's vacation at the ski resort next winter. He'd pull his son along on a toboggan and they'd throw snowballs. As the boat slowed, his mind jolted back to the reason he was out in the middle of a lake.

He'd observed Elias Miller with interest from behind his shades. Mirrored sunglasses were perfect for looking at people without them knowing. He could be the man Jenna had seen. Miller, was the correct height and approximate weight, had the same hair and beard. This man's beard was combed and tied with a band at the front. It did have gray streaks. He was much younger than Jenna described. Apart from the white in his beard, when he removed his hat, his hair was dark brown. The man's skin was weathered but he'd seen the same in a thirty-year-old cowboy and this guy lived in the forest. When they'd dropped anchor and Carter had cast his line, Kane used his phone to take a few photos of the lake, making sure to capture Elias Miller. He pushed the phone into his pocket and offered the man a beer from the cooler. He took a soda for himself and a beer for Carter. The first rule of extracting information is to create common ground with a suspect. "The storekeeper at the bait store mentioned you lived off the grid." He leaned back against the cabin and indicated to Carter. "I dragged Ty out of the forest a year ago, but I think he misses it." He held out the beer to Carter.

"Yeah, I miss it." Carter glanced over his shoulder and took the beer, setting it down in a holder on his chair. "I'm not big on the Man breathing down my neck." He snorted. "Black Rock Falls is safe, if you know what I mean?"

"This end of Stanton is practically untouched." Miller sipped his beer. "You can ride for miles and never see another soul. No one bothers you out there. Maybe you should try it?"

"Don't say a word." Carter gave Kane a warning glance. "We don't know this guy from Adam."

"Hey, I'm right here." Miller chuckled. "I meet all types on these charters. I'll forget you existed the moment you walk down the gangplank."

Shrugging, Kane smiled. He understood Carter's subterfuge perfectly. Adding a little more color to their story might extract information. "If he's off the grid, he's not a cop. Don't worry about it." He turned his attention back to Miller. "After fishing we're planning on taking a little expedition into the forest. I hear tell there are a few abandoned cabins in the west. Perfect for a weekend hideaway. We're looking for a secure place. Know of any?"

"Maybe." Miller shrugged. "Yeah, it's private, but I know of guys out there who'd shoot you and bury you so deep no one would ever find you. I built my own cabin. There are rumors, you know, of survivalists murdering guys living off the grid just to steal their cabins. You'll need to watch your back. It might be private but it ain't safe. The forest can be your worst nightmare."

"Where do you meet women around here?" Carter tossed back a fish and then wiped his hands on a rag before reaching for his beer. "The place looks dead."

"We have our ways." Miller shrugged and stared out across the lake. "I've never had a problem."

Sipping his soda, Kane relaxed enjoying the sun. "Ways?" He sniggered. "Do you lure them into the forest?"

"Tourists." Miller grinned. "The farrier organizes trail rides and campouts. There are only a few of us who know their way around the forest. Most of them are women, and some of them like the rugged outdoors types. It's like a big adventure to camp out with a rough guy."

Assuming Miller was pulling his chain, Kane went along with the ploy. "Right, so it must get pretty lonely over winter? Unless you can persuade one of them to move in?"

"I guess." Miller glanced at his watch. "Didn't you say you wanted to get back by noon?"

Kane nodded. "Yeah, our horses are at the farrier's. Once we saddle up, we're heading out on a trail ride to see if we can find a cabin."

"Best of luck. My horse is there too and I'd go along with you for a time, but I'm grabbing a bite to eat and some supplies before I head home." Miller wound up the anchor and winked at him. "Don't get eaten by a grizzly. There's been a few spotted in the area of late and they're protected in this region." He frowned. "People often go into the forest and never come out. I hope you've got no one waiting for you back home."

Rubbing his chin, Kane glanced at Carter. Was that a subtle

threat or a promise? He turned his attention back to Miller and shook his head. "Not at this time but we like it that way."

"Well, enjoy your weekend." Miller started up the engine of the boat and looked over his shoulder. "Maybe I'll see you around sometime?" He headed swiftly to the boat ramp.

"I'm sure you will." Carter grinned at him. "One thing's for darn sure, if we don't find a cabin, we'll be back. Best fishing charter I've had in a long time." He packed up his rod and lifted the cooler. "We'll be sure to ask for you by name."

"Well, you'll get me or one of the other guys they hire. It depends if I'm busy." Miller stared toward the forest and stroked his beard. "Sometimes, I don't leave my cabin for weeks."

As the boat bobbed and rolled beneath his feet, Kane glanced at his watch. "We've gotta go. Thanks for your time." He hurried from the boat and once out of earshot turned to Carter. "He's smooth and confident. Not anything like a survivalist or the usual off-the-grid silent type. I figure we have a contender." He smiled at Carter. "Unless we can swap him for you. Out there I figured you were the killer. You sure fooled me."

"That was the idea." Carter tossed a toothpick into his mouth. "I was hoping he'd mention living with someone, but if he did have someone holed up in a cabin, he's too smart to say anything. I agree, he's one for the maybe list."

THIRTY-SEVEN

The morning had been busy for Jenna. After making sure everything was arranged with Atohi Blackhawk and his cousin Chogan, Kane had called to tell her to meet him on the edge of the forest, in a parking area near the mouth of the lake. She'd spent her time on calls to Special Agent Jo Wells, the behavioral analyst out of the field office in Snakeskin Gully, and her computer whiz kid, Bobby Kalo, in an effort to unravel the current case. As Kalo hadn't been able to locate Wanda's father, she'd asked him to hunt down missing women across the state, as Wanda, the young woman she'd met in the forest, had mentioned other graves. If Wanda had been kidnapped, maybe there were more young people missing they weren't aware of. She'd asked him specifically to concentrate on teenagers missing from foster care.

After informing the local law enforcement in Bozeman about finding Wanda's body in Cottonwood Lake, she'd discovered the story Wanda had told her about going missing was recorded as a runaway by the foster parents. They'd insisted she'd often not returned from school and went missing for days at a time. They hadn't reported her missing for a week and when she'd dug a little deeper, she discovered that three previous girls from the same foster home had gone missing without a trace since Wanda disappeared. When she questioned these incidents, the local cop informed her runaways from foster care were frequent, as many as one in three. The usual welfare checks had been undertaken by the local social services and nothing was found to be amiss. Unable to understand the attitude, Jenna cleared her throat. She had personally made it her business to ensure every child in Black Rock Falls in foster care was well cared for. She either checked up on them personally or enlisted the assistance of Father Derry a very astute and caring member of the community who ran a number of shelters and assisted with Her Broken Wings Foundation, a halfway house she and Kane had established for people suffering from spousal abuse. "I watched a man beat Wanda to death with a baseball bat. I was a victim myself, after being hunted by the same man in the forest. Has it occurred to you that these missing girls might have entered the child exploitation trade?"

"*Of course it enters our minds, Sheriff Alton. What do you expect me to do? We have no evidence to follow. The problem is, after we find no trace of them and do the regular searches, they become cold cases.*" The cop sighed. "*If this Jane Doe is Wanda, it might take some time hunting down her father. I'll do a local search for any family members. The aunt you mentioned in your email passed over a year ago. I'll be in touch if we find the father.*" He disconnected.

Sighing Jenna leaned back in her chair just as her phone buzzed. It was Jo Wells. "Hi, Jo, what do you think about our latest killer?"

She'd sent over the case files and all the information she had on Wanda's killer earlier and followed up with a call. Jo had come back to her earlier than expected. She put the phone on speaker and stood. She needed to eat lunch before leaving for the forest and had just received a delivery from Aunt Betty's Café. She knew her team well and none of the men would have bothered to eat a thing since breakfast. Once the suspects left the lake, their trails would go cold, so she'd ordered a ton of takeout and packed it into coolers along with supplies for a few days. She'd kept out a bagel and cream cheese for her lunch and poured a cup of coffee while Jo spoke.

"Hmm, it's an interesting case. Obviously, child exploitation or sex slaves, from the details of restraint. The injuries sustained would certainly suggest it as well. Has Wolfe an autopsy report to back up the case?"

Jenna took her food back to the desk and sat down. "Not yet. He's performing the autopsy this morning. All I have is what I sent you, the preliminary report."

"That's graphic enough, and you witnessed the attack? Can you identify the killer?"

Sipping her coffee, Jenna shook her head as if Jo were in the room beside her. "No, not as in a lineup. Build, hair color is about all. It was at a distance, and even when he came close, I was head down, trying to hide under a bush. What are we dealing with here, Jo?"

"He lives deep in the forest, off the grid, right?" Jo's chair squeaked as if she was rolling it across the floor. "So we'll look at what we know. I'm assuming by the mention of graves, plural, he's been doing this for a time. Like you mentioned in your notes, he can't be finding these kids in the forest and just tripping over them. He must be getting them from a source. The FBI has been actively searching for a pedophile or sex slave ring that uses kids like a commodity. There was a case recently where a killer literally had a business going while he fed his lust for rape and murder. He'd kidnap two young girls, rape and murder one, and sell the other."

Jenna looked at her bagel and then swallowed hard and

placed it back on the plate. "Oh, that must be the case Carter mentioned earlier. Go on."

"He was a very organized and charismatic serial killer. The typical psychopath we've come to recognize. The man you're dealing with is secretive. He likes to hide his fantasy, but he isn't killing. He's organized to a point, as in these people who deal with children in this abhorrent way work the system of supply and demand in different ways. They buy or trade usually. So some of them would keep a girl until she is too old to attract them and sell them on to a slave trader. They don't make much money." She sighed. "Unfortunately, some of these young girls become pregnant. A baby brings big money on the black market, so that is another source of income. Remember, keeping a young woman as a sex slave is a form of domination. Killing them once he's finished with them is paranoia. He won't risk selling them, in case they tell someone about him and what he's done. The graves cement this profile because he doesn't want them escaping his hold over them."

Jenna nibbled at her bagel, keeping one eye on the time. She'd need to leave in under half an hour to meet Kane. "So we're not dealing with a psychopathic serial killer?"

"I'd need more to determine what he is." Jo cleared her throat. "He probably is a psychopath or sociopath. Both are possible. The fact he overkilled Wanda looks more like a crime of passion. Did you see it that way?"

Jenna washed the mouthful of food down with coffee. "No, not when you consider the first time he tried to kill her. Apparently, she disobeyed him and ran away. He'd hit her with a shovel and, believing she'd died, covered her face with a box and then buried her. The second time, I figure he was making sure he'd killed her. I saw rage at being disobeyed. There was no passion."

"How was he when he was speaking to her? Angry or nice?"

Allowing the terrifying moment to drop back into her mind,

Jenna thought for a beat. "He was quite charming, normal. He asked her to go back with him because he wanted her to train another girl for him. He promised she could go after, that he'd take her back to her family. He only got mad when she ran away."

"*Train another girl?*" Jo's fingers tapped on the desk. "*That proves my theory. He has a source to obtain girls, and from what you mentioned, it could be linked to some unscrupulous people in the foster care system.*"

Jenna chewed the last bite of bagel as Blackhawk came to the office door. "One second, Jo. Hi, Atohi, I'm on a call to Jo. I won't be long."

"What else needs to be packed into the truck?" Blackhawk looked around at the coolers. "All these and the box of Thermoses?"

Nodding, Jenna added a box of energy bars to the pile. "I think that's all. We packed everything else this morning."

"I'll take these and leave you to your call." Blackhawk indicated to his cousin Chogan to assist. "Keep one eye on the time. We don't want to miss the suspects."

Smiling at him, Jenna nodded. "Don't worry. If we haven't shown by the time Dave gets back to dry land, he'll find an excuse to delay them." She went back to her phone as the men left with the supplies. "I'm back, Jo."

"*Okay, going on what you're telling me, this killer is all about domination and power over his victims. He doesn't get his thrills from killing. He gets his thrills from humiliation, beating, and rape, all punishments. He'll be cold and deadly. I would say psychopath mainly because to inflict this treatment on a person, especially a kid, shows absolutely no empathy whatsoever. If he's selling her babies, it's a double whammy. That's his kid too, but he doesn't care. It's just income to him. A means for him to buy another slave.*" Jo blew out a long breath. "*He'll be in league with his supplier and buyer, whoever they are, so there will be* more people involved for you to find. We need to find the buyer and supplier. They might be part of a chain the FBI has been searching for. You'll need to interview him, Jenna. He'll be slippery and very smart. He won't be reasoned with, and to be honest, I doubt he'll give up his source."

Jenna pushed both hands through her hair. "Why?"

"Because he doesn't believe he's doing anything wrong." Jo sounded distant. "I've interviewed so many of these men. They always come up with an excuse. Like it's the victim's fault or God told them to kill. It's never their fault. Some of them believe they're doing a community service, particularly those who kill streetwalkers. He'll have some similar excuse to satisfy his reason. Maybe he takes foster kids because he gives them a home... Who can fathom the mind of a psychopath? I do my best, but with so many other psychoses affecting their reasoning, no two are alike." She blew out a long breath. "Just be careful. He won't be taken down without a fight. In his world you'll be invading his sanctuary. He'll try and use the castle law to get away with killing all of you."

Jenna stood and stared at the gun locker. "Okay, Jo. I'll talk to you later. Thanks." She disconnected and used her keys to unlock the door. She pulled out her rifle and laid it on the table with ammo just as the Blackhawk cousins walked into the room. She'd deputized them earlier that morning. "Help yourself to firearms."

"We have our own hunting rifles." Blackhawk smiled at her. "Kane insisted we keep back and out of the way once we have located the suspects. Although we'll be there if you need us."

Locking the gun safe, Jenna turned back to them. "Okay, that's good, but one word of warning: We haven't encountered a killer like this before. He has no feelings toward his victims. There will be no negotiations because he won't negotiate. This man is a monster."

THIRTY-EIGHT

The moment Kane's feet hit dry soil he called Rio. "Hey, my suspect is grabbing something to eat before he heads off. We'll do the same." He led the way back to town, with Carter ambling along beside him as if he had all the time in the world.

"We're already in the diner. Ours had the same idea. He mentioned grabbing some supplies before heading home, so he might be a time. We followed him here but we're not sitting anywhere near him. We know his horse is at the same place as ours and he'll need time to saddle up before he leaves." The low hum of conversation came from behind Rio. "We figured we'd head off before him and get to the edge of the forest. We'll give him a head start and then follow him. All we need now is Jenna to arrive with our tracker."

Kane stopped walking, turned, and stared into the distance. He could make out a horse trailer heading into town. "She's on her way and will meet up with us in the forest alongside the end of the lake. You'll see Blackhawk's horse trailer parked close by. Try not to make it obvious we're in a group. We'll give you time to move off before we head out. Use the coms the moment you hit the forest. Only use the satellite phones in an emergency or to text coordinates. Have them on vibrate, we don't want the suspects to hear us coming."

"Gotcha. Happy hunting."

Disconnecting his satellite phone, Kane turned to Carter. "It seems everyone is taking a lunch break, so we'll do the same and then leave before the suspects head off home. I'll ask Jenna to wait for us in the forest. We'll find her okay with the coms. We'll need to be out of sight when the suspects leave. I figure it's going to be difficult following them with the horses, especially Warrior. He likes to make his presence known."

"They know we're heading into the forest." Carter shrugged. "Telling them about our plans will avoid any suspicion if they do hear us. My concern is the third suspect, Josiah Washington. He is an unknown quantity and could be anywhere. If he is the killer, then we have a deranged man hellbent on mayhem roaming around. I've lived off the grid and, trust me, once the folks bury themselves deep, they'll take every precaution to stop intruders. Many of them are unstable or they're running from the law. They have nothing to lose."

Nodding, Kane pushed opened the door to the diner and went inside. The smell of chili cooking and fresh coffee filled his nostrils. He scanned the room, allowing his gaze to skim over Rowley and Rio sitting on the left side of the room, already eating their meal. A man who fit the description of Christopher Grant sat alone in a booth along one of the walls. He turned his attention back to Carter. "Jenna called Jo earlier, so we'll bring everyone up to speed before we leave. If I recall, there were two main trails heading into the forest. One ran along the creek and the other headed west. The only problem I can see is if both suspects head in the same direction. The storekeeper in the bait store didn't believe they all knew each other, so I doubt they'd travel together, and being secretive about where they live, having friends to rat them out wouldn't be an option."

"Yeah, that makes sense." Carter stared at the menu on a

chalkboard alongside the counter. "Let's hope they leave some distance apart. It would sure make life easier." He looked at the server. "Hamburger, fries, and onion rings." He paused a beat. "I'll have the apple pie and coffee."

Glancing around at the locals, Kane noticed all of them eating a steaming bowl of chili. It must be good. "Chili, apple pie, and coffee." He smiled at the server, a teenager of about seventeen with a serious expression. "Thanks." He headed for a table where he could keep his back to the wall and view the sidewalk.

Kane leaned back in his chair and waited for the server to pour the coffee. As he added the fixings, he looked at Carter. "The one thing we have in our favor is that summer is the time for tourists. We don't look like cops. We'll wear our Kevlar vests under our shirts but keep our badges covered unless we need to show them. Once we find the cabins, we can identify ourselves at that time."

"I have a call." Carter pulled out his satellite phone. "Carter." He listened for a beat. "Put all the info on a message and send it to everyone in the team. Anything at all on Josiah Washington? Has he ever gotten himself into trouble using the false ID?" He nodded and then disconnected. "That was Kalo. A girl has gone missing from foster care in the next county. A fourteen-year-old by the name of Naomi King out of Blackwater. What's that from here? An hour's drive maybe? She's never run away before. All previous reports of her foster families are that she's quiet to the point of being timid and never breaks the rules." He sighed. "If there is a foster care connection, this might be what we're looking for as it's a little too coincidental for her to go missing when we know Wanda mentioned the killer had another girl lined up."

The server returned with their meals just as Elias Miller entered the diner. Kane made a point of keeping his eyes lowered to the table, the last thing they wanted was to have him join them. As he lifted his spoon, Miller went to the counter, ordered his meal, and then drifted over to a booth not far from Christopher Grant. Kane picked up his spoon. "You could be right. That girl would be a magnet for the type of man we're looking for. Compliant and timid means easily dominated. She'd be too scared to try to escape and be suffering from Stockholm syndrome before the month was out. I hope she hasn't been taken by the killer, because by the time we find her she won't want to leave him."

"I just hope she's still alive and we haven't read this guy all wrong." Carter nibbled on a fry and sighed. "I'll be interested in hearing Jo's profile of Wanda's killer, because when I saw her body, it looked like a vicious thrill kill to me. If so and he has Naomi King, she's already dead."

THIRTY-NINE

A sense of foreboding surged through Jenna as she followed Blackhawk and his cousin Chogan into the forest. She rode an unfamiliar horse, one of Blackhawk's by the name of Toby. It was a strong gelding but placid enough. Her mare, Seagull, was somewhere in town with Warrior and Anna's pony. The latter would be used to carry supplies. Ahead of her, Blackhawk led a horse packed with supplies for the other team. It was a beautiful day, with sunshine and blue sky that spread across the heavens forever. If she hadn't been in a life-or-death struggle to survive, she'd have relaxed and enjoyed the peaceful surroundings. The forest carried a mixture of smells that were different from the Black Rock Falls alpine fragrance. This part of Stanton Forest held a mixture of botanical scents. The forest floor resembled an artist's palette. Winding between the trees, masses of wild-flowers danced in the breeze. There were many more blooms than she remembered from her visit. Pushing down her appre-hension, she moved forward into the threatening density of trees as Blackhawk led her through the forest, stopping only when they came to a fallen tree.

"This place is safe and we can wait here for the others."

Blackhawk pulled his horse to a halt and slipped from the saddle. He turned to his cousin. "Chogan, keep a watch out for the others and anyone else passing by."

"Sure." Chogan turned a full circle and then smiled. "There's no one in sight."

As Jenna dismounted and went to the saddlebags on the packhorse to retrieve a flask of coffee, she dropped onto a fallen log and passed each of them a cup. As she sipped the fresh brew, her phone vibrated in her top pocket. She pulled it out and found a message from Kalo. As she read the message her stomach squeezed. "Another girl has gone missing from foster care. This one is just out of Blackwater."

"How long ago?" Blackhawk looked at her with concern. "Do you figure the killer has her?"

Rereading the message, Jenna turned back to him. "I don't have the details but she was only reported missing three hours ago. The problem is that kids often run away from foster care, so the local authorities usually wait a time to see if they'll come back." She shrugged. "I would act without delay, but we also have the problem of the carers not reporting the children missing, even though the guidelines tell them if a child goes missing, they must call 911 without delay."

"Are you suggesting she could be in the forest with this monster already?" Chogan's eyes widened. "If the killer left the forest after murdering Wanda, he would have time to get to Blackwater if he had a vehicle."

Nodding Jenna grimaced. "Yeah, I agree. He knows the forest and could travel easily at night. He didn't appear to have any trouble when he was chasing Wanda down." She gripped her cup tightly and stared into the dense trees. "This makes finding his cabin all the more urgent. One night, let alone two, with a man like that could destroy a kid's life. No amount of counseling would remove the memories."

She used the GPS on her satellite phone to relay their coordinates to Kane and added a message about her concerns. She waited for his reply. It came a few moments later.

Aware of the consequences and urgency but both suspects are eating lunch. Leaving in five. See you soon.

To her surprise, it wasn't Kane and Carter who arrived first but Rowley and Rio. Blackhawk and Chogan headed to the perimeter of the forest to keep watch for the suspects. To save time, Jenna decided to wait for Kane and Carter to arrive before they brought them up to date with what happened on the boats. It was some time before Kane and Carter arrived and they took turns discussing the suspects. Surprised when both groups of men considered Elias Miller and Christopher Grant as suspects, Jenna needed clarification. "Okay, but I spoke to Jo this morning and told her what I know about the killer and how he behaved. She was able to give me a basic profile."

She gave them a rundown on her earlier conversation with Jo, emphasizing the danger this man possessed. She looked from one to the other. "Are you convinced both these suspects fit the profile?"

"Yeah, Carter baited Miller a little and he acted like I would expect for a psychopath. Cool, calm, and collected." Kane met her gaze. "We've dealt with too many of these men not to recognize the signs. His calm exterior said one thing, but his eyes told me another story. Miller is a definite maybe."

"Same." Rowley looked at Rio, who nodded. "From what you're saying, it could be either of them. Did you get a shot of Miller? Rio has one of Grant."

Taking the phones one by one, Jenna examined the images and shook her head. "It could be either of them. They both look similar to the man I saw in the forest. I can't be sure which one. I'm sorry."

"There's no need to be sorry." Kane frowned at her. "Both

fit the general description of the man who killed Wanda, so until we eliminate either one as a suspect, we follow the plan. Right?"

Jenna nodded. "Okay, but I'm changing the plan. We won't follow them. It will be too obvious. We'll take the well-worn trails and then hole up and wait for them to pass and then follow them back to their cabins. I hope we don't run into Washington. He's an unknown quantity, and if you see him, don't take any risks." She thought for a beat. "Have a reason for being in the forest. Not that it's anyone's business, but it's good to have something to say if you run into anyone."

Blackhawk's voice came through her earpiece. *"Christopher Grant is heading into the farrier's. Chogan is on his way back. No sign of Miller yet. I'm heading back now."*

Jenna glanced at her team. Everyone had heard the transmission. "Mount up. Call in every ten minutes. If you can't speak, just tap your earpiece. Rapid taps will mean you're in trouble. If so, message your coordinates. Got it?"

Rio and Rowley nodded. She had prepared them well for the mission. Both had liquid Kevlar vests under their shirts and were loaded for bear. She looked from one to the other. "Don't be a hero. If your guy is our man, call it in and we'll head to your position and surround him. We want him alive but he's dangerous. If all else fails, take him down. Do you understand?"

"We sure do, ma'am." Rio touched his hat. "You stay safe now." He turned his horse and followed Chogan into the forest.

In seconds, they'd vanished from view. She smiled at Kane. "How did Seagull behave with Carter?"

"She's been just fine with me." Carter stroked the mare's white neck. "She quickened her pace the moment she laid eyes on you. It's just as well I'll be riding Toby. I believe this little lady is jealous." He held out linked hands and boosted Jenna into the saddle.

"She is dainty in the way she steps but then an Arabian isn't built for rough riding." Kane mounted Warrior. "They're more elegant and she's the only one I've seen since living in these parts." He sighed and turned to Blackhawk. "Have you figured out which way we're heading?"

"Yeah, I used the satellite images of this part of the forest to discover suitable trails. I know where Chogan is leading the others." Blackhawk mounted a fine Appaloosa and led the way through the trees. "It is the most probable area for a cabin and we believe we've found a couple of clearings."

Underfoot, the scent of crushed flowers filled the air with each step deeper into the dense forest. As Jenna rode between Carter and Kane, the closeness of the dark shadows surrounding them didn't appear as daunting as her last visit. After riding for nearly half an hour, they came across a narrow trail leading to the west. All around Jenna had become very quiet. The sudden change in the noisy forest chatter set alarm bells ringing in Jenna's head. A shiver of apprehension ran down her spine. Someone or something was close by watching them. The change in the forest had alerted everyone and even Warrior started to dance and snort.

Sniffing the air, Jenna searched the deep shadows for any signs of a bear. Other animals could smell them immediately, although most times people couldn't unless they'd rolled in something dead. None of the pine trees held any of the distinct scratches usually left by a bear and the forest floor appeared to be clear of scat. Seagull's nostrils flared and she reared without warning, twisting like a cat landing from a great height. Jenna gripped hard with her knees and spoke softly to calm the mare and then came the distinctive sound of a shotgun being racked.

Cha-chung.

Ducking as chaos erupted around her, Jenna jumped from Seagull and dropped the reins, allowing the mare to follow Warrior deep into the forest. The other horses followed close behind weaving through the trees and vanishing into the shadows. Jenna headed for cover and ducked behind a rough trunk of a pine tree. Without a sound, Kane was beside her, weapon drawn. He indicated to their right and was giving hand signals to Carter, who Jenna couldn't see. When Kane's eyes slid to her and he held his hand up like a cop stopping traffic, she shook her head. When Kane mouthed the words *Cover me* and, without waiting for a response, vanished into the shadows, Jenna swallowed hard. She'd seen the damage a shotgun could do at close range and fear for his safety gripped her. In her ear, Blackhawk spoke so softly, she could only just make out his words.

"There's a boulder behind you, through the trees. I'm here. Come this way. It offers greater protection."

Heart pounding, she tapped her mic. Kane would have heard the transmission, and bending, she weaved between the trees and dived behind the boulder. Blackhawk pulled her to her feet and pointed in the direction Kane had vanished. She pulled her weapon from the shoulder holster and, using the top of the boulder to rest her elbows, aimed it in that direction. She could see clearly through the vegetation growing tall all around her. Protected by the solid lump of granite and concealed by the bushes, she peered into the forest looking for Kane or Carter. Nerves shattered by the sudden quiet, she took deep breaths. Her gut had been right, someone was out there but nothing moved in the shadows and no sound came from the direction Kane had gone. The forest was silent as if it were holding its breath and waiting for something to happen.

Boom!

Cha-chung.

Boom!

FORTY

The loud boom sent flocks of birds flying high into the air, and Rowley turned in his saddle to look at Rio. "That was a shotgun. What direction?"

"The echo makes it difficult." Rio reined up beside him. "From the direction Jenna was heading, I figure." He hit the button on his com. "Are you guys okay? We heard a shot."

The two taps that came back came through their coms, could mean they were fine and investigating or pinned down. He looked at Chogan. "That wasn't the reply I'd expect if they needed backup. We should keep going. It could be a disgruntled property owner and Jenna's team will handle him."

They moved on, winding through the forest, taking narrow pathways used by elk and deer. The deeper they traveled into the forest the cooler it became. The tall pines and dark shadows seemed to suck the warmth from the air. They followed a small creek, Chogan insisting that if there were any cabins in this part of the forest, they'd be near a water supply. After traveling for about twenty minutes, they arrived at a small clearing. The surrounding forest had been cut down, leaving stumps all over. Rowley frowned. It was illegal to destroy any part of the forest in this area, but it was obvious the wood had been used to build a rough cabin. It was difficult to determine if the cabin was inhabited. Apart from a pile of firewood stacked up in a lean-to, the building looked deserted. Not wanting to take any chances, Rowley dismounted and waved the others into the cover of the trees. He looked at Chogan and kept his voice just above a whisper. "Stay with the horses. We'll go take a look." He turned to Rio. "I'll take the left."

Rio gave him a nod and slipped into the trees to his right. Apprehensive and heart thumping a military tattoo in his chest, Rowley headed left, moving through the trees to approach the cabin from the rear. It was difficult in the dense vegetation and with each step branches clung to his clothes like long fingers trying to drag him back. He stumbled over exposed tree roots, grazing his knuckles on the rough pine bark. Eventually he reached the back of the cabin. The lean-to must be used for a horse as a pile of manure sat in a wheelbarrow, and the floor at the back was covered in clean straw. Rowley scratched his head at the sight. This place was in the middle of nowhere. Where did the straw come from? His question was answered when he spotted an old scythe leaning against the wall and roughly tied bundles of hay. It would be difficult cutting grass and drying it for enough winter feed. The area in front of the cabin was hardly enough to feed one horse let alone extra for a winter supply.

He walked round the back and met Rio heading toward him. "Someone lives here."

"So I gathered." Rio indicated to the other side of the cabin. "There's a vegetable patch and it's been tended recently. I peered in the window. It's empty as far as I can see. I figure we make ourselves scarce and watch. If one of our suspects is on his way home, he won't be too far behind us."

Needing to know if there were any signs of a woman in the house, Rowley nodded. "You go and keep a lookout. If the door isn't locked, I'm going inside to take a look. I know it's not legal, but if there're any signs he kept a girl in there, I want to know."

"It would be easier if we hunted around for the graves Jenna mentioned." Rio blew out a sigh. "What if he comes back? Do you really want a showdown with a serial killer?"

Shaking his head, Rowley looked at him. "We need to know." He walked to the front door and tried the knob. It turned and the door swung open with a soft squeak. He turned to Rio. "Go. I'll be five minutes. Use the com if you see anyone and ask Chogan to take the horses a ways away so they don't make a noise."

"Okay, but it's not following procedure." Rio stared at him hands on hips.

Frustrated, Rowley stared at him. "It's not like we can get a search warrant, is it? This place isn't on a map, and if one of our suspects lives here, it's owned by a dead man."

He ignored Rio's protests and stepped inside. The cabin was what he expected from someone living off the grid. Not overly tidy, dishes sitting in a plastic bowl on the kitchen table. It was primitive living until he caught sight of a CB radio set up in one corner. So this cabin had a power source? Going to the device, he followed the wires. No doubt a solar panel on the roof and a rechargeable battery. He searched the main room and then moved to the bedroom, opening the door slowly and peering inside. The unmade bed had sheets that hadn't been washed for a decade. He opened a few drawers and found women's underwear and hair accessories. He pushed the drawer shut and was just about to open the closet door when Rio's voice came in his ear.

"He's coming. It's our suspect, Grant, so he's going to recognize us." Rio swore under his breath. "He's coming in fast and he'll see you if you take the front door. Look for a window, or something."

Panic gripped him. "Copy."

Turning in a circle, Rowley went to the window and tried to push it open. It was stuck tight. Heart pounding, he moved to the door, not making a sound and closed it. It had been shut when he arrived, and he needed time. He heard the front door open and the sound of supplies being dumped on the kitchen table. Footsteps sounded across the wooden floor as Christopher Grant headed back outside. Rowley went back to the window and peered through the dusty glass and froze. To his horror he realized the bedroom looked into the lean-to and ducked away just as Grant led his horse into the makeshift stable. He had seconds to get out the front door before Grant unsaddled his horse.

Opening the bedroom door, Rowley headed across the floor to the front door. Halfway across, the sound of Grant coughing made him dive between a ratty old sofa set in front of the fireplace and a coffee table. Holding his breath as Grant carried more things to the kitchen table, he started to move the moment the man's footsteps left the wooden floor. Following so close, he watched Grant's back turn into the lean-to. Rowley headed in the opposite direction and pressed his back against the right side of the cabin, gasping for breath. Unable to make a break for it, and risk Grant hearing him running away, he crouched down and waited. It seemed to take forever for Grant to return to the house. He might live like a pig, but he obviously cared for his horse. He heard the sound of Grant moving through the grass, and then in the forest a horse whinnied.

Frozen to the spot and knees aching from crouching, Rowley peeked around the side of the cabin. Grant stood staring into the forest, scanning the vast expanse of trees for a long time. Finally, he turned and headed inside. The moment the front door squeaked shut, Rowley took off at a run into the forest and circled around to meet up with Rio.

"Well, that was the stupidest thing I've ever seen." Rio rubbed his chin. "I could just imagine explaining that to your wife if he'd shot you." He rolled his eyes. "Jenna will go ballistic when we give her an update."

Unfazed, Rowley followed Rio to where Chogan waited with the horses. "I found women's underwear and other stuff. Solid evidence."

"Yeah, maybe, but he heard the horses." Rio frowned and rubbed the back of his neck. "He knows we're here."

"We should move upstream and make camp before he comes searching for us." Chogan looked from one to the other. "Higher ground gives a better vantage point and we'll be able to watch him from there." He mounted his horse. "Take the horses into the river. We don't need to be leaving tracks for him to follow."

"Sure." Rio shook his head slowly. "Maybe it's evidence or maybe he buys it from yard sales. Whatever, it wasn't worth risking your life for, Jake."

Convinced they had a solid suspect, Rowley shrugged. "If I'm right about this guy, it was worth the darn risk." He snorted. "And I'd do it again."

FORTY-ONE

Cha-chung.

Boom!

The air filled with pine needles and shattered bark rained down on Jenna. In her ear came Kane's voice.

"Stay down. He's firing into the air. It's not either of the suspects we've met."

"Stay out of my yard." It was a man's voice. "I don't give no second warning."

"I figure he heard the horses." Carter sounded calm. *"Seems to me he must live close by."*

Shotgun pellets pinged on the rock and Jenna pushed under the curve of the boulder with Blackhawk. *"Copy. Hold your positions."*

Her eyes widened as a rider came into view through the trees. He was standing up in his stirrups looking around before riding off in the opposite direction. As Jenna turned her head, she caught sight of movement in the trees. She tapped her mic and dropped her voice so low she hoped the team could hear her. "We have company. On a parallel trail to where we are, he's coming from behind us. I can see him through the trees. I figure it's Miller. He's not carrying a shotgun."

"Copy." Kane was nowhere in sight. *"I have eyes on the shooter. He's moving west. Yeah, the other man is Miller. Don't anyone move and he'll go right past without seeing us."*

As the rider moved slowly along the trail, Jenna ran her gaze over him, trying to make out if he was the man who'd killed Wanda. The image in her mind wasn't clear and all she could see were the two photographs that Rio and Kane had shown her earlier. She dropped down behind the boulder and waited for Kane to signal when they could move. Ants crawled over her boots and started up her legs, but she didn't move and hardly took a breath as the jingle of the horse's tack pierced the silent forest. She hoped Warrior wouldn't start making a noise. With a strange horse close by and him surrounded by mares, Kane's stallion was getting overprotective, although he seemed to get along fine with Toby the gelding. Blowing out her breath as Kane's voice came through her com, she relaxed against the boulder and brushed the ants from her jeans.

"We're heading back to you. Stay down and don't make a noise."

Jenna nodded to Blackhawk, who smiled at her. She tapped her com. "Copy."

Moments later Kane and Carter emerged from the shadows and crouched beside her. Jenna looked from one to the other. "Did you see which way he went?"

"Yeah, right where Atohi figured." Kane indicated with his thumb over one shoulder. "I could hear water, so a slow-running creek. He must have a cabin close by. We'll go find the horses and then follow the creek. He should leave a trail we can follow. I figure we give him a head start, to avoid him hearing us." He turned and scanned the forest. "It's going to be difficult finding a black horse in the shadows, but he'll be leading them that's for sure."

"They went that way." Blackhawk stood slowly and peered into the forest. "Warrior isn't startled by gunshots, is he?"

"Nope, he's solid." Kane rubbed the back of his neck. "I hope he's not taking them back to town."

"I doubt it. He is loyal to you, Dave, and wouldn't have taken the mares too far." Blackhawk peered between the trees. "I'll be able to track them. The ground is soft between the trees."

"Great." Kane turned slowly, searching the forest. "I don't see or hear anyone. We're good to go."

Brushing pine needles and bark from her shoulders, Jenna nodded. "Okay, move out."

The way between the trees was narrow and dark. Jenna followed Kane and Blackhawk, and as if by agreement, Carter followed behind. It was obvious they were keeping her between them for safety as if it were an unwritten law or something. She smiled to herself. One thing was for darn sure, there was no taking the military out of either of them. They took their oath to protect very seriously and right now she'd become the focus of their protective shield. She spotted the ghostly outline of Seagull between the trees and sighed with relief. Hiking through a forest might be fun, but sore all over, she needed Seagull. They'd left their backpacks with their supplies on the horses to make it easier to move through the dense vegetation. Without them they'd be toast. Speaking softly to Seagull, she rubbed her silken neck and had taken hold of the mare's reins when Rio's voice came through her com.

"We've been listening to your transmissions and kept radio silence. We found Grant's cabin and had it under observation. He lives alone. We checked out his cabin before he arrived home, but now he's on the move. He was inside for half an hour or so and then shot out of the door as if his ass were on fire. We're following at a distance."

Jenna pressed her com. "Maybe he went to investigate the shots?"

"If he did, then he's heading in your direction."

Mounting Seagull, Jenna looked over at Kane. "Copy. We're following Miller, he just rode by but it wasn't him shooting. That guy issued a warning to stay out of his yard, and then took off. We're heading alongside the creek. I'll send the coordinates. If you've seen Grant's cabin and there's no girl there, he's not our man."

"Problem is, Rowley found women's underwear in his cabin, so either he's kinky or he's had a woman living there at one time. We looked around but found no graves."

"Stay on him. We'll need to know where he is in case he's a threat." Kane mounted Warrior, who was grazing nearby. "I wouldn't discount any of them yet."

Jenna nodded. "Me either. Keep me apprised of your position."

"Copy."

"That's all we need, three suspects in the forest at the same time." Kane shook his head and turned Warrior to follow Blackhawk.

A cool breeze whistled through the trees as they reached the sandy edge of a narrow creek. Miller's tracks were easy to follow in the sand, so they took a slow pace. Jenna looked at the creek with a different perspective than the last terrifying visit to these parts. Safe with Kane and the others, and riding with the sun on her after being in the cold dark forest, she only had the bruises to remind herself they were chasing down a killer. The water ran crystal clear and sunlight glistened on the wet rocks as it rushed over them. It was another small extension of Black Rock Falls, winding its way through the entire forest, giving a constant flow of water to the wildlife. It was remarkable and as if it had been carefully planned. Jenna stared into the clear blue sky above the cottonwoods alongside the creek and smiled. Maybe it had been planned.

Her mind went to Tauri. In her heart he was already her son and had been from the day they took him to the ranch. There had been no doubt he belonged with them. His happy smile and the warmth around her heart whenever she thought about him made her content. The way Kane played with him and involved him in everything. He was a great father and his love for the little boy shone from him. If she'd had a baby, Blackhawk wouldn't have considered them as possible parents. The offer to foster him with the chance of adoption would never have happened. She couldn't imagine missing out on having Tauri in their lives, and a baby could still come along. After all, it happened to many people who'd adopted first.

Her stomach gave a twist, remembering the final court date was fast approaching for the adoption. That day he would legally become their son, but it wasn't a done deal. It was nerve-wracking waiting for all the reports to be filed, wondering if they'd met all the requirements. Although they'd completed every prerequisite, the judge would consider all the reports and had the final say. Not knowing was tearing her apart, but she clung to hope. It had been helpful that Blackhawk had been made his legal guardian. His recommendation and the fact he and his family would be involved in Tauri's life had made it easier. If no one came forward to claim him, and they were deemed suitable parents, on that day he would become Tauri Kane.

Dragged from her thoughts when the horses stopped in front of her, she stared at Kane as he signaled for silence. When he slipped from Warrior and slid his rifle from the saddle holster, she dismounted and did the same. He waved everyone into the shelter of the trees. Jenna lowered her voice to a whisper. "What's wrong?"

"I smell smoke." Kane indicated behind him. "No one

would light a fire in the forest, it's too dangerous, so it must be a cabin. I figure we leave the horses here and go on foot to scope it out."

Jenna nodded. "Okay, what do you suggest? We spread out or stick together? How far do you think the cabin is from here?"

"Not far and it's definitely woodsmoke." Kane glanced at Carter. "If we stick together until we get a visual on the cabin and then I'll go one way and Carter the other, we'll be able to surround it. We use our coms to communicate our positions. The thing is, do we go right in and see if he has the missing girl or observe?" His eyes met Jenna's. "It's your call."

Thinking through the plan, Jenna nodded. "We observe because we have an unknown variable here, and that's the third suspect, Josiah Washington. We have no idea where he went. The cabin could be his, as he was concerned about 'his yard.' Miller could still be moving ahead. Unless we keep following his tracks, we'll never know."

"Take the backpacks." Kane unstrapped his from Warrior's saddle and shrugged into it and then helped Jenna. "We don't know what to expect or how long we'll be out there."

They walked along the riverbank for another hundred yards before the tracks moved back into the forest. The trail between the trees was evident and wide enough for two horses abreast. Increasing their pace, they moved in silence slowing when the trail led to a secluded cabin. It was a good size, with a front porch and a separate building. Out front, Miller's horse was tethered to a hitching post. The bulging saddlebags had been removed. The front door was open and voices drifted out toward them, but what they were saying was muffled. Jenna moved up close to Kane. "That's not a girl's voice."

"It sounds like the CB radio. Someone is calling him." Kane looked at Jenna. "Stay here with Blackhawk and watch the front door. We'll circle around and move in."

Jenna shook her head. "Use your scope and look inside the front door. If a girl is in there, you might see her."

"More likely she'll be restrained if she's in there." Kane narrowed his gaze at her. "If it's him, he doesn't care about her comfort, does he?"

They didn't get the time to argue about tactics when Miller came out the door dragging a teenager by the arm. The girl's hands and mouth were bound with gaffer tape. From the description Kalo had messaged her, it was the missing girl, Naomi King. When Miller shoved her roughly into the shed, slid the bolt securing the door, and then headed toward the cabin, Jenna went for her weapon. She moved forward and then reconsidered when Kane rested a hand on her arm.

"Wait. Someone warned him we were coming. So, he could have backup." Kane scanned the forest. "If he does, we'll need to keep the fight away from the shed to keep her safe."

Nodding, Jenna took in the surroundings. The forest came right up to the small clearing holding the cabin. It was so well hidden if they hadn't followed Miller, they'd have never found it. She turned to Carter, who was peering through his rifle scope at the cabin, "Okay, what's he doing now?"

"He's on the move, carrying a rifle and a box of ammo. He's heading into the forest." Carter pointed to the west. "Right now it's our chance to grab him. We know he's our man."

Making a decision on the fly, Jenna looked at Kane. "Go get him. I'll go with Atohi and release the girl. I'll bring her back here."

"Nah." Kane shook his head. "If you get the girl, head back to where we left the horses." He looked at Blackhawk. "Get Jenna and the girl to safety. We'll grab Miller and his horse and meet you along the riverbank." He gave Jenna a long look. "The girl is our first priority, right?"

Jenna nodded. "Yeah. Go!"

With a nod, Kane moved away from her, and in seconds, he

and Carter had vanished into the trees. Jenna looked all around and then turned to Blackhawk. "We'll use the trees for cover and circle around, just in case Miller doubles back."

"That works for me." Blackhawk smiled at her. "I'm glad we found her."

As they made their way through the forest, Jenna noticed a patch of sunlight and headed toward it, stopping dead at the sight of three graves and one open and ready for use. "This seals the deal with Miller. This is what Wanda described to me. We'd better keep going."

They reached the side of the small building, and Jenna stared into the shadowy forest, but nothing moved. She ran across the clearing and headed for the small building. As she reached out one hand to slide the bolt, a shot rang out and a bullet smacked into the door six inches away from her head. "I'm under fire."

"*On my way.*" She could hear Kane running through the forest, but would he get there in time?

As more shots pierced the silence, Jenna dropped and rolled. Out in the open with no cover, she didn't stand a chance. All around her the grass jumped as bullets smacked into the ground. Dust and hunks of soil splattered her face. Shots were ringing out all over. Her only hope was to keep moving. Pain from her bruised and scraped knees screamed as she rolled and tried to crawl away but there was nowhere to hide. The hail of bullets didn't let up and it was only a matter of time before one of them hit her. Kane would never make it on time. *I'm going to die.*

FORTY-TWO

Bullets whizzed past Kane, splitting the branches all around him. In his ear he heard Carter.

"Ambush. We're surrounded. I saw two muzzle flashes, one north and one south of our positions. I figure from the other shots, our third shooter is the one who has Jenna pinned down near the shed. Showing the girl was a ploy to get us out into the open."

Using a tree for cover, Kane slid down to sit on the floor. "Stay down. They don't know we have a backup team. Rio, are you hearing this?"

"Copy that." Rio sounded tense. *"Grant took off at a gallop in your direction. He knows the forest and took trails we'd never have found. We lost him but found his horse. We're on foot, ETA five minutes."*

"Copy. We'll take out the guy shooting at Jenna. I'll need you to keep Grant and Miller occupied for a time. Tell Chogan to take cover, then identify yourselves and return fire if necessary." Kane's attention went to Jenna. "Jenna, hang in there. We're under fire but on our way back to you. I'm not going to attempt to take the shooters down. Rio and Rowley are in the line of fire."

"It's only a matter of time before he hits me. He's shooting all around me." Jenna sucked in a deep breath. *"It's like he's playing with me."*

"That has to be Washington. He's crazy." Carter was his usual calm self, as if he were out on a picnic. *"You're female. He's a lonely old guy. He probably wants to keep you."*

"I'm not betting my life on that, Ty." Jenna gasped in a breath. *"Hurry, I've no cover out here."*

As shots rang out above him, Kane crab-walked through the trees heading to Washington's position. Moments later, he spotted Carter moving through the forest ten yards away from him. They moved in a parallel path toward Washington. It became obvious why the man was missing Jenna. Kane could smell the liquor on him and he was staggering from side to side as he waved the rifle around. Kane straightened, aimed his rifle, and raised his voice. "Sheriff's department. Put down your weapon."

"It makes no never mind." Washington spun around his rifle and aimed at Kane's head. "Law or not, you ain't allowed on my property."

"This ain't your property." Carter stepped out of the bushes. "FBI, and this land belongs to Black Rock Falls County. You're trespassing."

This close Washington wouldn't miss, but Jenna would want the man alive and it was obvious he wasn't planning on going quietly. Kane's attention moved to Washington's finger resting on the trigger. It twitched and Kane blasted a hole in his shoulder. As Washington fell backward with the force of the blast, Kane hit his com. "Jenna, Washington's down. If you watch the girl, we'll hunt down the others. Leave her in the shed and take cover. We have two shooters in the forest heading your way."

"Copy. Is he dead?" Jenna sounded out of breath. *"I've taken cover. Atohi is with me."*

Sighing with relief, Kane watched as Carter dragged Washington to a sapling and secured his arms around it and tied his ankles together with zip ties. "No. Dead drunk. He'll need medical attention, but it's a through and through. Carter is fixing him up. He'll do for now. We'll need to know your position at all times because things are going to get dangerous real fast. These guys have got nothing to lose."

"Copy."

The sound of a gunfight echoed through the forest. From the sound, Grant and Miller were on opposite sides and moving in on Rio and Rowley. Impatient to get moving, Kane paced as Carter pushed dressings over Washington's wounds. "Let's go or I'll have two dead deputies to explain to Jenna."

"I'm done here." Carter stripped off examination gloves and tossed them beside Washington, who was leaning against the tree, dead drunk or semiconscious. It was difficult to tell.

Summing up the situation and dropping into combat mode, Kane pointed to the opposite side of the forest. "We'll need to split up. Keep down to avoid friendly fire, and when you're behind one of the shooters, let me know."

"Copy that." Carter was swallowed by the forest.

As Kane moved toward the noise of gunfire, he stopped and listened. He could clearly hear Rio and Rowley's attempt to keep both men engaged but something was terribly wrong. Only one man was returning fire, not two. He hit his com. "Carter, have you got eyes on one of the shooters and can you identify him?"

"Yeah, I'm coming up on him now. Just a second, I'll pick him up on my scope." Moments passed. *"It's Grant."*

Miller is going back for the girl. Dammit, Jenna will try and stop him. Kane whirled around and, ignoring the bullets whizzing over his head, bounded through the forest. He hit his com. "Jenna, Miller is heading back in your direction. He'll kill the girl. He won't want a witness."

"He's not touching the girl."

FORTY-THREE

Calm determination filled Jenna as she listened to Kane's message. The rough bark of the pine tree pressed into her back as she caught Blackhawk's stone-faced expression. It was as if he could read her mind. "He won't be expecting me. I'll be able to get the jump on him."

"You know what he did to Wanda." Blackhawk shook his head. "He'll kill both of us without a second thought."

Stomach clenching, Jenna shook her head. Stiff from the grazes and bruises, she wouldn't be at her best, but determined to make him pay for what he'd done, she lifted her chin. "That's why I need to stop him. If I don't, he'll keep on hurting people."

The sight of Miller coming out of the forest startled her. It had only been a minute or so since she'd spoken to Kane. Miller made no sound and was bigger than she'd remembered. He moved with fluidity, holding his rifle shoulder-high and aiming in an arc. He reminded her of the way Kane and Carter used their weapons and the idea he was military trained chilled her to the bone. Heart pounding, she ducked back and pressed against a tree. Silently, she pulled her weapon. She'd have the element of surprise, but if he was military, taking him into custody alone would be difficult. She might train daily and had superior hand-to-hand combat skills, but life wasn't like TV shows. A military-trained man, fit and strong, could overpower her in seconds.

Indicating to Blackhawk to keep down, she peered around the tree as Miller approached the shed. When he turned slowly, aiming into the forest with his back to her, she had seconds to make her move, and taking a deep breath, she stepped out from behind the tree and aimed center mass. "Sheriff's department. Drop your weapon and put your hands on your head."

"Now, why would I do that, Sheriff?" The man whipped around and in a split second had his weapon aimed at her head. "First, I don't take orders from a woman, and second, I'll blow your head clean from your shoulders before you pull the trigger. Chances are, at this distance, you'll miss. The thing is: I don't miss." His lips quirked up into a smile. "You be a good girl and drop your weapon. I'll make it easy on you. There's no cavalry coming. You're all on your lonesome."

Don't miss? Just like Dave, huh? Was it the truth or a psychopath's guile to disarm her? She gave a toss of her head, but her eyes never left his face. She'd die before she gave up her weapon. Jenna swallowed hard. "I don't miss either. So, it seems we'll be here for a time."

"I'm coming." Kane's voice came through her com. "Get ready. I'll distract him and you'll have a split second before he kills me. Take him down. Jenna... for me."

With Kane heading her way, she had backup. Blackhawk was close by, but he'd made it clear that shooting a person wasn't an option and had left his rifle with his horse. Delaying the outcome was her only chance of survival in a no-win situation. She stared at the man's determined gaze and the hairs on the back of her neck stood erect. There could be no negotiating with a psychopath. It would be a battle of wills or who pulled the trigger first. She drew a deep breath. Just a few more seconds and Kane would be walking out of the forest. Panic gripped her and she pushed it down. It would be him or Kane. She grit her teeth. "Why don't you give up now? I have four deputies in the forest and they're all heading this way."

He ignored her and the rifle aiming at her head didn't waver. His eyes fixed on her, watching her with a fierce intensity. This was the last face Wanda had seen, the black unyielding eyes, the mouth set in a straight line. Panic threatened to rise up again and swallow her, but Jenna held her ground, holding her weapon in two hands and keeping her aim true. They stared at each other, and she sensed rather than saw Blackhawk moving toward the back of the shed. She hoped he wasn't planning on rushing Miller from behind. He wouldn't stand a chance.

"Look, it's nothing personal, Sheriff. You're in the way, is all." Miller's sudden change of demeanor didn't fool her. He smiled as if he was enjoying the situation. "I know you're scared. Your hands are shaking, I bet your knees are too. Your deputies are dead. The shooting has stopped, which means we've already won. You were sloppy, untrained, and we all knew you were in the forest." He chuckled. "I could smell you. Honeysuckle, right? Maybe I shouldn't kill you. You might come in useful. Me and the boys don't get too many women visitors."

Miller was standing in her line of sight, and directly behind him, Kane emerged from the shadows at the edge of the clearing. It was difficult to keep her eyes on Miller and not telegraph Kane was behind him. When Kane's fingers went to his lips and he let out a high-pitched whistle. Miller spun around and aimed the rifle at Kane. Without a second thought, Jenna pulled the trigger. Two shots rang out and Miller let out a piercing scream.

The rifle fell from his hand as he crumpled to the ground, blood pooling around him. She'd shot him in both calves, shattering his bones. She walked over to him and picked up his rifle. As he cursed her, she smiled at him. "Dammit, I missed. I was aiming higher."

FORTY-FOUR

Jenna turned as Kane came up behind her. The only sound was his gun sliding back inside his shoulder holster. "You have impeccable timing."

"Great shot!" Kane turned slowly to stare at Miller. "You're lucky. I wouldn't have been so considerate."

"You can all go straight to hell." Miller gripped his shattered legs, writhing in pain.

"It is good to see you, Dave." Blackhawk came from around the side of the shed carrying a length of wood the size of a baseball bat.

"See, I wasn't needed at all." Kane raised both eyebrows. "I've seen Atohi swing a bat. Home run every time." He nodded. "Right?"

"Maybe a slight exaggeration, but his head is much larger than a baseball." Blackhawk tossed the log aside and brushed his hands.

Her mind on the girl's welfare, Jenna left Kane to deal with Miller and went to the shed. She slid open the bolt and dragged open the door. As she stepped inside the dark recess, she stared into the terrified eyes of Naomi King. "I'm Sheriff Alton. You're safe now."

Having been bound with gaffer tape once herself, she recalled how painful it was to remove. Taking special care, she removed the tape from Naomi's mouth and slid her knife under it to cut through it. The tape was stuck fast to the girl's hair and would need a solvent to remove. She'd leave it until after a doctor had seen her. "There, I'll leave the rest and we'll get it removed later."

Taking a bottle of water from her backpack, Jenna handed it to the girl. "Sit down on the sack of potatoes and relax. It will be all right. Can you tell me what happened?"

"My foster father sold me to one of the men. They never used names. I had to call him Husband. It was terrible. He said he'd keep me for a time and then kill me. He's killed all his wives and buried them in the forest. He's crazy. They're all crazy."

The girl was covered in bruises and was wearing a short nightgown and nothing else. Jenna swallowed hard. She smelled really bad and the question she must ask caught in her throat. She laid one hand on the girl's shoulder. "Did he rape you?"

"They all did." Naomi stared into space. Not one tear ran down her cheeks. "I heard him screaming. Did you kill him?"

Sick to her stomach, Jenna shook her head. "No, I shot him and broke both his legs. Do you have clothes in the cabin?"

"I think so." Naomi was staring into space.

Keeping her voice conversational, Jenna took her arm. "We'll go and find you something to wear over the nightie. Don't wash, okay? We'll need to get a doctor to take some swabs to use in evidence against the men who hurt you. Once you're ready, we'll be riding back to town. You won't be going back to Blackwater. You'll be staying in Black Rock Falls. We have a special place for women who have been through similar situations and it's very safe. Not like foster care, more like a hotel. The other women are very nice and just like you. There are kids there with their moms as well. No one will ever hurt you again while you're in my town. I promise."

"You don't seem like the others. The do-gooders who figure they know what it's like. For them it's just a job." Naomi gave her a searching look. "You were abused once, right?"

Nodding, Jenna headed for the door. "Yeah, and I and my husband—he's the deputy outside—founded Her Broken Wings Foundation and we build places where abused women and men can live in safety. We have programs to get them into decent jobs and homes. They're protected by my department and have a hotline directly to me to call if ever they don't feel safe. We'll do everything to help you live a normal life. It will be your choice. You won't be thrust into a foster home unless it's with a family you like. The foster care system in my town is very heavily supervised. You're never a number or a case file."

"You'll want all the information on those men, right?" Naomi swallowed hard. "I'm not sure I can tell everyone in a courtroom what happened. All those people staring at me. I know what happens. They all believe I encouraged the men. I've watched TV shows. It's always the girl's fault."

Honesty was paramount at this stage and Jenna nodded. "If you want them put away for life, we'll need as many details as you can remember. Especially if they have any distinguishing marks, for instance, that are generally covered." She squeezed her arm. "We can arrange for a video link to the court, so you'll only see the lawyers. The defense lawyer will ask you questions, which may be distressing, but the prosecution will be on your side and he or she will speak to you beforehand and tell you what to expect. You'll need to be strong. Can you be strong, Naomi?"

"Yes." Naomi sighed. "They can't really do any more damage, can they?"

They walked out of the shed and Naomi pulled away from her. Jenna went to grab her, but Kane held up a hand to stop her.

"If she has something to say to Miller, it's best she has her say now." Kane beckoned Naomi closer, pulled his weapon, and aimed it at Miller's head. "Just give me an excuse."

"I'll bleed to death if you don't do something." Miller's face twisted in pain. "You have a duty of care. I know the law."

"Do I? According to the records, you're a dead man." Kane stared him down. "There's a grave already dug close by. No one would ever know and I wouldn't lose any sleep over scum like you or your buddies."

Jenna walked beside the girl as she approached Miller. She expected a tirade but Naomi didn't say a word. Calm and in control, she walked up to Miller and kicked him hard in one of his shattered legs. She stared at him as he yelped in agony and then spat in his face. Head erect, she turned and walked to the cabin. Shaking her head, Jenna went to follow.

"Give her some time alone." Kane stared after Naomi. "I figure she'll want some privacy to dress. You told her not to wash, right?"

Sighing, Jenna nodded. "Yeah, poor kid. She seems so remote. Shock most likely. I'll give her a few minutes to collect herself and then go and check on her." She blinked when Carter's voice came in her ear.

"We have Grant in custody." Carter chuckled. *"Well, he will be, but he's resting right now. You wanted him alive, so I just hit him from behind."*

Jenna smiled at Kane and touched her com. "Copy. Great job. We have Miller and the girl is safe."

"I heard the screams." Carter sounded amused. *"Isn't it*

strange how these abusers can't handle the other side of the coin?"

Jenna glanced at Kane, who was shaking his head. "Oh, I didn't abuse him, Ty. I could have killed him but instead I took out both of his legs, but the girl he raped wasn't so considerate." She paused a beat. "Are Rowley and Rio near your position?"

"Copy." Rowley's voice came through the com. *"We've found their horses. We'll collect the prisoners and bring them to the cabin."*

Looking down at the bleeding man, Jenna nodded. "Copy."

She removed her backpack and pulled out the first aid kit. Although seeing Miller in pain, seemed like Karma to her. He'd been right, she did have duty of care. Although he wasn't bleeding out, she'd need to bind his wounds, and one look at Kane's combat face told her not to ask him to tend the prisoner. Naomi was in the cabin getting dressed and would be fine for a few more minutes. Ignoring the pain from her own cuts and scrapes, she pulled on examination gloves and wrapped thick pressure bandages over each wound and then used zip ties to secure Miller's wrists. "You'll live, but the ride back to town is going to be painful." She stood and removed the examination gloves and rolled them into a ball. She looked at Kane. "When the others arrive, leave them with the prisoners and come and help me toss the cabin for evidence."

"Yes, ma'am." Kane's mouth turned up at the corner and his eyes sparkled with undisguised pride.

Walking on air, Jenna headed for the cabin, making mental notes on where to go from here. Three men in custody, and now it would take very careful questioning to discover the extent of their involvement. She'd need Wolfe's and Norrell's teams out to recover the bodies in the graves and maybe call in Jo to assist with the interviews. In fact, having Jo's expertise when it came to questioning Naomi might be crucial. The girl was obviously in shock, which wasn't surprising considering the ordeal she'd been through. It was great to be able to reach out to the local FBI field office for assistance and make use of their resources when necessary. As sheriff, she'd always be in charge in her county, not that it really mattered. Her team's involvement went deeper. Ty Carter, Jo Wells, and Bobby Kalo had become part of her extended family. Not bonded by blood but by a friendship second to none.

FORTY-FIVE

Black Rock Falls

The call came in from Jenna late in the afternoon. Wolfe rubbed his chin. A young girl raped by three men would need special care. She'd been there when the men were detained and traveled back to town with them. It must have been a harrowing experience for her, especially when she'd insisted on facing them and then formally identified them as the men who'd raped her. Her insistence that Miller was the man who'd taken her from the foster home had ensured they'd remain in custody pending further forensic results.

Wolfe walked from his office and made his way through to the other building. Forensic anthropologist Norrell Larson was, like him, a qualified doctor. After Jenna had fallen into the river, Norrell had abandoned her work at Bear Peak and had returned with only soil samples. The graves were deep and would take careful handling. Once Jenna and her team had completed the current case, they'd be returning to the old grave sites. He entered her examination room and waited by the door. His heart always missed a beat when he watched her working. Well, most times really. She was beautiful and it went right through. He'd never seen her angry. She seemed to be the most adjusted person he'd ever met.

"Shane." Norrell checked the clock on the wall. "Oh, is something wrong? I thought I'd missed dinner again. I get so absorbed in my work."

Wolfe smiled at her. He found himself doing that a lot these days. "Mind if we speak outside?"

At her nod, he headed for the hallway. When she followed, removing her gloves and looking at him with a concerned expression, he moved closer. "Jenna is bringing in a fourteen-year-old girl who informed her she was raped by three men. I figure as she wouldn't be wanting a male doctor examining her, you might be able to help out?" He blew out a breath. "I know you're busy and all, but we need this done right. Jenna has three men in custody and she believes one of them murdered Wanda Beauchamp. There are graves on the property as well. We'll need to exhume the bodies."

"Of course I'll examine the girl. My case isn't urgent." Norrell removed her scrubs. "By the soil samples, I'd say the remains in the grave at Bear Peak are at least six to ten years old. I'll get my team ready to roll in the morning. Where are we going?"

"It's the western part of Stanton Forest, out at Cottonwood Lake. It will be on horseback, so you might be back and forth a few times before we recover all the bodies, maybe three."

"Okay, fine. I'll have the team prepare what we need." Norrell narrowed her gaze. "I'll set up an examination room here for the girl. It will be stressful taking her to the morgue. I have plenty of warm rooms. I'll get my team to set one up, so send Jenna to my back entrance. I'll make sure to meet them when they arrive if you give me a heads-up."

Wolfe smiled at her. "Thanks. I'll process all the evidence. I'll need the whole ten yards: swabs, nails, images of bruises or contusions, and blood and saliva samples."

"So, the usual?" Norrell touched his face and kissed him. "Thanks for bringing me in on this case. I really feel like part of the team."

Wolfe chuckled. "You're part of the family now." He pushed a strand of white-blonde hair behind one of her ears and sighed. "I'm so glad you came to Black Rock Falls."

"Trust me, I had more than work on my mind when I accepted your offer." She grinned and her smile lit up her eyes. "I think you did as well."

Nodding, Wolfe was suddenly sixteen again and awkward around girls. "Darn it and I thought I was being subtle." He stepped away from her as one of her team emerged from a nearby room. "I'd better be heading back. I'll call you when Jenna is close by."

"Okay. Is Emily in today?" Norrell smiled at him. "It would be better than a male assistant, if the girl is in shock."

Wolfe checked his watch. "She'll be here before you start. She usually drops by after class. I'll call her and make sure. I'll come by and collect the samples. We'll need to process them without delay." As one of her assistants was hovering in the hallway waiting to speak to Norrell, he gave her a nod and headed back to the mortuary.

He made the call to Jenna and arranged for his daughter Emily, currently studying for her medical degree, to assist Norrell. He checked his watch and went to wait in his office.

Twenty minutes later, Jenna and Kane walked through the door. He looked at both of them. "You look exhausted. How are you feeling, Jenna?" He stood and fed three pods into the coffee machine and placed cups under the nozzles.

"Surprisingly elated." Jenna smiled at him. "We both shot suspects, so would appreciate you checking us out and making sure we're fit for duty."

Waiting for the machine to hiss and bubble, Wolfe looked at Kane, who shrugged. "Give me the circumstances of your shoot."

"Washington was shooting at Jenna, and he had her pinned down. He'd been drinking and was acting like a crazy person. I identified myself and he refused to comply, so I shot him in the shoulder. Carter was with me and we gave Washington immediate care."

Nodding, Wolfe made notes on a file. "A righteous shoot. Did the fact he was shooting at your wife come into your decision?"

"Honestly?" Kane smiled at him. "The husband in me wanted to take off his head, but the cop in me disarmed him, so we could haul him in for questioning. He'll recover. If I'd wanted him dead, he'd be dead and it would have still been a righteous shoot." He leaned back in his seat. "We sent the three suspects to the hospital with Rio and Rowley. Once they're cleared, we'll question them. They've all been read their rights."

Wolfe stood and added fixings to the coffee and handed the cups around. Debriefing Kane was unnecessary. In the field he was as stable as a rock. He nodded. "I can't see any reason why you can't continue with the investigation."

"Thanks." Kane saluted him with his coffee cup.

Wolfe moved around the desk and asked Jenna to stand. He examined her eyes, the cuts and scrapes. Finally checking out the bruises all over her back and ribs, he sighed. "You, on the other hand, need to be resting. You've been through a tough time." He returned to his desk and opened up her file. "Okay, you didn't kill anyone. What happened?"

When Jenna explained she had a fierce sparkle in her eyes. The defender of abused women was always there smoldering under the surface. Bringing three to justice was a triumph and right now she was running on adrenaline. "Did you want to kill the suspect?"

"Not at any time, no." Jenna's gaze didn't falter. "I wanted him alive to answer questions. This child exploitation group goes deeper than I ever imagined. I know predators infiltrate everywhere to get to kids, but selling foster kids is about as low as they can go. I need to get these guys and shut them down." She sipped her coffee and raised one eyebrow. "He had a rifle aimed at me, when Kane whistled and he turned around, I had less than a second to take out his legs. If I'd missed, I doubt either of us would be sitting here right now."

Typing, Wolfe glanced at her. "Blackhawk called. He said you're brave like a cornered wildcat protecting its young." He stopped typing and leaned back in his chair. "I know asking you to rest is wasting my time, but do your best. In my opinion, I don't believe the shootings will impact your work." He sighed and reached for his coffee. "Now tell me what you know about the graves and their tie-in with Wanda Beauchamp and this young girl."

FORTY-SIX

After meeting Jenna and Naomi at the back entrance to her building, Norrell waited outside the bathroom for the girl to disrobe and place all her clothes into evidence bags. These were collected by Emily and labeled and dropped into a plastic container. She'd given her scrubs to wear and wanted to make the examination as unobtrusive as possible. It must have shown on her face as Naomi followed her into an examination room.

"The sheriff told me you don't usually examine rape victims but wanted me to feel comfortable." Naomi looked up at her. "Thank you. It's been a long time since anyone cared about my feelings. I appreciate you."

The need to keep a professional façade straightened Norrell's back as she led her to a gurney. "My specialty is forensic anthropology but I'm a qualified doctor, so I do know what to do." She indicated to Emily. "Emily is studying to be a doctor and will be here for support too. We both understand how traumatic this has been for you and we don't want to make it any worse."

"Okay." Naomi's head nodded like a bobblehead toy. "What's first?"

"I'll take samples from under your nails." Emily pulled on fresh gloves with a snap. "Then I'll need to take photographs of all your injuries. I know it seems intrusive, but I'll keep your face out of the shots and just focus on the injuries. These are essential to bring these men to justice and you'll be protected at all times."

"Do what you must." Naomi held out her hands. "I scratched one of them for sure, all down one side of him." She looked at Norrell. "I bit one of them on the shoulder and drew blood. I could taste it in my mouth. After that I couldn't do much. They tied me up and beat me."

Sick to her stomach, Norrell took swabs from the girl's mouth and any contact injuries. She collected samples of blood and urine. Taking it at a steady pace to avoid giving Naomi time to think, she helped her remove the scrubs and Emily swiftly recorded every bruise and contusion on the girl's battered body. After she'd completed a full examination and ran through all the necessary tests and paperwork in a rape kit, she patted the girl on the arm. "Wrap yourself in the sheet and Emily will take you to the bathroom. You can take a nice hot shower and wash your hair. Emily has brought you some of her sister's clothes to wear. She's just about your size. We thought it would be better than wearing scrubs when you go to Her Broken Wings. When you're done, we'll have a little chat and I'll fill in some paperwork. It's up to you if you want to talk to Sheriff Alton today. She'll need to ask you very detailed questions about what happened."

"I don't mind talking to her. She's very nice." Naomi followed Emily into the bathroom.

It had been some time since Norrell had worked on a live patient, as in collecting forensic swabs. She'd helped out alongside Wolfe during various crises in town but usually her victims never talked back to her. It was disturbing and she realized why she'd taken an interest in forensic anthropology. She liked digging for answers and could feel herself being dragged into this case. The cold case and the graves Blackhawk had discovered would be her next priority. She removed her gloves and mask and tossed them into the garbage and then went to her office. She found Wolfe inside, patiently reading through files on his iPad. "Naomi is okay, no permanent physical damage at least. She has information to give Jenna. I need to do a medical history and we're good to go."

"Is there proof she was raped?" Wolfe placed his iPad on the desk and frowned. "The images Emily sent are extensive."

Filling a cup from the coffee machine, Norrell turned and leaned against the counter. "Yeah, there was enough damage to indicate multiple rapes and I found seminal fluid. They didn't worry about using protection. She'll need to be tested for sexually transmitted diseases and later a pregnancy test. The swabs and evidence I've collected are labeled and ready for you." She held up a finger. "She scratched one man down his left side and bit another on the shoulder. You'll need to do a rush on examining them before they get the chance to bathe, and from what Jenna mentioned, it's not something they do frequently."

"It's too late." Wolfe opened his hands wide. "For two of them anyway. Both are in surgery with gunshot wounds." He shrugged. "Kane and Jenna have taken the horses back to the ranch. They should be back by the time you've concluded your interview. Carter has flown back to Snakeskin Gully to collect Jo. Jenna wants her in with the girl for the interviews."

Sitting in her office chair, Norrell sipped her coffee and sighed. "They could have cleaned the scratches anyway and the bite. I just hope we have enough evidence to make a case against them."

"I think so." Wolfe stood and refilled his cup and then went back to his seat. "Kane gave me some information. Naomi identified the men in custody as those who'd raped her and pointed out Elias Miller as the man who'd taken her from the foster home. When they searched Miller's cabin, they grabbed some of his clothes. He had blood on a pair of jeans and it came back a positive match for Wanda Beauchamp. It's damning evidence." He rubbed his chin. "I'll take my team through the cabin. From what Jenna said, it is a smorgasbord of evidence. It's likely we'll find traces of other women he's taken there and murdered. There could be graves all over the forest."

Nodding, Norrell considered the implications. "I guess it comes down to how far he was prepared to carry the body." She frowned. "Although, that's no indication either, as he had a horse. Also, he might have let them go and the three of them hunted the girls down for sport. That's happened before, so it's within the realms of possibility that the three graves they found are the tip of the iceberg. The problem is, in such a vast forest, finding them would be near impossible."

"We can organize a search around the three cabins and some ways around, but as you say, finding them would be difficult." Wolfe sipped his coffee and sighed. "Maybe Jenna can work on a deal with one of them. If he tells where the bodies are buried, she'll put in a good word with the DA or something?"

Checking her watch, Norrell stood. "I'd better go. I have the evidence packed and ready for you." She smiled. "I hope you find something Jenna can use."

"So do I." Wolfe followed her out into the hallway and Norrell handed him a sealed plastic evidence box. He smiled at her. "Thanks. I'll see you tonight."

FORTY-SEVEN

MONDAY, WEEK TWO

In normal circumstances, Jenna would have worked Sunday, interviewing the suspects and Naomi. Instead, she had a seventy-two-hour holding period before the DA needed to issue arrest warrants, which gave her two days to interview the suspects. In this time, she could arrange lawyers if required and get clearance from the hospital to say that all her suspects were fit to be interrogated. Waiting also gave her victim time to recover a little, and for Carter to return with Jo. She had to admit, she needed a little time to recuperate as well. She ached all over and the ride into the forest hadn't helped her battered and bruised body one bit.

Wolfe and Norrell's teams had returned for the second day to exhume the bodies in the graves. They'd found the remains of two victims and would bring back the third sometime today. Wolfe's team had finished a forensic sweep of the cabin and taken over two hundred samples to the lab for analysis. This morning, he would be moving his team to the cabins owned by Grant and Washington.

Jenna leaned back in her chair. She'd wanted a legal representative for Naomi and had spoken to the DA about the case. As an abandoned child, her legal guardian was in fact the social services in Blackwater. It had taken the DA less than ten minutes to convince them to transfer the guardianship to Black Rock Falls and arrange for a female prosecutor to be present during Naomi's interview with Jenna. She'd be arriving by ten. After contacting the local defense lawyer, Samuel J. Cross, he'd arrived earlier and was speaking to Miller. He also would be standing by if charges were laid against the other two of her three suspects. As for the three men being involved with the rape case, Cross might take them all under his wing, but she had also contacted attorney Jeremiah Ash, just in case he was required. She already had an arrest warrant for Elias Miller, after supplying the DA with the evidence against him for his involvement in Wanda Beauchamp's death and the abduction of Naomi. The charges would be upgraded the moment any forensic evidence came to light.

As a witness to Wanda Beauchamp's death, Jenna had excused herself from the Miller murder case and regretfully handed it over to Rio rather than Kane. With Kane being her husband, she couldn't risk the case being thrown out of court due to conflict of interest. However, she and Kane would be in, boots and all, when it came to the rape case. It would be tried separately and there was no conflict of interest. The other two detainees had already arrived and were in holding cells. Once Aurora Greenway, the prosecutor, arrived she could proceed. Hopefully by eleven Rio would be speaking to Miller. Her phone buzzed. It was Maggie on the counter. "Yes, Maggie."

"I have Ms. Greenway to see you. She said you are expecting her."

Jenna smiled. "Yes, send her up and can you please contact Father Derry and ask him to bring Naomi into the office for the interview? He'll be waiting for the call."

"Sure thing." Maggie disconnected.

Standing and walking to the door, Jenna glanced at Kane working at his desk. "The police prosecutor, Aurora Greenway, is on her way up."

"Okay." Kane pushed to his feet. "She's the new one, right?"

Nodding, Jenna walked out onto the landing and waited for Aurora to climb the stairs. She was willowy, with dark hair in a swept-up style, wearing a black suit and low heels. As she looked up and smiled, Jenna looked into a remarkably beautiful face. She wondered how experienced she was. The woman looked under thirty. "Ms. Greenway. I'm Sheriff Jenna Alton and this is my deputy, Dave Kane."

"Nice to meet you." Aurora shook hands with them and took the offered seat in front of Jenna's desk. Kane sat beside her. "I've heard so much about Black Rock Falls. It sounds like a more interesting place to work than where I started, in Sunshine." She placed an iPad on the desk. "I've read the case file. How is she holding up? Will she be able to tell us what happened?"

The idea of asking the emotionally damaged girl questions, concerned Jenna. "Yes, I think she will if she's handled correctly. Jo Wells is on her way. She is a behavioral analyst and very experienced in interviewing."

"I'm here." Jo appeared in the doorway. "Carter dropped me at the ME's office and I walked over. He's going to the ranch to get the dogs. He'll be driving back, so will be a time."

"Okay." Kane stood. "I'll take you down to the interview room, so you can set up. Jenna will meet Naomi when she arrives and bring her through. I'll stay here. I don't figure she needs men around her right now."

Standing, Jenna led the way to the door. "She likes you and thinks Father Derry is lovely, so she's not off men for life, thank goodness." She headed downstairs.

Naomi arrived with Father Derry shortly after. Pale and with bruises showing on one cheek, her eyes looked huge as she stepped through the glass doors. Jenna smiled at her. "How are you settling in?"

"It's lovely and just like you said it would be." Naomi hugged her chest, obviously nervous. "I like the games room and the other kids are great."

Nodding at Father Derry, she indicated to the kitchenette at the back of the office. "Do you want to wait here? We have fresh coffee and plenty of takeout from Aunt Betty's Café or would you rather we call you when we're done?"

"Call me. I'll be at the shelter. It's only a few minutes' walk away." Father Derry patted Naomi on the shoulder. "God be with you." He hurried out the door.

Jenna took Naomi to the interview room and introduced her to Jo and Aurora. "We're all on your side, so you can speak freely. Aurora will be in court and making sure the men who hurt you go to jail."

It took every ounce of willpower for Jenna to sit through the interview. The details were horrendous and brought back bad memories of her own. Jo was remarkable and kept Naomi talking.

"Was there anyone else at the cabin when you arrived?" Jo looked across the desk.

"Yes, two men." Naomi folded her hands on the table.

Jenna laid twelve photographs on the table, within them were the three suspects. The positive ID was needed on tape, although the girl had accused the men at the cabin as the three men who'd assaulted her. "If any of those three men are here, can you point them out to us, please?" She nodded to the girl. "Pick each one up and hold it up to the camera."

When Naomi, selected the three suspects, Jo continued. She asked her what happened next and extracted every painful detail, including distinguishing marks. Naomi had a very clear memory of everything and only hesitated a few times. There were tears and anger, but she made it through.

Breathing a sigh of relief, Jenna handed Naomi a box of tissues and gave her time to gather herself. She looked at Aurora. "Is there anything else you need?"

"Not for this case, but although it's hearsay and not admissible, it might be interesting to know if they mentioned anyone else apart from Wanda." She turned to Naomi. "Do you recall any other names at all they might have mentioned?"

"Only one, but it might not mean anything because they told me my new name was Grace." Naomi sipped a soda and sniffed. "This one." She indicated to Washington. "He asked me if I could make pancakes. He said the one thing he missed about Della was pancakes." She squeezed the can and it crinkled under her grasp. "He said his day was Wednesdays. I'd stay with him and clean his place and make him pancakes."

"That could be very helpful." Aurora looked at Jenna. "Something you might bring up in an interview. If they think we know all about them, they often sing like a canary."

Trying to swallow the bad taste in her mouth, Jenna stood and stopped the recording. She needed to take a few deep breaths or maybe scream into a pillow. "We'll step outside and give you some alone time to chat. I'll call Father Derry to escort Naomi back to Her Broken Wings."

Outside in the hallway, she looked at Jo. "I do my best to bring these animals in alive, to get answers. I had the chance to kill him and I chose not to. After hearing what he subjected that child to, I wish I had."

"Well, we'll make sure we have a solid case so none of them slip through the net." Jo smiled at her. "It's perfectly normal to be angry, Jenna. It makes you human, is all."

Shaking her head, Jenna looked at her. "You recall the Tarot

Killer? The vigilante who hunts down people who get away with crimes like this?"

"Vividly." Jo nodded. "It's an ongoing case."

Jenna leaned against the wall. "You know, at first the Tarot Killer made me angry, by taking the law into their own hands, but now I understand them just fine."

FORTY-EIGHT

Carter had returned with the dogs. His Doberman, Zorro, had become quite sociable due to the constant visits and usually sat almost to attention beside his master, but Jenna bit back a giggle when he tried to squeeze into Duke's basket in the corner. His long thin legs seemed so delicate as he trod gently around Duke's rolls of fat trying to find a space to sit down.

"Zorro." Carter rolled his eyes skyward. "With me."

"Just a minute." Kane headed out the door returning moments later with another basket. "We keep this one in the conference room for Duke. "Is it okay if Zorro uses it?"

"Oh, go on." Jo gave Carter a soft punch in the arm. "Be flexible for once in your life. We're all relaxing. He should be able to as well."

"Go lie down." Carter pointed to the basket.

Zorro stepped inside, turned around three times, and dropped with a sigh, looking up at Carter with undisguised love. Jenna grinned. "Aw, that's lovely."

"Hey." Aurora Greenway knocked on the door. "I've finished speaking to Naomi and she's left with Father Derry. I believe she is going to be fine. I've explained everything that will happen and told her it might be some time before we go to trial, if we go. I'm sure, with the amount of evidence, we'll be able to persuade a guilty plea. Time will tell."

"Hi, we haven't met." Carter stood and removed his hat. He held out his hand. "Special Agent Ty Carter out of Snakeskin Gully."

"Aurora Greenway. I'm the prosecutor." She smiled. "Are you involved in this case?"

"I am indeed." Carter nodded slowly. "Anytime you need to be brought up to date with the investigation, call me." He handed her his card.

"Oh, okay thanks." Aurora backed out of the room. "I'm needed back at the office." She hurried away.

"Oh, that was smooth." Kane shook his head. "She practically ran out of the room."

"It's my charm is all." Carter grinned. "She'll call."

The phone rang and Jenna picked it up. It was Sam Cross in the interview room. "Hi, Sam, who do you want first?" She listened. "Okay, we're on our way."

She looked at the others. "Miller wants to talk about Naomi, so we're all involved. When we're done, he'll speak to Rio. Jo, do you want to speak to him about Wanda as well?"

"Yeah, Ty will too." Jo looked at her partner. "We're here as consultants and Rio will probably appreciate the support."

Jenna nodded. "I'm sure he will."

They headed down to the interview room and all went inside. After listening to Naomi's taped description of what occurred, she glanced at Kane. "You and Jo take the lead."

"Okay." Kane gave her a concerned stare and sat down opposite Miller, seated in a wheelchair, with Jo at his side. Turning on the recording devices and giving the date and time, plus who was present, Jenna sat down. Carter leaned against the door, chewing casually on a toothpick.

"You've been charged and read your rights." Kane leaned on

the table, his hands resting on each side of a legal pad containing a few notes. "It might interest you to know that Naomi's foster parents, Chad and Carol Brimmer, have been taken into custody by the Blackwater sheriff's department, and all their computers, phones, and any other communication devices confiscated."

"So?" Miller shrugged. "I have a question for you: Why did you pretend to be tourists and hire a charter boat? Did you want to question me without legal representation?"

"It was a coincidence, is all. We wanted to go fishing and at the time we didn't know Naomi was missing or that you'd be our captain for the day." Kane shrugged. "Did I, at any time, ask you about abducting young women?"

"Nope, but you did say you wanted a cabin where you could hole up for a time." Miller glared at Carter. "Like you wanted to take a woman there."

"Not that it's any of your business or relevant to the case, I'm single and, yeah, I'd like a hideaway to take a date for the weekend down there by the lake. Being an FBI agent has its restrictions." Carter moved the toothpick over his lips. "It's not a requirement to show you our creds when we go fishing. If you recall, when we saw you at the cabin, we all identified ourselves and you started shooting. I'm a federal officer, and that carries jail time."

"Getting back to the case." Kane sighed. "How many girls has Brimmer sold you over the years? He is ready to make a plea bargain, so ask Mr. Cross here if it would be in your best interests to reply."

"Go ahead." Cross gave Kane a quizzical stare. "They have solid evidence against you, Mr. Miller. I'm sure you'd rather distance yourself from a child exploitation ring."

Jenna's phone vibrated in her pocket and she looked at the message. It was from Emily. The sheets on Miller's bed had given all three men's DNA, plus Naomi's and Wanda's. The

DNA under Naomi's nails matched Grant, and Washington had a bite mark so deep it clearly showed her chipped tooth. There were traces of DNA all over the cabin. If they linked them to the bodies in the graves, they had all three men. She showed the message to Kane and then pushed the phone back into her pocket.

"Four, maybe five." Miller shrugged. "No one else wanted them. So why are you worrying so much? They're like dogs. You get one and if it don't work out or gets old, you shoot it and get another one."

"How did you pay for them?" Kane made a few notes on the legal pad and then raised his gaze back to Miller. "I'd assume a young girl would be expensive. Or did you exchange her for something of value?"

"Oh, what do you think?" Miller laughed and stared at the ceiling. "You stupid or something? Why do you buy pigs?"

"I don't know, to eat maybe?" Kane's mouth turned into a flat line. "You didn't eat the girls, we know that for sure. We've already collected the bodies from the graves in your backyard. Why do *you* buy pigs?"

"To breed them." Miller shook his head. "Do you know how much I can get for a baby? Everyone wants a baby. People are so desperate they'd pay any price. That's how I get the money to buy more pigs." He laughed hysterically at his joke.

"So, Grant and Washington were involved in this scheme as well?" Jo crossed her legs and leaned back in her chair. "Did you have one girl each?"

"Nah." Miller glanced at Cross, who nodded. "We didn't take more than one at a time and, yeah, the guys were involved, but you know that already, right? They were protection, is all. I negotiated everything and gave them a percentage. We shared the girls around, so no one knew who the baby's daddy was, just in case one of them got sentimental and wanted to keep it." He gave Jenna a long look. "I don't get sentimental."

Bile rushed up the back of Jenna's throat. They had what was close to a confession. She took a deep breath, wanting to bring the interview to an end. "We have DNA evidence against all of you. May I suggest you discuss a deal with your lawyer. You might find a more lenient judge if you plead guilty." She looked at Cross. "Not for the sake of your client, but to save the victim from reliving this over and over again."

"I'll discuss it with my client." Sam Cross gave her a small smile. "Is that all? I'll need to confer with Mr. Miller."

"Yeah." Kane turned off the recorder. "All for now."

"Wait!" Miller glared at him. "I'm in a wheelchair because of your sheriff and I haven't eaten today apart from the slop at the hospital." He looked at Cross. "They have to feed me, right?"

Jenna nodded. "Yeah. I'll organize something."

FORTY-NINE

Jenna led the way back to the main office and leaned against a filing cabinet. "That was intense." She looked at Carter. "The media devices that the Blackwater sheriff's department confiscated tie in with our case. How do we get our hands on them?"

"There's an FBI task force working on a child exploitation ring. I contacted them personally because this might be another arm of a massive, well-organized group buried in the dark web. I asked Kane to send them a copy of Naomi's interview as it's crucial evidence." Carter sighed. "We have a top cybercrime team working on it and I persuaded the sheriff to hand over the evidence to them. The team will check it out without tipping off the kingpin. If they find anything incriminating, they'll take over communications as if nothing happened to see if they can trace the organizer."

Shaking her head in dismay, Jenna stared at him. "That information is crucial to our case too. You know as well as I do that these monsters have auctions. They sell kids, most times into slavery or, worse, for snuff movies. We can't possibly allow Chad and Carol Brimmer to walk free." She swallowed hard.

"It's being taken care of, Jenna." Jo touched her arm.

"Another FBI team is on its way to assist the Blackwater sheriff. There will be other charges laid to keep them in custody for as long as it takes to go through their devices. The other charges will follow. They won't walk away with anything, and your DA will have the option to extradite them so they face jail time here as well."

Raising her hands up and dropping them to her sides in dismay, Jenna headed for the front desk. The foyer was filled with reporters and Rio was issuing a statement. Edging her way through the crowd she looked at Maggie. "I need a meal for Miller, and arrange something for the other two as well, and then we can ship them off to County."

"Okay, leave it with me. I'll get sandwiches delivered. I took a box of takeout to your office just before. Kane ordered it for lunch." Maggie eyed her critically. "You, okay, Sheriff? You look sheet white. Nasty interview?"

Jenna nodded. "Yeah, the kind nightmares are made of." She pushed away from the desk. "Grant is next."

"Do you want to take a break?" Kane walked up beside her. "Rio is next with Miller. When he's done, I'll have Rowley take him back to his cell. I'll arrange for County to collect all of them. We can't care for Grant and Miller here. Not with their injuries. Washington can go too. I figure he's an alcoholic."

Pushing her hair from her eyes, Jenna nodded. "Okay. Tell Rio to let them know they can eat directly after the interview. I don't want any duty-of-care issues with them." She smiled at him. "You ordered lunch. I guess we'd better eat it. We can watch the interviews on the screen in my office."

"That sounds like a plan." Kane grinned.

It seemed surreal watching the interviews and not being involved. Rio with his retentive memory didn't need notes and conducted the interview with an almost bland expression. Jo asked a few questions, but it was evident that Cross had discussed the statement Jenna had given about Wanda's murder and the consequent DNA evidence with Miller. When Jo asked him a few questions about how he felt about killing Wanda, the pure psychopathic traits blossomed.

"I enjoyed it." Miller shrugged. "She was useless and I already had a replacement." He stared at Jo. "It was a business. Like I said before. You can't think about them as pets. They're not pets. Just like every farm animal, they serve their purpose for a time and then you replace them."

When word came that Grant and Washington had refused to talk, Sam Cross arrived at their office. Jenna waved him inside and offered him a cup of coffee. "They won't offer any defense for their actions?"

"Seems that way." Cross scratched his chin. "They figure if they plead guilty, the judge will go easy on them." He looked at Jenna and sighed. "Seems to me they were a little afraid of Miller."

"I figure no one can scare you into raping a child." Kane shook his head. "I hope they throw the book at them. The DNA evidence against all of them is damning. Wolfe has identified one of the girls in the graves as Della Gooding, another Blackwater missing person from six years ago. She wore a silver bracelet with her name inscribed on it, and the dental records confirm it was her." He sighed. "The other remains we turned over to Norrell. They're older, buried maybe seven to ten years ago. It will be a time going through records and trying to match her to a name. These girls seem to come from all over."

"Well, I'm done here." Cross drained his cup and stood. "I'll follow up at County. I'm sure the DA will be in touch about future court hearings and a trial. Unless Miller decides to plead guilty. I hope so for the girl's sake."

Jenna nodded. "Me too. Thanks, Sam."

When he'd left, shutting the door behind him, Jenna pushed both hands through her hair. "It's been a horrific day, but we got them. Within the hour they'll be on their way to County and out of our hair. I'll be glad to see the back of them."

"Me too." Kane's phone buzzed and he read a message. "Next Wednesday is the final hearing for the adoption." He smiled at her. "I'm excited and nervous at the same time."

Nodding Jenna sipped her coffee. "Same." A shiver crawled up her spine. "They can't take him from us, can they? I mean, if they deny the adoption, we can still foster him, can't we?"

"Jenna, for four years the social services scoured the country looking for his father." Kane reached across the desk and took her hand. "Tauri was destined to remain in foster care for life if Atohi hadn't agreed to take him. His main reason for the DNA search was to link Tauri to one of his people. He used his contacts, including Wolfe and Carter to search everywhere before he found the link to Annie. There is no one who can claim him. I just wish we'd found him sooner."

FIFTY

It was one of those opportunities that comes once in a lifetime for someone like me. I have a good reason to be making a fast visit to Black Rock Falls, and I don't need much time. What I need is opportunity. I've been watching Chad and Carol Brimmer's activity on the dark web for a time in an effort to discover the identity of the kingpin in the child exploitation ring. It is far reaching, and touching them when they are part of an FBI investigation would be suicide, but the arrests of Miller, Grant, and Washington in Black Rock Falls caught my interest. By hacking into the interview of Naomi King and reading Sheriff Alton's files, my course is set. My, how those files are protected, but not well enough to prevent me from following the case in real time. The monsters are planning on dealing their way out of jail time and I can't allow that to happen.

I'm just waiting for one tiny error or scrap of information I can use to get close to them. Right now, I have no idea if I'll be able to find justice for the unknown quantity of girls the men have raped and murdered, but I'm here and must at least try. Sometimes, it's as if fate guides my hand and justice hands me the green light to go ahead, so I wait in the foyer of the sheriff's office for that one chance. My baseball cap pulled down over my eyes and wearing a jacket I'd pulled from the local shelter's donation box. I stand, notebook in hand, in the guise of a reporter listening to the media report, blending into the surroundings. Out of the blue, the sheriff herself arrives and asks the receptionist, Maggie, to order takeout to be delivered for Miller and the others. How extremely fortunate. I duck through the crowd and head along Main to the local diner pulling on gloves. The CCTV camera over the counter blinks red and I push on sunglasses, pull down my hat, and slip into Aunt Betty's Café. The place is busy, with servers dashing back and forth. When one of them heads my way, before she has the chance to duck behind the counter, I turn my back to the camera and smile. "I'm here to pick up the sandwiches for the sheriff's office, Maggie thought you might be busy."

"We are but they're ready. We had some prepacked." The woman grabs a box from behind the counter and hands it to me.

I don't have much time. Minutes tick away, leaving me no room for error. He'll be searching for me soon and I must be right where I said I'd be. Keeping my head down, I carry the box out the door and head back along Main. The alleyway beside the shelter is empty, with a staircase leading to an upper floor. No cameras to worry about this time. I drop the box on the steps, peel open the plastic packets, and open the sandwiches. In my purse, disguised as a lipstick is a slow-acting poison. I shake the contents over each sandwich and replace them in the packets. Inside a fold of the cardboard carton, I slide a tarot card, carefully pleated into a neat square and undetectable unless they look very closely. By the time they do, and I'm sure the medical examiner will be thorough, I'll be long gone, leaving another mystery behind.

Satisfied, I go to the shelter's donation box, return the jacket and baseball cap, grab a large floral blouse and a straw hat. I put them on and head back to the sheriff's office. Going inside will be fraught with danger, now the press has gone. I slow my stride as two middle-aged cowboys walk past and head for the glass doors. Another perfect opportunity and one I hadn't expected. I hurry toward them before they reach the steps and smile at them. "Could you drop this takeout at the counter for me? My baby is in the truck and I don't like leaving her alone." I glance over my shoulder toward a line of parked vehicles and sigh. "It's urgent and Aunt Betty's is too busy to deliver it right now."

"Sure thing." One man takes the box and heads for the door.

I flee, running down back alleyways and depositing clothes into dumpsters on my way. I drag my hair down and run my fingers through it. My reflection in the store window looks just fine. With my jacket over one arm, I slide into a store with the name Bygone Days and select a vase. I browse a little more, as a man steps out from the back and waits at the counter. Planting suggestions in the storekeeper's mind is a ploy I always adopt. Say it and that's what they remember. "I'm sorry to take up so much of your time. There are so many wonderful things here."

"Take all the time you need." The storekeeper smiles benevolently. "That vase is an antique. Hand-painted porcelain. There are another few nice ones to your left."

I nod, looking around as if interested in everything in his store. "Yes, I looked at those, but I like this one the best."

I place the vase on the counter and pay in cash. Always in cash. I'm about to leave, when as if on cue, a familiar face peers through the door. It's time to leave and fly far away from Black Rock Falls. Heart pounding, I smile and wave my purchase. "I found just what I needed. It's perfect."

My cover is complete. My job done. It's a good day.

FIFTY-ONE

TUESDAY, WEEK TWO

"Kane." Frowning, Kane listened to the prison warden on the other end of the line. "No, the sheriff isn't here just now. I'm her deputy. What seems to be the problem?"

"The three men you sent over yesterday died overnight." The warden sounded agitated and was breathing heavily.

Astounded, Kane pushed a hand through his hair. "Died? What happened to them?"

"We're not sure. There are no signs of foul play. The doctor can only suggest poison. They ate the same as everyone else on remand last night, and no one else died." He cleared his throat. *"I've called you first. The doctor is on the phone to the medical examiner. I imagine he'll take the bodies back to Black Rock Falls."*

Kane looked up as Jenna walked into the office. "Okay, I'll follow up from here. Thanks for letting us know." He disconnected and stared at Jenna. "Miller, Grant, and Washington died last night. The prison doctor figures they might have been poisoned. They had the same food as everyone else at the prison last night, so it might have happened here."

He retrieved the CCTV footage of the cells from the

previous day and they watched Rio carry a box to the cells and hand sandwiches and sodas to the prisoners. He ran it forward to when the men left and Rowley pulled on gloves and collected the garbage and tossed it into a can. "No one touched the food. I can't believe it happened at Aunt Betty's."

"They ate from Aunt Betty's same as we did, so it can't be what we gave them." Jenna frowned. "I haven't called in the cleaners yet. Maybe we should go and check out the garbage, so we can eliminate the diner from the investigation?"

Kane grabbed gloves from the desk drawer and tossed her a pair. "I doubt anyone got to the food before they ate it, Jenna, but be careful."

"I'm always careful." Jenna took a pile of evidence bags from a shelf and headed down to the cells. They went along each one before checking the bin in the hallway. "We have the wrappers but no food. I guess we'll take them to Wolfe." She dropped them into an evidence bag.

Kane picked up a cardboard carton. "They must have come in this box." He examined it for any smears or powder and then spotted the corner of something printed shoved into the bottom. "There's something here." He pulled out the folded piece of card and held it up to show Jenna. "I believe we have our answer." He opened out the card. "The Tarot Killer strikes again."

"Oh, not again." Jenna gaped at the card. "How did the Tarot Killer get to the food between Aunt Betty's and here? How did they know the food was for the prisoners?"

Bewildered, Kane shook his head. "The *why* he did it gets me. The prisoners were caught and in custody and likely facing life imprisonment. Justice was served."

"Oh, that's spooky. After hearing what happened to Naomi, I was just saying to Jo how I understood why the Tarot Killer seeks vengeance on men like Miller." She frowned and stared at Kane wide-eyed. "You don't figure Jo is involved, do you?"

Rubbing the back of his neck, Kane stared at her. "Not unless she can teleport or something. She's been right here all the time. None of us have left the building and she never went near the cells at any time." Bewildered by the enormity of what had happened, he stared into space. "I hope Wolfe can find some answers because I'm out of ideas."

"This case has to go deeper than we imagined. Maybe there are more graves out there?" Jenna chewed on her bottom lip. "Maybe the Tarot Killer knows more about that trio than we do and figured that jail time wasn't enough punishment. Who knows? All I know is we solved the case and brought the men to justice."

Trying to get his mind around the enormity of the situation, Kane gave himself a shake. "We'll ask Maggie who delivered the takeout and then head down to Aunt Betty's."

They hurried downstairs and went to the counter. "Do you recall who dropped the prisoners' lunch by yesterday?"

"No, can't say that I do." Maggie frowned. "I was in the bathroom. It was on the counter when I returned, and Rio picked it up and took it down to the cells."

"Thanks." Jenna headed for the door. "Well, it's not Rio. He was here all the time too and we'd have seen him tampering with the food. Drive down to the diner, I think it's starting to rain." She hurried for the Beast.

The smell of barbecue ribs made Kane's stomach growl as he opened the door to the diner. He followed Jenna to the counter. When the manager, Susie, came out from the back room, he smiled at her. "Do you recall who delivered the second box of takeout to our office yesterday?"

"I was off yesterday." Susie frowned. "Was there a problem with the food?"

"We're not sure." Jenna smiled. "We just need to know who delivered it."

"About what time?" Susie waved them into the back room where the CCTV screens were set up.

"Around one, one-thirty I think." Jenna looked at Kane. "Was it that time?"

Kane nodded. "I think so. We were all kinda busy."

They watched the video flash by until Susie slowed it at twelve-thirty and moved forward slowly. Kane narrowed his gaze as a figure came into view and turned away from the camera. One of the servers gave them a box and they walked out the door. The film went on for another hour without anyone else collecting a meal. No one left with a delivery. "Go back to one-ten and zoom in." He waited. "Is that a male or a female?"

"I can't be sure. Young male, twenty to twenty-five maybe. The shirt looks Western, maybe a ranch hand?" Jenna leaned closer. "There's no way we can identify that person from behind. They knew about the cameras and avoided them."

"That's Wendy talking to them. I'll go and ask her." Susie stood and headed out the door.

Bending and staring at the screen, Kane shook his head. "Unless Wendy can identify this person, we don't have anything to go on. We know the Tarot Killer is a master of disguise. What baffles me is how they always seem to be in the right place at the right time. How did they know you would order food for the prisoners?"

"Well, if they'd been watching and knew we had them in custody, they'd only have to hang around the office at lunchtime." Jenna shrugged. "With the media crawling all over the place, they could have mingled with the crowd. Maggie would have raised her voice to be heard over the noise when ordering. If we knew how the Tarot Killer gets their information, we'd be able to catch them, but that's a mystery no one can solve. The FBI has been chasing them for years and found nothing but shadows and dead ends."

Kane rubbed his chin. "It can't be an inside job. Wendy

would recognize one of our team. I mean, Jo is the only person apart from you who comes close to the height of that guy and neither of you are that broad. Although, it could be the jacket, I guess."

"The problem is someone got to the prisoners on our watch." Jenna looked stricken. "With every security precaution we've implemented, this vigilante got to them." She shook her head. "You ordered takeout this morning. What if it had been us, any of us, who'd eaten food meant for them?"

Nodding, Kane stared at her. Things would have to change and right now. He cleared his throat. "Honestly, if this vigilante is as smart as we believe, then they'll know we'll implement precautions to avoid this happening again, but from now on, we collect the food."

"I've spoken to Wendy." Susie came back into the room. "It was busy. She recalls someone, maybe a young guy, picking up the takeout. He mentioned being sent by Maggie, but that's all she remembers."

"Okay, thanks." Jenna squeezed Susie's arm. "Someone poisoned the food."

"What! Poisoned the food? Is this a prank?" All the color had drained from Susie's face. "We're ruined."

Shaking his head, Kane rested a hand on her arm. "We know who did this. What we need to discover is how they did it. You haven't gotten any new staff lately, have you?"

"No, same as usual." Suzie frowned. "Look from now on, I'll ask the chef to pack everything into a box and seal it, so no other hands touch your food. You trust him, right? He's been here for twenty years."

Kane thought for a beat. "Yeah, we trust him. I have an idea."

He hurried out to the Beast and collected a pile of tamper-proof evidence stickers from the forensics kit and carried them inside. He handed them to Susie. "Here, ask him to seal the cartons with these."

"That's a great idea and we'll make it a policy not to hand out your deliveries to anyone but people from your office. It will only be me or Wendy handling deliveries when you're busy." Susie shivered. "Are you sure news of this won't get out?"

Kane shook his head. "Not exactly, as it's under investigation. Right now, we know the food was tampered with when it left here, and the men died in jail. Wolfe is handling the forensics. I can't see any reason to involve Aunt Betty's."

Jenna looked at Kane. "I guess we get a copy of this footage and give it to Carter. He can add it to the ton of other useless information they have on this guy."

"I'll get a copy for you." Susie sat at the desk. "If you want to wait, the ribs are on special." She grinned at Kane. "Cherry pie fresh from the oven." She suddenly frowned. "That's if you still trust our food?"

Kane exchanged a look with Jenna and smiled. "I figure if someone wanted to poison us, we'd be dead by now. It sounds delicious. We'll wait."

EPILOGUE

WEDNESDAY, WEEK TWO

Standing on the front porch in the sunshine, Jenna stared into the distance, taking in the view of the snowcapped mountains and everything green and lush in between and feeling grateful for the chance to live in such a beautiful home surrounded by people she loved. Her stomach had been flip-flopping all night. With the hearing for Tauri's adoption at noon, sleep hadn't come easy and she'd seen Kane staring at the ceiling for most of the night too. She pushed her nerves aside and breathed in the fresh-scented summer air. It was always so clean and crisp early in the morning and she enjoyed doing the chores and working out before Tauri woke. Life had certainly changed with him in their lives. It was as if that empty space in her heart had finally been filled.

Her mind wandered to the events of the last week or so. Although the case had ended abruptly, all investigations going forward were out of her hands. She'd turned over all the evidence to Wolfe and the footage to Carter, who in turn forwarded it to the FBI task force chasing down the Tarot Killer. At least they'd hunted down everyone involved in Naomi's case. The investigation into Wanda Beauchamp was complex, and although her office had handled the investigation into her death, the Bozeman police department would be proceeding with her abduction or sale by her foster parents, and arrests had already been made. Jenna would be kept in the loop of the outcome as a courtesy, but she wouldn't be involved.

The autopsy report on Wanda would be through this morning, although she doubted it would differ much from Wolfe's initial findings. The same with the report of the victim in the grave, a young girl by the name of Della Gooding, closing a cold case going back some years. The body had been buried in sand and was well preserved. Due to the caseload, she'd asked badge-holding deputy and Wolfe's assistant, Colt Webber, to stand in for her during the autopsies. The missing babies Miller had crowed about selling had troubled her, but with him dead, the only possible leads would be via the foster parents of the girls. All were out of her jurisdiction, but Carter had stepped in to place the investigation into the correct hands within the FBI, and whoever was involved would be brought to justice.

Footsteps came from inside and the door swung open. Duke bounded out, followed by Kane and Tauri. They'd planned to keep today as normal as possible for their little boy, but he would be going to court with them at noon. This morning he'd attend kindergarten as usual and then they'd drop by and collect him before the hearing. Jenna's stomach clenched again as she swung him into her arms and kissed his cheeks. "You know Mommy loves you, right?"

"Love you too, Mommy." Tauri wriggled to get down. At four he was becoming very independent. "Daddy told me about going to court. I'm not scared." He smiled at her and squeezed her hand. "You must be brave too. It's going to be just fine, you'll see."

"I thought it best to be honest with him." Kane's attention followed Tauri across the yard with Duke lumbering along beside him. "I told him the judge will ask him some questions and not to be scared. We'll be right there and so will Uncle Atohi." He slipped one arm around her and squeezed. "The last six or so months have been like a lifetime."

Two butterflies danced by, and Jenna watched them for a second, wondering if they'd escaped from her stomach. It was as if she had a swarm of them inside her. She leaned into Kane and nodded. "It has but everyone has been positive. We can only hope no one has claimed him in the meantime. Although I know that's an entirely selfish thing to say, I honestly believe he is meant to be with us."

"The authorities have been searching for four years." Kane pushed on his Stetson and shrugged. "If his father knew about him and walked away leaving him in foster care, he doesn't deserve him. Although if anyone does come forward as the years go by, we'll discuss visitation rights then. It will be Tauri's choice if he wants to see them or not. When we sign the papers, he will be ours legally. No one can take him from us, not ever."

Willing the day to turn out right, Jenna headed for the garage. "Carter and Jo left early. They had a few things to do. They would have left yesterday but for the court hearing."

"I'm glad to have their support." Kane opened the door of the Beast and swung Tauri into his car seat, followed by Duke. He climbed behind the wheel. "At least we have no cases today. That has to be a bonus."

Jenna smiled at him. "I'll close the office at eleven. Rio can handle the 911 calls. We all need some downtime."

"Maggie won't budge from behind the counter." Kane backed out and headed for town. "You know she likes to provide a public service from eight to five."

After dropping by the kindergarten with Tauri, they headed into the office. Jenna made sure her deputies were updating their files and would be sending them the autopsy reports when she received them. She climbed the stairs to her office to find

Kane at his desk. Wolfe had sent over a ton of information. "Any new findings?"

"Yeah, and I'm only up to Wanda's autopsy report." Kane's brow wrinkled into a frown. "He says there are signs of multiple births. She had many old broken bones. A twist fracture of one arm was a significant injury. The back of her head showed a blunt force trauma injury that might have caused her amnesia. I could go into more information, but from what Naomi told you, it would make it ten times worse." He paused and scanned the next document. "The body of Della Gooding was well preserved and he found similar abuse. She died from strangulation. A knotted rope was used and it was still on the body."

Appalled, Jenna shook her head. "The Tarot Killer must have been following these men. Whoever this person is, they seem to find the very lowest form of monster and take them out." She sighed. "What else does it say?"

"As we can blame the Tarot Killer for the deaths of Grant, Miller, and Washington, Wolfe is analyzing the blood samples of the prisoners with his sights on herbal slow-acting poisons. These seem to be the Tarot Killer's choice when poisoning someone. The remaining food in the men's stomachs was prison food and that returned as nontoxic. He has a few poisons in mind to find a match but he's thinking belladonna or wolfsbane. Nothing that can be purchased in Black Rock Falls or surrounds. A full analysis will take weeks."

The reports were very depressing. Jenna dropped into her office chair. "I hope they trace the baby sellers. Carter seems to think the task force will hunt them down. I hope the people responsible will rot in jail." She checked her emails and smiled to see one from Naomi. "I have an email from Naomi. She says her blood tests came back negative. She didn't catch anything from the men who abused her. She's settling in fine and met another girl her own age. She is starting school again next Monday and is looking forward to making friends."

"That's wonderful." Kane leaned back in his chair. "Make sure to tell her we'll always be here for her."

Jenna smiled at him. "I will."

Eleven came so fast Jenna jumped to her feet when she glanced at her watch. "We have to go and pick up Tauri. It's nearly time and we don't want to be late."

They arrived at the courthouse twenty minutes before their case was due to be heard in the family court and greeted their lawyer. To Jenna's surprise, waiting outside the court room was all her substitute family: Wolfe and his girls; Rio and his brother and sister, Cade and Piper; Rowley, his wife, Sandy, and the twins. As she took a seat and pulled Tauri onto her lap, Carter and Jo walked along the hallway with Colt Webber.

"Maggie said to tell you she's here in spirit. She has a lineup of people waiting to pay fines from Kane's day on speeding duty. Same with Kalo. He is handling our office." Carter grinned around the toothpick in his mouth. "Blackhawk is just parking his truck, and his mom is here too."

The time had come for the decision that would change their lives and goosebumps crawled up Jenna's legs. She took one of Tauri's hands and Kane took the other. They walked into court and took a seat with their lawyer. Behind them, friends and family followed in silence. When the judge came into the room and saw the crowd, his attention went straight to her.

"Do you consent to having these people in the courtroom?" The judge sat down and stared at them. "These proceedings are usually conducted in private."

"They're our family." Kane smiled. "Our support team."

"Very well." The judge perused the documents in front of him. "I can see there has been an extensive search to find a relative to Tauri and I've read the reports from the social services about the prospective parents. Now I'd like to hear from Tauri."

He looked at the little boy. "Do you want to go and live with Jenna and David Kane? Are you happy with them?"

"Yes." Tauri looked from one to the other and then back at the judge, his face serious. "I am happy. I love Mommy and Daddy."

"Very well. I hereby grant the petition to terminate parental rights. From this day forward no other claims to this child will be accepted by law. I have considered the petition for adoption and hereby sign the documents to finalize the process." He signed documents and handed copies to the clerk, who handed them to the lawyer. "Congratulations, Tauri, you are now legally the son of Jenna and David Kane." He looked at the people cheering. "Come on in and congratulate them."

Tears streamed down Jenna's face in uncontrolled joy. As she picked up Tauri, Kane enclosed them in a bear hug, his eyes wet with tears. As their family surrounded them, Jenna looked into Kane's loving expression and grinned. "We have a son."

A LETTER FROM D.K. HOOD

Dear reader,

Thank you so much for choosing my novel and coming with me on another of Kane and Alton's thrilling cases in *Where Hidden Souls Lie.*

If you'd like to keep up to date with all my latest releases, just sign up at the website link below for my newsletter. An email from me will arrive about my latest release. I will never share your email address or spam you, and you can unsubscribe at any time.

www.bookouture.com/dk-hood

As you know if you read the series in order, I follow the seasons. *Where Hidden Souls Lie* is set during summer in Black Rock Falls, so the next story will be set in fall/autumn. Which brings us back around to Halloween. In *Where Hidden Souls Lie,* I mention the old graves Atohi discovered in the forest, and I figure Halloween is the perfect time for Kane and Alton to be stirring up ghosts of the past. Some say you should never poke a sleeping tiger... but danger has never stopped them from getting to the truth. Halloween in Black Rock Falls always carries an extra serving of spooky, so when their investigations reconnect a deadly circle long broken by time, and a killer stalks Black Rock Falls, no one is safe. Get ready for chills down your spine in book twenty-one.

If you enjoyed *Where Hidden Souls Lie,* I would be very grateful if you could leave a review and recommend my book to your friends and family. I really enjoy hearing from readers, so feel free to ask me questions at any time. You can get in touch on my Facebook page or Twitter or through my webpages.

Thank you so much for your support.

D.K. Hood

http://www.dkhood.com
dkhood-author.blogspot.com.au

 facebook.com/dkhoodauthor
twitter.com/DKHood_Author

ACKNOWLEDGMENTS

During the writing of this novel, I had some serious health problems and required an operation that knocked me off my feet for three months. This was followed immediately by a life-threatening family health issue. It has been amazing to feel the love and support from other authors, my readers, and especially the amazing team behind me at Bookouture. Honestly, having a company that understands and actually cares about me is remarkable. I am well, my family is well, and I'm able to keep writing far into the future. Thank you and God bless you all.

3-24
c mor

Made in the USA
Middletown, DE
26 October 2023

41439483R00161